# LEFT TO VANISH

(An Adele Sharp Mystery—Book Eight)

BLAKE PIERCE

**Blake Pierce**

Blake Pierce is the USA Today bestselling author of the RILEY PAGE mystery series, which includes seventeen books. Blake Pierce is also the author of the MACKENZIE WHITE mystery series, comprising fourteen books; of the AVERY BLACK mystery series, comprising six books; of the KERI LOCKE mystery series, comprising five books; of the MAKING OF RILEY PAIGE mystery series, comprising six books; of the KATE WISE mystery series, comprising seven books; of the CHLOE FINE psychological suspense mystery, comprising six books; of the JESSE HUNT psychological suspense thriller series, comprising nineteen books; of the AU PAIR psychological suspense thriller series, comprising three books; of the ZOE PRIME mystery series, comprising six books; of the ADELE SHARP mystery series, comprising thirteen books; of the EUROPEAN VOYAGE cozy mystery series, comprising six books (and counting); of the new LAURA FROST FBI suspense thriller, comprising three books (and counting); of the new ELLA DARK FBI suspense thriller, comprising six books (and counting); of the A YEAR IN EUROPE cozy mystery series, comprising nine books); of the AVA GOLD mystery series, comprising three books (and counting); and of the RACHEL GIFT mystery series, comprising three books (and counting).

An avid reader and lifelong fan of the mystery and thriller genres, Blake loves to hear from you, so please feel free to visit www.blakepierceauthor.com to learn more and stay in touch.


ISBN: 978-1-0943-9112-0

**BOOKS BY BLAKE PIERCE**

**RACHEL GIFT MYSTERY SERIES**
HER LAST WISH (Book #1)
HER LAST CHANCE (Book #2)
HER LAST HOPE (Book #3)

**AVA GOLD MYSTERY SERIES**
CITY OF PREY (Book #1)
CITY OF FEAR (Book #2)
CITY OF BONES (Book #3)

**A YEAR IN EUROPE**
A MURDER IN PARIS (Book #1)
DEATH IN FLORENCE (Book #2)
VENGEANCE IN VIENNA (Book #3)

**ELLA DARK FBI SUSPENSE THRILLER**
GIRL, ALONE (Book #1)
GIRL, TAKEN (Book #2)
GIRL, HUNTED (Book #3)
GIRL, SILENCED (Book #4)
GIRL, VANISHED (Book 5)
GIRL ERASED (Book #6)

**LAURA FROST FBI SUSPENSE THRILLER**
ALREADY GONE (Book #1)
ALREADY SEEN (Book #2)
ALREADY TRAPPED (Book #3)

**EUROPEAN VOYAGE COZY MYSTERY SERIES**
MURDER (AND BAKLAVA) (Book #1)
DEATH (AND APPLE STRUDEL) (Book #2)
CRIME (AND LAGER) (Book #3)
MISFORTUNE (AND GOUDA) (Book #4)
CALAMITY (AND A DANISH) (Book #5)
MAYHEM (AND HERRING) (Book #6)

**ADELE SHARP MYSTERY SERIES**
LEFT TO DIE (Book #1)
LEFT TO RUN (Book #2)
LEFT TO HIDE (Book #3)
LEFT TO KILL (Book #4)
LEFT TO MURDER (Book #5)
LEFT TO ENVY (Book #6)
LEFT TO LAPSE (Book #7)
LEFT TO VANISH (Book #8)
LEFT TO HUNT (Book #9)
LEFT TO FEAR (Book #10)

**THE AU PAIR SERIES**
ALMOST GONE (Book#1)
ALMOST LOST (Book #2)
ALMOST DEAD (Book #3)

**ZOE PRIME MYSTERY SERIES**
FACE OF DEATH (Book#1)
FACE OF MURDER (Book #2)
FACE OF FEAR (Book #3)
FACE OF MADNESS (Book #4)
FACE OF FURY (Book #5)
FACE OF DARKNESS (Book #6)

**A JESSIE HUNT PSYCHOLOGICAL SUSPENSE SERIES**
THE PERFECT WIFE (Book #1)
THE PERFECT BLOCK (Book #2)
THE PERFECT HOUSE (Book #3)
THE PERFECT SMILE (Book #4)
THE PERFECT LIE (Book #5)
THE PERFECT LOOK (Book #6)
THE PERFECT AFFAIR (Book #7)
THE PERFECT ALIBI (Book #8)
THE PERFECT NEIGHBOR (Book #9)
THE PERFECT DISGUISE (Book #10)
THE PERFECT SECRET (Book #11)
THE PERFECT FAÇADE (Book #12)
THE PERFECT IMPRESSION (Book #13)
THE PERFECT DECEIT (Book #14)
THE PERFECT MISTRESS (Book #15)

**BOOKS BY BLAKE PIERCE**

**RACHEL GIFT MYSTERY SERIES**
HER LAST WISH (Book #1)
HER LAST CHANCE (Book #2)
HER LAST HOPE (Book #3)

**AVA GOLD MYSTERY SERIES**
CITY OF PREY (Book #1)
CITY OF FEAR (Book #2)
CITY OF BONES (Book #3)

**A YEAR IN EUROPE**
A MURDER IN PARIS (Book #1)
DEATH IN FLORENCE (Book #2)
VENGEANCE IN VIENNA (Book #3)

**ELLA DARK FBI SUSPENSE THRILLER**
GIRL, ALONE (Book #1)
GIRL, TAKEN (Book #2)
GIRL, HUNTED (Book #3)
GIRL, SILENCED (Book #4)
GIRL, VANISHED (Book 5)
GIRL ERASED (Book #6)

**LAURA FROST FBI SUSPENSE THRILLER**
ALREADY GONE (Book #1)
ALREADY SEEN (Book #2)
ALREADY TRAPPED (Book #3)

**EUROPEAN VOYAGE COZY MYSTERY SERIES**
MURDER (AND BAKLAVA) (Book #1)
DEATH (AND APPLE STRUDEL) (Book #2)
CRIME (AND LAGER) (Book #3)
MISFORTUNE (AND GOUDA) (Book #4)
CALAMITY (AND A DANISH) (Book #5)
MAYHEM (AND HERRING) (Book #6)

**ADELE SHARP MYSTERY SERIES**
LEFT TO DIE (Book #1)
LEFT TO RUN (Book #2)
LEFT TO HIDE (Book #3)
LEFT TO KILL (Book #4)
LEFT TO MURDER (Book #5)
LEFT TO ENVY (Book #6)
LEFT TO LAPSE (Book #7)
LEFT TO VANISH (Book #8)
LEFT TO HUNT (Book #9)
LEFT TO FEAR (Book #10)

**THE AU PAIR SERIES**
ALMOST GONE (Book#1)
ALMOST LOST (Book #2)
ALMOST DEAD (Book #3)

**ZOE PRIME MYSTERY SERIES**
FACE OF DEATH (Book#1)
FACE OF MURDER (Book #2)
FACE OF FEAR (Book #3)
FACE OF MADNESS (Book #4)
FACE OF FURY (Book #5)
FACE OF DARKNESS (Book #6)

**A JESSIE HUNT PSYCHOLOGICAL SUSPENSE SERIES**
THE PERFECT WIFE (Book #1)
THE PERFECT BLOCK (Book #2)
THE PERFECT HOUSE (Book #3)
THE PERFECT SMILE (Book #4)
THE PERFECT LIE (Book #5)
THE PERFECT LOOK (Book #6)
THE PERFECT AFFAIR (Book #7)
THE PERFECT ALIBI (Book #8)
THE PERFECT NEIGHBOR (Book #9)
THE PERFECT DISGUISE (Book #10)
THE PERFECT SECRET (Book #11)
THE PERFECT FAÇADE (Book #12)
THE PERFECT IMPRESSION (Book #13)
THE PERFECT DECEIT (Book #14)
THE PERFECT MISTRESS (Book #15)

THE PERFECT IMAGE (Book #16)
THE PERFECT VEIL (Book #17)
THE PERFECT INDISCRETION (Book #18)
THE PERFECT RUMOR (Book #19)

**CHLOE FINE PSYCHOLOGICAL SUSPENSE SERIES**
NEXT DOOR (Book #1)
A NEIGHBOR'S LIE (Book #2)
CUL DE SAC (Book #3)
SILENT NEIGHBOR (Book #4)
HOMECOMING (Book #5)
TINTED WINDOWS (Book #6)

**KATE WISE MYSTERY SERIES**
IF SHE KNEW (Book #1)
IF SHE SAW (Book #2)
IF SHE RAN (Book #3)
IF SHE HID (Book #4)
IF SHE FLED (Book #5)
IF SHE FEARED (Book #6)
IF SHE HEARD (Book #7)

**THE MAKING OF RILEY PAIGE SERIES**
WATCHING (Book #1)
WAITING (Book #2)
LURING (Book #3)
TAKING (Book #4)
STALKING (Book #5)
KILLING (Book #6)

**RILEY PAIGE MYSTERY SERIES**
ONCE GONE (Book #1)
ONCE TAKEN (Book #2)
ONCE CRAVED (Book #3)
ONCE LURED (Book #4)
ONCE HUNTED (Book #5)
ONCE PINED (Book #6)
ONCE FORSAKEN (Book #7)
ONCE COLD (Book #8)
ONCE STALKED (Book #9)
ONCE LOST (Book #10)

ONCE BURIED (Book #11)
ONCE BOUND (Book #12)
ONCE TRAPPED (Book #13)
ONCE DORMANT (Book #14)
ONCE SHUNNED (Book #15)
ONCE MISSED (Book #16)
ONCE CHOSEN (Book #17)

**MACKENZIE WHITE MYSTERY SERIES**
BEFORE HE KILLS (Book #1)
BEFORE HE SEES (Book #2)
BEFORE HE COVETS (Book #3)
BEFORE HE TAKES (Book #4)
BEFORE HE NEEDS (Book #5)
BEFORE HE FEELS (Book #6)
BEFORE HE SINS (Book #7)
BEFORE HE HUNTS (Book #8)
BEFORE HE PREYS (Book #9)
BEFORE HE LONGS (Book #10)
BEFORE HE LAPSES (Book #11)
BEFORE HE ENVIES (Book #12)
BEFORE HE STALKS (Book #13)
BEFORE HE HARMS (Book #14)

**AVERY BLACK MYSTERY SERIES**
CAUSE TO KILL (Book #1)
CAUSE TO RUN (Book #2)
CAUSE TO HIDE (Book #3)
CAUSE TO FEAR (Book #4)
CAUSE TO SAVE (Book #5)
CAUSE TO DREAD (Book #6)

**KERI LOCKE MYSTERY SERIES**
A TRACE OF DEATH (Book #1)
A TRACE OF MUDER (Book #2)
A TRACE OF VICE (Book #3)
A TRACE OF CRIME (Book #4)
A TRACE OF HOPE (Book #5)

# CHAPTER ONE

At night, the reddish hue of Castle Sforzesco could just be glimpsed amidst surrounding trees in the arms of Milan. Signora Calvetti admired the view as her sedan pulled through the gated driveway, stray gravel crunching beneath the tires.

The driver glanced in the mirror, tipping his hat once. "Are you sure you don't want help with the luggage, Signora Calvetti?"

Gianna pulled her single blue suitcase close, patting it affectionately with a gloved hand, and shook her head, silver curls shifting about her high cheekbones, feeling her diamond earrings swish. "Thank you, Enrico, but no. You might think me old and ill-abled, but I can carry this small thing myself."

Her driver flashed a starlight smile. "You don't look a day over forty, signora."

"Fifty-eight last month, and don't you forget it!" Calvetti chuckled softly, shaking her head and opening her own door before Enrico could hop out and open it for her as he was oft to do.

She pulled the suitcase behind and hefted it in one hand. No wheels, nor extending handle. Gianna refused to allow her life of creature comforts to extend so far it ruled out a little bit of healthy exercise. And with how often she traveled for work, there came plenty enough opportunities.

She hefted the small blue case and looked up, admiring her home. Though, perhaps most might call it an estate. Beige and cream siding mimicked seaside sandstone and the cobblestone walkway hinted at a bygone era beneath the railed terrace of the mansion which overlooked the tennis courts, private pool, and small guesthouse lodged up against an encircling marble wall.

Gianna waited as Enrico circled the car around the marble fountain roundabout and slowly made his way back up the drive toward the gates again. She watched him leave, the blue suitcase still gripped firmly in her gloved hand. The day be damned when she needed someone else to carry her own burdens.

She nodded resolutely, then turned toward the mansion. The place was a lot more spacious since the children had moved out and she'd gotten rid of that sorry excuse for a husband nearly three years ago.

She pressed her lips together and was approaching the doors of her home when a flicker of light caught her attention.

Gianna paused, frowning, one foot on the lowest step. She glanced over toward the guesthouse. Another flicker in the window… Hesitantly, she lowered the suitcase to the first step, releasing her grip and staring in the direction of the smaller guesthouse.

Not a flicker. A light. Difficult to spot due to the cast iron lampstand between the houses. As she'd passed from one side to the other, the light had flashed on either side of the metal protrusion. She wrinkled her nose—how had a light been left on?

The gardener?

She frowned deeper now, beginning to move in the direction of the guesthouse.

If that damned wastrel and his brood were squatting in the guesthouse again, she'd give him a scolding to be remembered. She wouldn't fire him—no, he'd been loyal to the family. But one must have boundaries in life.

She picked up her pace, leaving her blue suitcase behind her against the lowest marble step, gravel crunching beneath her shoes as she stalked toward the guesthouse.

"Hello?" she called out, feeling a mild annoyance rising.

She'd wanted to come home, relax in the hot tub, drink some wine, and doze off watching whatever new recommendation she could find in the romantic comedy genre. Now, though, beneath the glare of the moon, her own scowl intensified.

"Hello?" she called louder.

No answer.

Perhaps her children had been through. Though she'd made it clear that now they had their own places they ought to announce any visits. She sighed. They'd often been the most unruly of kids. Especially given how much attention the nannies had lavished.

She stalked toward the guesthouse, clearing her throat and approaching the front door.

The door had been left open too.

She paused now, hesitant. "Hello?" she called, voice louder. "Is anyone in there?"

Her eyes darted to the security cameras on the marble wall directed toward the driveway. Even from here, she could see the glinting blue lights of the alarm system up at the main house. She'd never bothered to place a system in the guesthouse. No one had lived here for years.

Now, though, she was beginning to regret this security blind spot.

She hesitated, swallowing and standing on the cobblestones facing the door. A slow shiver crept up her spine, and for a moment, she thought to turn back, to call the police…

A soft, moaning sound echoed from the guesthouse and she yelped instinctively, jolting back.

She watched as the open door widened further, the moaning coming from the creak of the hinges as the wind caught the frame. The light was on in the entryway. No one inside. No sign of a disturbance at all.

The gardener. He'd probably gone in to use the restroom.

She nodded to herself. Yes. The gardener. She shook her head once and then walked with purposeful strides back toward the open door. Just a quick look around to make sure nothing had been taken. Then she'd lock up and give the old family employee a stern talking to.

Boundaries. They mattered. She'd always known it.

Muttering to herself, though not quite falling into the crime of grumbling, she approached the open door. Business on one side, gardeners on the other… It would be nice to have a getaway at some point where others took care of her for a change. Maybe a hotel in the countryside. Or, perhaps, to her own summer home in Aquitaine.

She stepped into the house, carried by the relief of a future hope.

"Hello?" she said a final time, just in case.

But her query was met only by the whining hinges and the whispering breeze. The bright entryway light, which she'd spotted through the window, glared down at her, illuminating the small hallway. No sign of disturbance. No shoes by the door. Nothing.

She nodded resolutely and approached the light switch on the opposite side of the hall. As she moved into the guesthouse, up the hall, a floorboard creaked.

She frowned. The hinges of the door behind her groaned. She began to turn, hesitantly, one finger extended toward the light switch.

And then, the sudden sound of sprinting feet.

She yelped, whirling around. Rough hands shoved her hard against the wall. Her eyes widened and she tried to scream, but leather-clad fingers jammed into her mouth, holding back the sound. She tried to bite down, but the fingers jerked back, pushing her face against the cheap wallpaper.

Heavy breathing, a soft growl. And then something around her throat. She choked, gasping, trying to yank free. A shadow—a strong shadow—was behind her, pushing hard, holding her in place. She gasped, strangling, trying to scream but finding her breath was now in short supply.

It felt like… beads around her neck? A single black emblem, hard to discern, dangled from the edge of a gloved hand, attached to whatever was strangling her. She stared, her eyes bulging, fixated on the dangling ebony as the strange beads tightened on her throat.

A hoarse voice whispered in her ear. "Did you miss me?"

And then, darkness came calling.

## CHAPTER TWO

"I don't know," Adele murmured softly, shaking her head.

"My uncle spoke highly of you," said a soft voice near the fireplace. "Is there anything he might have told you?"

Adele's lips felt numb and she brushed her blonde hair from her eyes, her gaze hazy as it moved from the cold fireplace up to where Brigitte Henry watched her. She'd never met Robert's niece before the funeral. Now with it over, she wasn't sure she ever wanted to see the young woman again. Brigitte had the same eyes as her uncle, oddly solemn and mischievous all at once. A searching, knowing gaze. An exposing gaze.

And Adele *felt* exposed, standing in the study of her old mentor's mansion, before a cold fireplace, one hand braced against a leather chair.

"I don't mean to trouble you," murmured Brigitte, attempting a smile, but then seemingly deciding this wouldn't help matters, so she left it and just watched Adele. "Only, yesterday, when I asked if you'd be willing to help settle some of this, I didn't realize Uncle might have changed the will."

Adele winced, shrugging again. "I really don't know. I'm very sorry."

Brigitte sighed, turning to face a pile of cardboard boxes where some of Robert's books had been stowed. Adele had overseen this task personally. The books had been Robert's favorites. Very few things were valued by the man as much, and she was determined to see them packed properly.

Adele felt her fingers against the leather spine of another tome. Some third volume in a historical treatment of the Roman Empire. She glanced down at the nearly indeterminable golden scrawl on the front of the cover and tried her best to smile.

She couldn't manage it, though.

What was the point of memories without the source of them? It felt ike warming in the sparks of an already doused fire.

"Hmm?" Adele said, looking away from the book toward Brigitte. "Sorry, what was that?"

Robert's niece did smile this time—a soft, sad smile. "The lawyer is talking with my father in the other room," she repeated. "Did you want to join us? Amendment or not, you're in the original will."

Adele breathed slowly, closing her eyes in thought. Robert had left her something?

Did she deserve it?

Did it matter?

She felt a flash of guilt realizing how very little she wanted anything to do with tokens or heirlooms, sentimental or otherwise. Yesterday, the funeral had been difficult enough. She hadn't allowed herself to cry. She'd refused.

Tears wouldn't bring him back. Tears wouldn't bring him justice.

She glanced out the window, into the garden beyond, her eyes tracing the single marble statue of the angel. The marble features had been washed with a hose now, clearing the mud from the angel's eyes. She shivered, remembering that night three weeks ago.

Remembering how she'd found Robert on the floor.

He'd died horribly.

"I… I… sorry," she said, reflexively. "I just… I'll be there in a moment if you don't mind. Just…"

Brigitte hesitated, one foot turned toward the open kitchen, where Adele could hear voices as the estate details were being settled by lawyers and relatives. "Thank you," Brigitte said at last, quietly.

Adele frowned. "For what?"

"I know how much Uncle cared for you… We, well, when we moved—three hours away and, well, just… I didn't visit as much as I would have liked." Brigitte winced, shaking her head. "I know he cared for you."

"I moved too," Adele said softly. "And not just east of Paris." She thought of her sojourn to California, working for the FBI. It seemed a lifetime ago now. She remembered Robert's many letters, his invitations to visit. It had taken her years to summon the courage to return.

Years she'd left behind. Years where she could have spent time with him.

Years she might have used to find the bastard who'd done it.

She felt another cold prickle along her back and glanced out the window again.

He was out there still… somewhere, biding his time. Her mother's killer had targeted Robert because of her. That much was obvious now.

She hadn't seen it coming. Maybe she hadn't wanted to. What sort of investigator missed something this obvious? Robert had been tortured to death because of her. Because she'd been too slow…

She closed her eyes, still facing the window. Perhaps the mud splashed in the marble angel's eyes had been a mercy. See no evil?

And yet Adele hadn't been afforded that same courtesy. She'd seen again and again what the man they called the Spade Killer had done. Her mother, now Robert… His other victims had fared just as horribly.

Worst of all, she knew the killer was still nearby… probably even in Paris. But she didn't know how to find him. She had no leads. Anyone close to her was in danger—that much was obvious. A task force of a sort had been assembled back at the DGSI—at least, so she'd been told. Of course, she'd been left out of the line-up as well as anyone connected to her. Probably good, anyway. When the task force inevitably failed to turn up anything new, at least she wouldn't know the source of the inevitable failure. The Spade Killer was a ghost. She'd gone through those files more than anyone, gone over them again and again. Everything they had on the murderer.

Nothing new. Nothing new *ever* came up. They were stuck. The path forward was murky at best, invisible at worst.

Even at this thought, she took a hesitant step away from Brigitte, more reaction than anything. She thought of how she'd treated John at the funeral yesterday. He'd tried to talk with her twice, and both times she'd given him the cold shoulder. It was for his own good. At least, that's what she wanted to believe.

She remembered the last text message to her father. *Lie low for now. Lock your doors. Get a patrol car to watch your house.*

At least in Germany, her father might be afforded some level of safety. But that was no guarantee where the Spade Killer was concerned. She'd considered asking Renee to do the same, but she'd known John would never comply with such a directive.

"Adele?" Brigitte's voice poked through her overcast thoughts. "We're just sorting the last details out. Mr. Ozil is asking for you."

"The lawyer? I'll… be right there. You go on. Just finishing up."

Robert's niece nodded politely, dipping her head, then she turned, moving behind the red leather chair, past the cold fireplace and into the kitchen.

Adele slowly lowered the leather-bound book into one of the boxes, setting it neatly on top of its cousin volumes. She looked toward the open kitchen doorway, listening to the soft murmur of voices.

She didn't deserve anything Robert had left her. She'd failed him to the point of death.

She felt a flash of disgust. No… She needed out.

Trying to move as quietly as possible, Adele headed in the opposite direction of the kitchen doorway, moving toward the hall that led to the front door. As she left, hastening with each haunted step through the familiar mansion hall, her phone began to buzz.

Adele frowned, glancing down.

But even as she picked it up, it rang along with the vibration. Wrinkling her nose, she stared at the device.

Two incoming calls.

She blinked in surprise.

Two calls simultaneously, both from numbers she recognized. The first, from Agent Leoni—the Italian she'd grown fond of over the last few months. She pictured the handsome agent's features in her mind—his perfectly sculpted nose and Superman curl of dark hair against his forehead. She felt tempted to smile, staring at the buzzing number.

Did she want to talk to him, though?

*Everyone close to you is in danger,* whispered a small voice in her mind. *Everyone who draws near will die!*

She shivered and instantly hung up on the call from Leoni. No… Not now. That would have to wait. Still, the second phone call was a welcome one. Another number she knew.

Work.

With a flooding sense of strange relief, she pushed out the front door, stepping into the small, gated garden and moving past the marble angel with its pristine features. With a rasping voice, Adele answered, "Adele."

"Agent Sharp?" said the familiar, growling tone of Executive Foucault, her boss at the DGSI. "Have a second?"

"Yes, sir," she said, quickly. "A case?" She winced at how eager she must have sounded.

She continued toward the black gate outside Robert's mansion and pushed out onto the street.

"No rush," Foucault said, his expression indeterminable over the call. "How are you feeling?"

"Sir, do you have a case for me?"

"Answer my question first."

"Feeling, sir?"

"Dammit, Sharp, I know you and Henry were close. Are you up fo a—"

"Yes sir," she said quickly, her back to the hedge encircling Robert's home. "Very much so, sir."

Executive Foucault paused on the other end and Adele waited on tenterhooks, hoping she'd sounded convincing enough. She couldn't continue like this. From the funeral to estate management and back to her apartment. It had been weeks since the death. She was an investigator, a bloodhound. It felt like she'd been kenneled against her will. Plus, she needed a distraction. Anything to get her mind off the dark thoughts, the swirling, looping anxiety.

"Am I going to regret this, Sharp?"

"No sir. Definitely not. I'm tip-top of my game, sir."

"Tip-top? Hmm?"

Adele coughed delicately. "The funeral was yesterday, sir. I've dealt with it."

This, she knew, was a lie. But she couldn't remain like a dinghy in a stormy sea with nothing to do, nowhere to go.

Foucault sighed on the other end. "All right. I'm taking your word on this one, Sharp. But I'm warning you, if I get a whiff that your head isn't on straight—"

"Straight as a pin, sir."

"Right. Well, in that case, yes, Agent Sharp. I have a case. And it's a strange one."

# CHAPTER THREE

Adele leaned back in her work sedan, eyes closed, feet on the dashboard where she'd parked around the corner from Robert's estate. Her full attention now was directed toward the buzzing sound coming from her cell phone's speaker.

"Both of them wealthy, sir?"

"Yes, and both in their fifties."

"Strangled, you say?"

"That's what it looks like. We're waiting for the full report, but it seems straightforward enough."

Adele lowered her feet from the dash, her eyes still closed, as she considered this. "Two wealthy women, both in their fifties, killed within three days of each other. By strangulation. Is that about it?"

"That's what it looks like."

"And we're sure they're connected?"

"Again, we're not sure, but that's what it looks like. If I had all the answers, I wouldn't be calling you. Besides, we're a bit short staffed over here at the moment."

"Oh, why?"

An awkward pause. And she realized with a sickening jolt. "Oh," she said, dully. "The task force, right? How are things on that front?"

Foucault sniffed. "I'll keep you informed of any developments."

Adele didn't say it, but she knew this was boss code for *we've got shit all.* For a moment, she felt another sickening thought. Was this just a ploy to get her out of the way, to prevent her from interfering with the investigation? She closed her eyes at the thought, shaking her head.

"Well, Sharp, are you in?"

She swallowed back the rising tide of nerves, focusing on the simple need for a distraction more than anything right now. "Of course. Just, sir, the UK—I haven't worked a case there in a while."

"But you have in Italy. I'm sure your Interpol connections will pay off. I'm simply the liaison here, Agent Sharp. The initial murder, the one in the UK, seems like the killer's first. But now, the same MO in Italy three days later suggests he's picking up the pace."

"And we're sure it's the same MO?"

"Yes. The ligature marks from the strangulation are… well, here, this is what the coroner in London said, and I quote: 'peculiar and bizarre.'"

"How so?"

"Coroners in both places say it looks like some sort of beaded material was used. Not exactly a strangulation weapon of choice. Suggesting—"

"The same killer."

"Exactly. Well, final chance, Sharp. Are you in? If these kills are connected, we have a problem. The killer avoided two security systems, managed to travel internationally, and had the fitness and strength to kill two women with his hands. We need you focused if you're in."

Adele opened her eyes, staring out the windshield at the gray skies above Paris, frowning over the cars parked in front of her along the sidewalk. The city felt darker now. The clouds above grayer, the sunlight dimmer. She nodded, not that he could see, and said, "Yes sir. I'm in. Very much so. Just…"

"Just what?" He sounded suspicious now.

Quickly she said, "Just if possible, could I have another partner for this one?"

"You don't wish to work with Agent Renee?"

"Not this time, sir."

"Did something happen—"

"No. Nothing. Just, well, sir, it's two wealthy women."

"So? Adele, I told you if you didn't think you could handle—"

"I can!" she protested quickly, feeling her stomach twist. She couldn't afford to lose this case, not now. If Foucault took it from her because he suspected her of being too emotionally distraught, she wasn't sure how she'd survive another three weeks of cabin fever and listlessness. She *needed* this case, but she also couldn't work with John. Anyone close to her… Everyone was in danger. She needed a partner who could take care of themselves, and who even the most neutral onlooker wouldn't suspect of harboring any sort of fondness for Adele. Besides… the person she had in mind also could bring a unique insight into this particular case.

"It's nothing like that, sir," she pressed. "I figured I could benefit from someone in the victim's age group. Someone who might be able to think like them."

Foucault didn't say anything at first and Adele looked at the phone, making sure she hadn't lost the connection.

"Sir?" she ventured.

"You want another partner in the victim's age group…"

"Yes sir." Adele coughed and blinked. "How about Agent Sophie Paige, sir?" She winced, waiting. Sophie Paige *loathed* Adele, ever since an incident when Adele had last worked at the DGSI, years ago. She'd reported missing evidence, which Paige had taken to protect her then-husband. Adele hadn't known who'd taken the evidence at the time. In the end, all parties had been cleared of wrongdoing, and Foucault had gone to bat for Agent Paige.

It was still something of a mystery why the Executive was so protective of Agent Paige. Some whispered infidelity, others thought blackmail. Adele wasn't so sure, though.

Either way, Paige hated Adele's guts. Even the Spade Killer wouldn't be stupid enough to think Sophie Paige was a friend or a worthwhile target. In a strange twist, Sophie's hatred of Adele would keep her safe. It had to. Adele couldn't think of any other options.

"You're sure?" said Foucault. And even the Executive, who knew the extent of the division between the older and younger agent, couldn't keep the note of surprise from his tone.

"Yes sir, very sure. Agent Paige will be perfect on this case."

"All right, Adele. I'm giving you a bit of leeway on this one. Remember, though, even a *whiff* of baggage, and I'm pulling you."

"Got it."

"I mean it. I know you lost someone, Sharp. But our job can't afford distractions. Already, two women have been killed in their homes. Mothers, both of them. The killer is escalating. Two dead in three days."

Adele bit her lower lip. "I understand, sir. If another body drops, it's on me."

"Let's just make sure that doesn't happen. You'd best get going now. I'll have Agent Paige meet you at the airport with the tickets and itinerary. Good luck, Agent Sharp. Catch this bastard before he kills again."

***

Adele wasn't quite sure where to look. For one, on her open laptop which rested against the lowered tray, she had the gruesome crime scene photos. On the other, she could feel the ghoulish glances Sophie Paige kept shooting in her direction where she sat next to Adele in the aisle seat.

Sophie Paige was middle-aged with silver hair and severe features like a nun from the fifties, or a stern substitute teacher. She was also one of the more experienced DGSI agents in the branch.

Their elbows had brushed once, in the first few minutes of the flight, during take-off, and Adele had practically banged her head against the window, trying to distance herself.

Now, Agent Paige and Adele had settled into a sort of game of cat and mouse with their elbows and the shared armrest. Each of them doing their best to avoid any sort of physical contact with the other, despite the crowded nature of the airplane's seating.

The twin nozzles of air above were in opposite postures. Adele had turned hers on, which had promptly seen Agent Paige turn hers completely off. Adele's reading light was on, which meant Paige's was off. Adele's laptop was open, her tray table down, which meant Paige was now scrolling through her phone, leaning back and shooting reproachful glances toward the younger woman.

"Well?" Paige said, gruffly, breaking a silence that had lasted an impressive five minutes this time. "Anything?"

Adele blinked a few times, wincing, feeling how dry her eyes were from the steady nozzle spray of air conditioning. Then again, she refused to turn it off and give Paige the satisfaction. So, determinedly tilting her head down to avoid the brunt of the air nozzle, she refocused on the crime scene photos once more.

"Beads?" Adele murmured, zooming in on the ligature marks of the first victim's neck. She winced at the red and purplish bruising around the throat.

"Why would a killer use beads?" Paige asked, her tone icy.

"Don't know. Any guesses?"

"No."

"Do you see anything?"

Paige sighed, but then scrolled through her phone again. She tapped the device with a straight, manicured finger sans polish. "Might be pearls," she said. "Both of them are wealthy. Seems like the sort of thing people in their income brackets might use."

"Pearls? I didn't think of that. Do you think they're being targeted for theft?"

"I don't know, Agent Sharp. It's a theory."

Adele pursed her lips, feeling a strange sense of ease at the clear disdain emanating from Paige. Clearly, old grudges still carried weight where the senior DGSI operative was concerned.

"Let me ask you another thing," Paige said.

Adele looked over now, meeting the middle-aged woman's severe gaze. Such a strange thought that a woman like this had raised five children of her own, while simultaneously having a successful career with the DGSI. From all the stories she'd heard, Paige was an excellent mother. Which only made her hatred for Adele all the more odd.

"Yes?" Adele said.

"Foucault mentioned you requested me, specifically."

"I—yes."

"Why? It's no secret that…"

"You don't like me?"

"You don't like me either."

"I don't have a problem with you, Agent Paige." This was actually true. Adele sometimes felt uneasy around the other agent, but from everything she knew, Paige was a capable crime-solver.

Sophie snorted. "Why?"

Adele hesitated, shrugging. "I felt like you could bring something to the case."

"Foucault said it was because you think I'm old. Like the victims."

Adele winced. "I didn't say that."

"That's what Foucault said." Paige turned back to her phone now, scowling as she scrolled through the coroner's initial report.

Adele sighed, returning her attention to her laptop and settling in for a long flight, pressed tight against the iciest of shoulders. The pictures showed the means of murder. But if they wanted to nab this guy before he murdered again, she needed to see the crime scene itself.

What sort of killer avoided security systems, crept into a guesthouse to strangle a wealthy woman? A clever man, for one. A vicious man. A strong one—to be able to choke life from a body. What else, though? What specific sort of sickness had motivated the bastard?

She supposed she'd have to wait and see the scene of the crime before reaching a conclusion.

# CHAPTER FOUR

Adele whistled softly as the taxi pulled up the driveway, through the enormous estate's open gateway. Ahead, in the nighttime glow, the mansion cast against the outline of Milan seemed a looming, regal thing. Her eyes darted from the open terrace on the third floor, to the metal mesh of the tennis court next to the natural pond-shaped private pool. The trees themselves, scattered throughout the estate, looked a hundred years old.

The trip from the Malpensa Airport had reminded her of Agent Christopher Leoni again. She'd been tempted to call, but once more had held back. Everyone was in danger when near her. Everyone she felt a fondness toward was inevitably put in harm's way. Which, she supposed, was why having Agent Paige along, despite the scalding glances and scornful looks, was a blessing in disguise.

The taxi driver pulled past the two officers guarding the gateway. Adele flashed her credentials through the open window and said, "DGSI with Interpol," and the Italian police waved her through.

As they trundled slowly up the long drive toward the giant mansion and its smaller guesthouse, Adele felt a rising sense of anticipation.

Her stomach twisted and for a moment she frowned, glancing off out the window and watching the neat rows of small conifers pass by. She shifted uncomfortably, putting a hand to her stomach and pressing against the odd, nearly painful sensation.

Sophie Paige didn't even glance over, preferring to bark directives at their driver. As they neared the old mansion and the location of the second victim's home, Adele realized with a start what she was feeling.

Stage fright.

She blinked in surprise. It had been years since she'd faced this particular demon before stepping onto a crime scene. Anxiety, fear, worry all came as part of the job, but this sensation now had only been an issue when she'd first started at the DGSI.

But the nearer they got to the roundabout at the end of the drive, the more her stomach twisted and churned. She kept her hand against her abdomen, pressing as if to hold back the rising tide of unease. She could feel her breaths coming in quick patterns and consciously forced herself to inhale for four seconds, hold it for four, then exhale for four more.

The vehicle skidded to a halt, and by the guesthouse Adele spotted more Italian police lingering on the steps, or moving in and out of the smaller home.

"You coming?" Paige grunted, one leg already through her open door.

Adele inhaled once more, this time holding the breath and feeling the twisting, unnerving sensation spread. What was happening?

An image flashed across her mind.

The crumpled, frail form of her old mentor, lying in a pool of crimson across from a red leather chair near a cooled fireplace. She shivered, closing and opening her eyes like the lens on a camera.

She'd known Robert's death had affected her. But this was her first case back on the job. She couldn't fall apart, not now. A little bit of unease, a little bit of nervousness was bound to happen. She tried not to let the frustration show and pushed open her own side of the taxi and slid out onto the cobblestone drive.

"Coming," she murmured, taking a breath of cool evening air outside Milan.

Sophie Paige was already striding purposefully across the drive, toward the guesthouse and the gathered *polizia*. Adele adjusted her sleeves, brushing a length of blonde hair behind one ear, and then followed close behind, inhaling four seconds, holding, exhaling four seconds as she walked.

"Agent Paige," said a voice from the doorway of the guesthouse. "And Agent Sharp, I presume?"

A rail thin man with a bony face and spectacles was standing in the door, looking down at his phone and then glancing up at each of them in turn as if comparing them to some picture.

"Agent Mariano," Paige called, taking the lead as Adele tried to catch up.

"Yes, glad to meet you," the ghoulish-looking man said, his French discernible, but clouded by a thick Italian accent.

Paige wrinkled her nose and came to a halt at the base of the stairs in front of the small guesthouse. A couple of *polizia* moved past her, hefting twin forensic bags and murmuring beneath their breaths.

Adele's Italian wasn't up to scratch, but she caught a couple of words. "…Blind spot…" and "… tonight…"

The two forensic investigators moved toward the main mansion, still muttering and ignoring the French agents entirely.

Agent Mariano tapped a bony finger against his pale lips, still outlined in the open doorway as he was and cleared his throat. "Signora Paige," he said, glancing from his phone to the older woman once more. "I was told you'd be arriving an hour—"

"Agent," Sophie interrupted.

"*Mi scusi?*"

"Agent Paige is fine, Agent Mariano," she said, testily. "And yes, our flight was briefly delayed."

"Apologies," Adele added over Sophie's shoulder.

The older woman ignored this input and said, still gruff, "What do we know about the victim?"

Mariano raised a crooked eyebrow, stretching his pale skin in strange ways, but then crossed his thin arms across his bony chest and, still standing upright in the doorway, he said, "Signora Gianna Calvetti was on the board of directors for L&L Italia."

"What's that?" Adele asked.

The ghoulish-faced man's gaze shifted slowly like a strand of moonlight in a graveyard, moving from Paige to Adele. "How you say… manufacturing. Industry manufacturing."

"An Italian manufacturing company?" Adele said, her own voice shaky in her ears, her stomach still twisting. She fought the urge to flinch, though, and through tight teeth, pressed. "So if she was on the board of directors of this company, might that have played in the motives of the killing?"

The Italian agent blinked once, thick eyelids falling over bulging eyes. "Possible."

Paige cleared her throat, stepping forward and, perhaps coincidentally, directly in front of Adele, regaining Mariano's line of sight. "I can't help but notice the security cameras," Paige said, waving a hand toward the mansion and then toward a couple of fixtures Adele had also spotted on the encircling wall behind the guesthouse. "Do we have the film?"

"*Si.* However, nothing was caught. The killer avoided security cameras. State-of-the-art security system, too. Not a cheap one. And yet, the murderer was careful to avoid them entirely."

Adele frowned, glancing back at the mansion, toward the lenses on the gates. She clicked her tongue, and then, allowing Sophie to stand in front of her regardless, she said, "Maybe that's why he chose the guesthouse. There are no blind spots leading up to the mansion, but over here…"

"Yes," Paige interrupted. "I was going to say the same thing. Over here, there seems to be less security."

"Indeed," replied the Italian. He stepped back, extending an arm toward the open hall. "The deed was done just here. The house-cleaners found the body and called it in—just against the wall. Obviously, the corpse is now at the morgue, but, see what you will, my French colleagues."

The man continued gesturing with a wave toward the hall and Adele stepped past Paige and moved up the stairs first. Sidling along Agent Mariano, she caught a whiff of what smelled like moth balls and urinal kegs.

She winced, but then peered along the small, cramped hallway. No sign of blood, no sign of any murder. Just an empty hall with cheap wallpaper.

"Just there?" Adele asked, picturing the crime scene photos in her mind.

Again, her stomach twisted and again she breathed slowly, waiting for the Italian's response. Paige waited on the drive, watching from the base of the stairs.

"*Si*, signora. Just there. No cameras inside the guesthouse, though."

Adele glanced back, wrinkling her nose at another whiff of mothballs. The middle-aged, pallid Italian watched her from thick-lidded eyes.

"The killer did his homework," she said.

"*Si*."

"He knew about the security system. Knew the cameras. Means he cased the joint before."

Mariano nodded once, his head above his black suit bobbing like a pale buoy in dark water. "We have discussed such possibilities with Signora Calvetti's eldest daughter." He nodded toward the mansion. "She is still answering questions up at the house."

Adele looked back, then glanced at Paige. She held the older agent's hostile gaze for a moment and said, "Think we should talk to her next?"

Paige's tongue probed the inside of her cheek, but then she nodded stiffly.

"Say, signoras, er *agents*," Mariano amended at another look from Paige. "Is this true what I hear—a serial killer?"

Adele began to answer, but Paige interrupted. "We can't confirm or deny at this point. We're looking into all possibilities."

"But there was another murder. In London, no?"

Adele didn't even bother to answer this time, once more allowing Paige to take the lead. "A similar murder, yes. Matching ligature marks, but we can't assume anything more than a coincidence at this point."

Adele staved off a slight frown at this. She wasn't so sure in this regard, but also didn't see the point in objecting, and so she moved past Mariano, down the steps again, and toward the large mansion.

If it was a serial killer, it meant he'd already claimed two victims. Had he stalked them before making his first kill? How many victims did he have planned?

Two already… or two disconnected cases?

Her stomach twisted and she winced against the physical bout of nerves.

Could she trust her instincts on this one at all? Had Robert's death really taken so much out of her? He'd been her mentor, her instructor. And the Spade Killer had hunted him anyway. If anyone should have seen the knife in the dark, it would have been Robert.

And now, Adele felt alone, out in the cold, driving blind on a highway in a blizzard. She could only hope she didn't go careening into anything too important while fumbling around in the dark.

A serial killer. Had to be, yes? Or was she now biased?

She swallowed back her nerves and picked up her pace, her shoes clicking against the cobblestones as she hastened toward the mansion.

The eldest daughter would have answers. She would have to. On this case, Adele had a niggling suspicion that she would need all the help she could get. One body, two bodies… three? More?

# CHAPTER FIVE

Adele settled slowly at the ornate, oak dining room table beneath a miniature chandelier likely intended to convey unpretentious, but rather settling for something closer akin to watchful and rigid.

The many crystal baubles reflected the bright yellow light stretching from within the confines of the bulbs and cast shimmering patterns across the lacquered surface of the antique table.

A round woman with pleasant eyes and a blue turtleneck sat across the table, small hands folded daintily over each other, her rosy cheeks flushed in the bright light and due, in no small part, to the series of questions she'd endured over the last half hour.

Now, as Adele took in the dining room, she cleared her throat politely, glancing from the woman to the two police officers who were rising from their seats nearest her.

"Anita?" Adele asked, cautiously, her voice inquisitory.

Agent Paige crowded in behind Adele, offering no small talk and moving directly toward the table. "Hello, Ms. Calvetti," she said in accented English. "I was told you can speak *inglese*. Yes?"

Anita Calvetti, the eldest daughter of the deceased, glanced uncertainly from the Italian detectives who were now scraping past Paige, along an ornate bookcase and moving back into the hall. Her eyes then darted to Adele and Agent Paige.

"I… yes," she said, with no trace of an accent. "I studied in America. Who are you?"

"DGSI," Paige said, softly. To Adele's surprise, the gruff, older agent's voice was gentler now. And one of her neatly manicured hands reached out, covering half the distance from where she'd sat toward where Calvetti's hands were still wringing each other. Paige stopped though, before quite making contact, allowing the gesture to simply linger as a placating one.

Adele settled into the cushioned, ornate chair at the head of the table, beneath the chandelier and facing Anita's nervous form. The victim's daughter was quite pretty, with pure black hair and dark, intelligent eyes.

"I don't know what DGSI is," said Anita, frowning. "I just finished speaking with the police."

"We're not Italian," Paige said, still surprisingly gentle. "Sorry for the inconvenience."

"DGSI is French," Adele supplied.

"Oh… Well. Okay then. How can I help you?"

"Would you like a glass of water?" Paige asked. "I know how exhausting these things can be."

"I—actually, yes. Water would be great."

Paige nodded, rising to her feet and moving around the table. "Kitchen this way?" she asked, pointing toward a side door.

"Last room on the left," Anita mumbled, still staring at her wringing hands. The younger woman shook her head slowly as Paige hurried from the room, now leaving Adele and Anita seated across from each other, facing opposite sides of the enormous oak table.

Adele closed her eyes a moment, trying to place her thoughts. They weren't so distant from Anita's, she imagined. The woman couldn't have been much past her twenties. The same age Adele had been when…

When what?

When it had all collapsed.

"I'm very sorry for your loss," Adele said, feeling some of her nerves fading to something akin to a sense of familiarity.

"Thank you, Agent…"

"Adele. You can call me Adele."

"Yes. Well, thank you. I'd be lying if I told you I was very close with my mother. She was a hard woman. Brave, but hard." Anita sighed again, glancing off at the bookcase with reflective glass doors.

"I see. And did she have any enemies you can think of? Anyone who might…"

"Want to strangle her to death? My mother wasn't a soft woman, Agent Adele."

"Just Adele is fine."

"All right, Adele. My mother had a reputation of being ruthless in the board room. She was cutthroat to get there." Anita shrugged.

"So you're saying there were many who might have a motive?"

"Yes. I guess I am saying that."

"Anyone in particular you can think of?"

Anita chewed the bottom of her lip, glancing off for a moment and sighing to herself. Her short-cut, dark hair shifted as her eyes fixated once more on Adele. "I suppose the man she replaced on the board of directors didn't think too fondly of her."

"She took someone's job?"

"The exact words he used, I believe, before security escorted him out was, 'you stupid, ugly bitch, I'll make you pay.'" Anita bobbed her head once, showing no emotional reaction to the harsh words.

"He said that?" Adele didn't let her own thoughts show. Clearly, however, the victim was a woman who knew how to raise tempers.

"Ask anyone at that meeting. He wasn't happy when they voted him out and my mother in. She was behind it, of course. Like I said, cutthroat."

"You sound impressed."

Anita sighed again, smiling softly and staring at the back of her soft fingers. "Impressed? Maybe a bit. Angry… that too. My mother wasn't a very understanding woman either."

"Anyone else you can think of?" Adele asked, wincing sympathetically, but pressing the line of questioning."

"My father, I suppose."

Adele blinked, but before she could continue, Agent Paige returned, carrying a glass of water and placing it in front of the young woman. Anita accepted with a grateful nod and sipped from the glass, sighing in contentment before placing it on the table next to a coaster.

She stared at where the cool glass met the old antique before looking up again. "Will that be all?" she said. "I'm quite tired."

"One last thing," Adele said, grateful Paige allowed her to continue without interruption. "Your father had a grudge against your mother. Any reason in particular?"

"They're divorced now," Anita said, following another sip. She swallowed. "I guess passion was often a mark of their relationship. Never did one hear such loud altercations when they were angry, nor such emotional reunions when they made up."

"But it did end?"

"Yes. Divorced, like I said. Probably for the best…" Anita trailed off, frowning against what seemed a rehearsed line. "Maybe not the best anymore. But my father didn't love my mother. Spoke harshly of her since…" She trailed off again, blinking as if suddenly realizing what she was saying. She stammered, looking quickly from Adele to Sophie, "Not that I think he did anything. No, sorry. I was just processing. Both of them were quite angry with each other. But I never felt like they might…" She swallowed. "Harm anyone."

"Right," said Adele. To her surprise, facing across the table and watching Anita, she felt some of the unease from earlier had melted like ice in sunshine. She knew what it was to lose a mother at that age. But it didn't sound like Signora Calvetti was anything like Elise Romei. Adele's own mother had been her best friend. A kind, compassionate woman. Not cutthroat in any way.

She wondered if it was easier or harder to have lost someone she loved, rather than someone she'd only respected.

Adele listened as Agent Paige asked another question, but she couldn't quite make out the words. She just watched, not quite seeing. Listened, not quite hearing, her own mind plagued with memories, images… *Bleeding, bleeding…*

And now, Robert gone too.

Paige patted Anita on the back of the hand, and Adele blinked, focusing once more and realizing she was being addressed.

"Pardon?" Adele said, looking at Paige.

The older Frenchwoman frowned slightly but said, "I think we best go, yes? Ms. Calvetti has been through a lot."

Adele released a breath but nodded quickly. "Right. Yes. Thank you, Anita, for your time."

The two agents pushed slowly up. Adele felt a sense of disappointment they hadn't managed to exact any further information. She supposed the next stop would be the coroner. Hopefully that way—

"How dare you!" a voice suddenly erupted from behind them.

All three figures in the dining room spun around, eyes widened instinctively and fixating on the man standing in the door. He had a thick finger jutting into the room and his eyes blazed with fury. "You have no right! None!" he yelled. He stamped his foot hard against the floor, his face reddening even further, and for a moment, Adele thought he might very well explode.

# CHAPTER SIX

Adele watched as Agent Paige's hand darted to her sidearm, but she didn't draw, her eyes narrowed on the man in the doorway. Continuing in broken English, the man made himself heard with increasing gusto. "No right! How dare speak me daughter without me? How dare!" Spittle actually flung from his lips, speckling the magnificent oak table. He wagged a finger around, nearly as round as a polish sausage.

Anita winced as the man screamed, trying—it seemed to Adele—to sink further into her chair and hide beneath the table.

At last, though, she groaned softly and got to her feet, interrupting the diatribe.

"It's fine, Dad," she said, raising her voice. Then hurriedly she rattled off something in Italian.

The man paused long enough to draw a deep, gulping breath, his cheeks reddened and his chest protruding like some strutting hen. He wore muttonchops of silver and gray, and had a wobbly chin that moved when he spoke.

He turned to his daughter, shaking his red face adamantly, and replying in a burst of Italian himself.

The daughter replied again, then, with an apologetic wince, switched back to English. "I am sorry, Agent Adele, but this is my father. He is not pleased you have spoken with me."

Adele frowned at the man in the doorway. "I'd gathered as much," she said. "Excuse me, Mr. Calvetti," she began, but she didn't make it far.

"Signore Herrera," he snapped, returning to English. "You little French girl, why speak to me daughter?"

Adele blinked, her eyes narrowing slightly. She'd long grown accustomed to blustering men throwing her gender back in her face as some sort of cudgel. Normally, she knew how to maintain her calm. She'd dealt with such barbs over the course of her career on countless occasions. The criminal elements, international or otherwise, often broke windows but weren't exactly shattering glass ceilings.

Now, though, as she paused, staring at the red-faced man, she could feel her own temper rising. Her lips formed a thin, firm line. "Signore

Herrera," she said, slowly trying to keep her rising anger in check. "I understand your daughter is an adult. She can speak for herself, yes?"

She glanced toward Anita, who nodded quickly but looked nervously at her father as she did.

"No!" Herrera snapped, wagging his finger now and stepping forward so he was pointing the offending digit beneath her nose. "No!" he repeated, seemingly stuck on one of the few English words he'd mastered. "This is no. My daughter speak not to you! Horrible, horrible French girl."

Another lance of rising anger jolted through Adele. She tried to count to ten in her head, calming herself as best she could.

"You leave her alone. Anita, come—we go!"

"Hang on," Agent Paige called out. "We'll say when you can leave."

The man turned to Sophie now too, sniffing dismissively and shaking his red face. "No," he said, returning to familiar lingual territory. "I think no. Come, Anita."

The round, pretty-faced girl winced, glancing from her father's beckoning fingers toward Adele and Agent Paige. Though Anita appeared in her mid-twenties, she seemed little more than a chastised child under her father's fury.

Again, Adele could feel her own temper rising… Counting to eight… nine… ten…

The counting was supposed to reduce one's temper, but she could only feel her fury rising all the more at the stupid look on that red face and behind those beady little eyes. Besides, hadn't Anita let slip her father's loathing for his wife? Divorced three years ago, no love lost. Now, Mrs. Calvetti was dead.

And if anything Signore Herrera didn't seem much broken up about it.

"Come!" Herrera called with a final stomp of his foot.

"No," Adele said, rising from her seat now and facing the Italian. "You wait right there," she said, finding her own voice, losing some of the normally calm facade she'd grown so accustomed to displaying in such volatile conversations.

The man blinked at her in surprise, likely ill accustomed to anyone talking back beneath his tidal wave of personality.

"You're the victim's ex-husband, yes?" Adele said, speaking slowly so he could track the English.

"No!" he cried, shaking his finger.

"He is," Anita sighed, softly.

Her father's ire rounded on his daughter and he yelled something in Italian which this time went ignored.

"I'd like to know what you were doing last night," Adele said firmly. "When did you find out about your wife's murder?"

"Ex!"

"Excuse me?"

"Ex-wife," snapped Herrera, still puffing his chest.

Part of Adele wanted nothing more than to take a large pin and pop him like a balloon. She could feel her anger still swelling and was breathing heavily now as if after a long jog. She'd been able to get morning runs in most days during the weeks leading up to Robert's funeral, but now she felt trapped, stuck in place as if glued to the floor.

"Right," she amended, her tone harsher than she might have liked. "Ex-wife. Where were you?"

"Excuse me?"

"Where were you last night. It's a simple question, sir. I'm afraid if you don't have an answer, we can—"

"Stupid girl," he snapped. "Do you know who me are? Hmm?"

"*Who I am*, Dad," Anita said, sighing. "She's an agent with the DGSI. Just answer her."

Adele took a step forward, standing nearly chin to chin with the short man. Her own eyes narrowed, meeting his beady gaze. He didn't seem to have the good sense to step back though, and smelled of an entire bottle of expensive cologne. Her eyes began watering at such proximity to the noxious odor and she glanced aside, inhaling deeply through her nose for the simple benefit of fresh air.

"I don't know who you are," Adele said, growling now. "I don't care." She jammed a finger into his chest and the man suddenly yelped as if he'd been stabbed. He held his chest, making a big show of reeling back and thumping against the opposite wall. His eyes widened in horror. "Attack!" he screamed. "Assault! *Polizia!*"

"Shut up," Adele snapped. "Answer my question or I'll lug your fat ass to a jail cell for a couple of days and then maybe you'll figure out how to answer a simple question."

The moment the spiel fell from her lips, she blinked in surprise at the content of her own words. She could feel Sophie Paige watching her now, off to the side. She noted Anita shift uncomfortably, one hand pressed against her mouth as if trying to hide a gasp of surprise or a creeping smile.

Mr. Herrera though, looked like he'd been slapped. He gaped at her a moment, meeting her eyes as if giving her a chance to take it all back.

But Adele was in too deep now. Even without John Renee around, she seemed to find a way to piss off their witnesses. Then again, as far as she knew, this man was a suspect.

At last, he waved his fingers, adjusting his shirt with an air of wounded pride. "I was not here," he said. "I in city—Milan." He waved a hand airily up the hall in the direction of the great city.

"I know what Milan is," said Adele. "Do you have proof?"

"I prove? I with girlfriend," he snapped.

"You were with your girlfriend."

Anita coughed, waving delicately. "He always spends the night in the city with her," she said. "They usually post about it online." She glanced at her own phone, and then, with a little sigh of relief, she hurried over, patting her father consolingly on the arm and extending her device beneath Adele's nose. "See," she said. "Look. That's them right there. Look at the date."

Adele glanced down, watching as Anita scrolled through a series of social media photos dated from the previous night. Mr. Herrera was unmistakable, accompanied by a much, much younger woman with a sculpted nose. Both of them were laughing and drinking in the pictures, equal parts bar-hopping, it seemed, and driving around in a bright red Ferrari.

Adele resisted the urge to roll her eyes and instead checked the timestamp on the photos.

The pictures ranged from ten p.m. through midnight. In each of the photos, Herrera was accompanied by his younger girlfriend.

She glanced from the phone to Agent Paige, raising an inflective eyebrow and nodding toward the device. Paige stepped in, glancing over Adele's shoulder at the phone in Anita's hand, frowning even deeper as she too read the dates.

"Your wife's passing," Adele said, turning back now. "Any idea who might have wanted her dead?"

"All want dead!" he declared, smiling now and wagging his head. "Yes. Here," he said, suddenly reaching into his pocket, pulling out a wallet and peeling off two crisp hundred-euro notes. He flung them at Adele. "Give gift to killer. Hmm? Thanks him. Thanks! Very thanks!" He grinned now, nodding quickly and wiggling his fingers toward the bills fluttering to the ground.

"You don't seem too upset about it," Adele said, feeling her own frustration still pulsing in her chest.

He snorted and reached for his daughter now, trying to tug at her. Anita reluctantly joined her father, patting him consolingly on his hairy arm and trying to pull him through the doorway.

"We didn't say you could leave," Adele snapped.

The man hesitated, framed in the door, glancing sidelong at his daughter, back to Adele, and then licking his lips slowly.

Adele paused, considering it all for a moment. The social media photos suggested the man had spent all night with his girlfriend. An accomplice? Given the state of them, and the redness of his cheeks, though, he was still wearing off a hangover. Was that the sort of man to plot out a route through a security system, lure a smart and competent woman, and kill her without leaving a trace?

Looks could be deceiving. Time stamps, less so. She couldn't fully cross the infuriating man off the list, but he wasn't at the top. Besides, she'd already made a scene.

Her nerves, her temper—all of it felt out of whack. She felt like a rookie again, wishing someone was around to show her through the ropes once more. She missed John… missed Robert… But sometimes, no amount of wishful thinking made an ounce of difference.

"Now you can go," Adele said, pointedly glaring at the red-faced Herrera.

He turned before she'd even finished, dragging his daughter toward the door and muttering a series of Italian words Adele didn't need a dictionary to interpret, leaving the DGSI agents standing in the otherwise abandoned dining room.

Adele traced a finger along the oak table, wincing against a headache but at last looking up to meet Agent Paige's frown.

"Not protocol, Sharp," Paige said slowly.

Adele shrugged. "Sorry. I'll do better. Just a bit of jet lag."

"Right, jet lag…"

Adele winced, but nodded. The last person she'd confide in was Agent Paige. Besides, Paige was close with Foucault, and the Executive had made it clear: any whiff of unprofessional behavior and he'd take her off the case.

Adele needed the work. She needed this and so she just nodded, trying to force a smile at Paige and saying, "Don't think it's him. Doesn't seem the sort."

"The pictures aren't an airtight alibi."

"No. I guess not. But they're enough that I think our next stop should be the coroner." Adele half expected Paige to protest, if only to be contrarian. So it was much to her surprise when the older woman paused in thought, but then nodded once, adjusting her suit and brushing past Adele. She strode with clicking footsteps down the hall and toward the front where the taxi driver was still running their meter.

Adele stood in the old mansion, beneath the fake chandelier…

Robert's house was a bit smaller, but not by much. And his sense in décor was infinitely better. Or, at least *had* been.

Was the coroner the best step?

Maybe talking to some of the board? What about the first victim in London?

So many options. Adele winced, trying to think it through. She heard the front door open and shut as Agent Paige made her escape from the old house.

Normally, Adele wasn't the type to endlessly second-guess. But now she wasn't sure. The coroner? The victim in London? The board?

At last, she sighed and just shook her head, rubbing at the bridge of her nose. Maybe it really was jet lag… If not, she was beginning to feel unraveled.

One step at a time. That's all. Every case was one step at a time. What other choice was there? Lives were on the line. Nothing to boost a mood like staring at a corpse.

Adele shivered and turned slowly, walking up the hallway in the direction of the roundabout and the waiting taxi. Coroner it was. One step…

…At a time.

One kill at a time.

She'd just have to keep up.

# CHAPTER SEVEN

Agent Paige leaned down, glancing through the window. "Tip is included," she said, frowning toward where the driver waited expectantly. The man's features twisted into a scowl which Paige was happy to return. She made a shooing motion. "Go. We're done with you."

The man muttered darkly a couple of times, and then with a screech of tires peeled away from the curb, moving back out into the night.

Paige turned now, facing the small coroner's office on the outskirts of Milan, bordered by an old, blocky industrial building and a row of small eateries with names she couldn't pronounce. She turned with stiff motions, approaching the door to the coroner's where Agent Sharp waited, one hand braced against the glass, her eyes staring off into the distance as if tracking some weather pattern on the horizon.

Paige approached the younger woman, frowning as she did.

Agent Sharp had never been her favorite person, especially not after that business nearly ten years ago. The younger woman had nearly ruined Paige's career. Adele had protested her innocence more than once, but some betrayals were unforgivable regardless of an apology.

Now, though, as she approached the door held open by the younger woman, Paige couldn't help but examine Adele where she stood.

The young agent was headstrong and often shirked protocol, but she was a competent operative. Competent enough, at least. Naive and inexperienced, in Sophie's opinion, but still with an acceptable closure rate… Well, perhaps if she was being fair a bit more than acceptable. The only person who had a better closure rate in the DGSI was the late Robert Henry, Adele's mentor.

Paige hesitated on the sidewalk before brushing past the younger woman without comment, stepping into the dingy lower level of the small coroner's office. She resisted the urge to glance back at first, but when no sounds came in pursuit, Paige paused in a doorway, regarding Sharp.

The woman remained in the frame, the vacant look in her eyes.

"You coming?" Paige said, raising her voice.

Adele didn't seem to hear.

"Hey!" Paige snapped. "Are you coming?" she enunciated.

Adele blinked and looked over. She nodded swiftly and stepped into the dingy hall, allowing the glass door with the golden lettering to swing shut behind her. Paige kept her lips pursed as Adele hastened over.

The younger woman was behaving strangely. She seemed on edge, nervous even. The way she'd lashed out at Signore Herrera was only one from a slew of alarming interactions. Paige studied Adele's flustered expression as the younger woman approached. Adele was taller than Paige by a few inches, and had an exotic beauty about her which Paige in her younger years might have envied. Now, though, there was nothing about the dark clouds behind her eyes which Paige coveted.

Robert was dead.

Everyone at the agency knew.

Adele had been close with her mentor. *Very* close. Some of the younger agents gossiped about their relationship behind closed doors with coy winks and nods. Paige hadn't participated in such tawdry rumors, but she wouldn't have put it past someone like Adele. Agent Sharp was always willing to play her own game, indifferent to the opinions of others.

But now Robert was dead. And it seemed to be weighing on Adele's mind…

Rumors swirled about the agency about the killer. A copycat, some said, from Agent Sharp's past. No one knew for sure, though. For a moment, as Adele approached, moving toward the door into the deeper portion of the lower-level coroner's office, Paige thought to pause and ask.

But then, as Adele looked up, Sophie decided against it.

At least one of them had to be a professional. Besides, if Adele acted up further, she would have no qualms about contacting Foucault to yank the upstart off the case.

Paige nodded to herself, smiling as she did, and then pushed through the office door.

"Ah, DGSI?" came a voice—mercifully speaking French—from the back of a low room lined with sinks. The space looked like a Laundromat, minus the machines, replaced by large floor-to-ceiling silver coolers.

"Agent Sharp," Adele said, swallowing. "This is Agent Paige."

"Come, come. I've been expecting you—over here!" The coroner waved the two of them over from where he stood by a low sink in the back of the room. The sound of splashing water cut off, and then a large man built like a powerlifter spun around. He had no neck, his head seemingly a part of his shoulders, wide as they were. He was forced to turn completely to acknowledge them, unable to glance back it seemed by the sheer musculature of his upper frame.

The man was bald, save a wisp of hair combed to one side. He flashed a thumbs-up at the women, smiling congenially. "Hello! Hello!" he said, chipper and cheerful. "Come, my dear audience, and allow yourselves to witness this humble production." He hummed, clapping his hands together and skirting over toward the one of the lockers, his gray and white coat swishing against a silver table.

"We're here about Signora Calvetti," Agent Paige said, standing next to Adele, equal parts amused and alarmed by the coroner's large frame and flamboyant speech.

The powerlifter chuckled and rapped his knuckles against a metal door. He leaned in and whispered, "Hello in there? Wakey wakey. Anyone home?" He chuckled and held a finger to his lips, waiting, and then declared, "No! I guess not. Oh well! Come closer—they won't bite. Though I might. Here, here, pull up a seat." He gestured toward one of the silver tables.

Adele and Paige both looked at the indicated metal surface. Was that a streak of blood in the center? Paige shivered and decided to remain standing, as did Adele. Though both of them did take tentative steps forward.

The large coroner pulled open the metal door and yanked out a metal stretcher, upon which rested a body beneath a blanket.

"And here she comes," he declared, "our star actress. Spotlights shine, the crowd watches with alarm!" With a dramatic flourish he pulled down the top of the blanket, revealing two cold feet with purplish toes.

He winced. "Aha, slight technical malfunction." He pulled the thin fabric down again and hurried over to the top of the stretcher. Again, he reached up and this time, slowly, one eye closed as if he were peeking, he pulled down the sheet, revealing a cold face with closed eyes.

"There we go," he said. "No more surprises for our audience. Come closer, come closer, you won't see a thing from the bleachers. Front row seats. Splash zone! Aha!"

Paige quirked an eyebrow, but reluctantly, straight-postured and full of unspoken cynicism, she approached the large coroner and the corpse.

Adele lingered behind simply watching.

"Here we go, here we are. A plot twist indeed!" He tapped a thick finger against the corpse's pale flesh, sans gloves. "See that, my shrewd-eyed watcher? Hmm? See that right there?"

Agent Paige leaned in, frowning as she did. The same bumpy ligature marks she'd seen on the crime scene photos were now displayed across the victim's neck. Signora Calvetti was paler and older than she'd seemed in other pictures lying naked and dead beneath a tarp. Her throat was ringed in an angry red loop, with small bubble-shaped indentations along the wound.

Sophie looked up at the coroner. "She died by strangulation, yes?"

"Yes, yes. Very much so. You guessed the ending beforehand. Haha. Spoiler alert, though, am I right?" He winked at Paige with a cheerful smile.

She returned a stony, ice-cold glare which didn't seem to bother him in the least.

"Beads, pearls?" Paige asked, tight-lipped.

"Could be," he said. "Well… maybe. Beads, though…" He frowned, glancing off at the ceiling, tracing a gray crack in the cement, and paused. "Can't recall ever seeing *beads* used to kill."

"Beads are usually on string," Adele murmured.

The large coroner and Paige glanced back toward where the agent was standing, her arms crossed now, her eyes more alert than they'd been earlier. She was staring at the corpse, frowning.

"What's your point?" Paige asked.

Adele took a shaky breath, but then nodded as if trying to reach a conclusion herself before giving voice to it. "Strings break, yes? Something like pearls might have a more reinforced cord. But beads? Beads would break, no?"

The coroner nodded slowly, tapping his chin with the same finger he'd poked the dead woman's neck. "She raises a good point." He glanced toward Paige as if waiting for her to respond.

"Still might be beads," she said, coolly.

"Could be," Adele replied. "But…" She frowned, shaking her head. "Never mind."

"No, dear," said the coroner. "Tell us, what were you thinking? There are no stupid questions in the arts."

Adele swallowed. "I wouldn't say—never mind. Just, it's nothing, just a thought."

Paige sighed. It was just like Adele to drag it on. She often enjoyed the attention.

At last, though, Adele said, “What about a rosary? Stronger twine than beads… Not as valuable as pearls.”

“Signora Calvetti was not a religious woman,” said Paige frowning.

“Not Calvetti’s rosary. The killer’s. What if he brought it?” Adele nodded more firmly this time as if carried by a surge of momentum. “Maybe the killer has religious motivations…” She paused now, though, a look of doubt crossing her features, and she sighed, shaking her head. “Maybe not, though.”

The coroner clicked his tongue like a doting mother.

Paige frowned at Adele’s theory. There was no evidence of a rosary, only an outline. Young agents often jumped to conclusions too early. Paige would have to keep an extra tight lid on this investigation if they wanted to get anywhere meaningful. “Anything else?” Paige asked, looking at the enormous man.

He nodded, chipper and cheerful. As he opened his mouth to respond, though, Paige snapped, “Cut it out with the metaphors and get on with the point. This isn’t art. It’s murder.”

The man blinked, taken aback. His smile faded a bit, but then, frowning from beneath his whisked hair, he muttered, “Definitely death by strangulation. Couldn’t have taken more than a minute. She didn’t suffer much.”

“I’m sure that will console someone,” Paige said. “But how about evidence, clues? Little red fibers or some button…” She waved a hand. “Anything?”

“Little red fibers?” The large man wrinkled his nose. “No, I’m afraid nothing like that.” This time was it her imagination or had he flashed her a condescending look? Her eyes hardened, glaring at him, but he just glanced off, feigning ignorance.

“Fine,” Paige said, growling. “Agent Sharp, I’ll be phoning for another taxi outside. This was a waste. We have nothing new.” She said it loudly, so the large galoot could hear, then, with one last look toward the victim, she turned on her heel, marching back toward the door.

“Where next?” Adele asked, her voice faint.

Paige didn’t look back, just nodded once, approving of Adele’s willingness, at least for now, to hand over the reins to the investigation. Paige was the senior agent after all.

“London,” she snapped. “Nothing useful here. Might as well go see what we can find about that first victim. Maybe it is a serial case.”

“What about the board member Anita mentioned?”

Paige snorted, waving a hand. "I've been in boardrooms like that. Behind closed doors, far worse has been uttered. Besides, that board member wouldn't have any reason to visit London. No, we have our next step."

Adele said, "All right then, if you're sure. How soon can we get a flight to the UK?"

"An hour, two tops. Foucault will set it up himself."

Paige then stepped into the hall, out into the cold gray corridor and toward the front door again. She heard a soft muttered apology behind her and then the sound of quickened footsteps as Adele made to give chase.

The large coroner's voice boomed out after them, "Break a leg!"

## CHAPTER EIGHT

Gianna stared at himself in the reflection of the small hostel's glass window, his eyes tracing the bucolic country scene against the ridge of firs. He smiled softly to himself, one hand gripping the handle. The other hostel guests would be out until evening. He'd asked early the previous day, so he could plan out his own particular getaway.

"Gianna Calvetti…" he murmured softly. His new name. The last one he'd only had for three days. This one wouldn't last much longer either.

He always took their names when he released their souls to perdition. "Is anyone there?" he whispered in a soft, feminine voice, watching the way his lips moved in the reflection of the glass. "Is anyone in there?" He grinned to himself. He was getting better at emulating the voices of his camouflage.

"Fifty-eight! And don't you forget it!" he declared, nodding at the glass, his voice still soft and lilting. Just like hers had been. His fingers tightened even more against the handle. "Don't you forget it! Fifty-eight! Don't you forget!"

And then he gritted his teeth, swinging the whip *hard.* The small pieces of bone embedded in the thick cords gouged into his back and he hissed in pain.

"Not a day…" he gasped. "Over…" He struck himself again. A whirring sound, a snap, the pain. "Fifty-eight!" he screamed.

He stood there, breathing heavily, shirtless in the window, watching the countryside with wide eyes.

"I'm sorry," he whispered to the glass. "I'm sorry, oh great Judge! I'm sorry, your eminence!" He screamed the prayer at the ceiling as the whip came whistling back again, scoring Gianna's shoulders. "I'm so sorry," he sobbed.

He'd killed the original Gianna, taken her soul and name. She'd deserved to die, of course. But even as an instrument of righteousness, an instrument of the mighty Judge, he still had to atone for the taking of a life.

Another whistling sound, another dull *thud*, followed by spittle falling from clenched teeth. He was on his knees now, feeling the warm blood spilling down the crease of his back. "Anyone there?" he whispered, still lilting and soft. "Anyone in there?"

Another strike.

She'd blasphemed the Judge. Blasphemed his holy ground. She hadn't deserved her skin. Nor had she deserved the gift of a soul.

"Is anyone there?" he whispered. "Yes," he snarled back in a much deeper, darker voice. "You stupid whore. I'm here… I'm here for you!" He gritted his teeth, whipping himself with the bone-tipped flail again. He yelled once more, but this time smiling as warm blood dripped down his shoulders, down his back, to his waist. "I'm here for you," he whispered.

He nodded adamantly, gasping, his chest heaving as he stared out the small German hostel's window. No longer in Italy. No. The next stop was here. Only five miles down the road.

Of course, he'd already memorized the security system, memorized *her* schedule. Gianna was clever when she needed to be. Gianna was careful. He'd been planning this for years now…

They should have left him alone. They shouldn't have done what they did. Mothers, they called themselves. A flock of black geese. They'd whipped him then, too.

Nearly fifty years ago. Only five… He'd only been five…

But he'd understood pain then, and he understood it now.

"Is anyone there?" he whispered, tears now falling from his eyes. "Is anyone?"

A whistle. A *snap.* A howl of pain.

Yes… Yes, he'd atone now and then atone again when the time came. Only five miles away for his next stop. Five miles for the vengeance of the Judge to descend in fire and brimstone. To descend on those who dared to speak for the ever-watcher, and the judge of millennia. Only five miles away…

He smiled again, despite the tears, despite the pain, despite the warm trickle down his back, streaking him, baptizing him. Soon, so deliciously soon.

A whistle. A snap.

A scream.

## CHAPTER NINE

Exiting the airport taxi, Adele stepped out into the evening, beneath gloomy skies. Again, she found herself facing a mansion. Her feet crunched against gravel, and her eyes traced the stone and pillar facade of the old, looming manor.

Adele heard the car doors slam behind her as Paige and the two accompanying officers also exited the vehicle. Ahead, a row of yellow and black caution tape cut access to a courtyard driveway across from a three-car garage. The garage itself was larger than most houses.

Few trees surrounded them. Rather, this estate, in contrast to the Italian one, seemed a combination of trimmed hedges in strange shapes and a large lake behind the house itself, the swishing blue reflecting off the large parlor windows.

"Just this way, Agents," said one of the police officers, dipping her head politely and waving a hand. Adele half expected her to click her shiny black shoes.

She fell into step behind the officers, gravel crunching beneath her feet as she followed along with Paige toward the old mansion.

"And she was found outside here, yes?" Adele asked, grateful to be speaking in English once again, now having hopped the pond to London.

The second officer glanced back, tipping a black-billed hat. "Just in the private nursery," he said, nodding. "Over here—this way."

He led them toward a small glass nursery, with more caution tape out front. An officer was standing by the glass, playing on his phone. He looked up and quickly coughed, stowing the device and standing to attention, suggesting, perhaps, he was low on the local totem pole.

Adele nodded politely, then followed their guides beneath the caution tape into a small, humid nursery. Rows of potted plants in orange ceramic bowls lined wooden shelves. Two particularly large garden beds centered twin plastic sheets beneath an array of sprinklers jutting from a thick black pipe that spanned the entirety of the nursery.

For a moment, standing in the glass nursery, as if beneath some large magnifying lens, Adele felt a shiver up her spine. She swallowed, glancing back toward where Agent Paige was wiping a finger along one of the shelves, leaving a trail of dark in dust.

"She was found just over here," murmured the female officer, pointing toward a couple of scattered ceramic pots and some shattered orange clay. Twin piles of dirt and wilted greenery suggested some of the nursery denizens hadn't fared much better than their late caretaker.

Adele approached the disheveled area, frowning as she did.

"He attacked her late at night," said the officer, quietly. "Best we can guess—right after she got home."

"Husband?" Adele asked.

"Deceased. A few years earlier. Her fortune was inherited."

"I see." Adele frowned, her eyes moving from the scattered and broken pots toward a dark alcove beneath two rows of wooden shelves. She bent over, hands on her knees, frowning into the corner.

Just large enough for a person.

A hiding place, perhaps?

"Security systems?" she asked, straightening up again.

"Only on the main house, not in the nursery, unfortunately. We checked."

Adele nibbled her lip, glancing toward Agent Paige. "Another blind spot."

The older agent grunted once, brushing a hand through silver hair. "Looks like our killer does his homework."

"When was the body found?" Adele asked.

The officer cleared her throat. "The next morning, by one of the victims' bible study partners."

"Bible study?" Adele asked, frowning and feeling a flicker of excitement. She thought back to the bead marks on the victim's neck. A rosary after all? She swallowed, avoiding Paige, who seemed to be watching her suspiciously. Adele asked, "Was the victim religious?"

"A staunch Catholic. She donated time and money to the church—a lot of money." The officer didn't bat an eye, but by the emphasis of the words, it seemed she thought this part important.

"Where there's money, there's often murder," Adele said softly. She glanced toward Paige, then back. "Any known connection with the victim in Italy?"

The officer frowned, nibbling her lip, but shook her head quickly. "Something about that was mentioned, but no connection we know of on our end. Did you find something?"

Adele shook her head, crossing her arms and feeling her suit's sleeves crinkle.

Both wealthy, both in their fifties, both living somewhat alone in old houses. Both strangled to death with odd ligature marks. But that was where the similarities ended. The murderer didn't seem to be stealing anything. So while wealth was a connection, money wasn't the motive. At least not at first blush. As for the first victim's religion—a devoted Catholic. But the second victim had no church affiliation. One religious, one not. Both wealthy.

Adele shook her head, trying to make sense of it. "I… I need whatever you have on Mrs. Churchville," she said, glancing toward the officer. "Even details that might seem unsubstantial. No stone unturned."

Paige frowned from where she stood in the glass doorway. "What are you hoping to find?"

"A connection," Adele murmured. "Between this victim and the other. Some reason the killer chose them in particular."

"We have what you need back at the precinct," the officer volunteered. "It isn't far from here."

Adele weathered Paige's stormy gaze and instead nodded at the officer. "Appreciated. And I do mean *anything* related to the victim. No matter how inconsequential you might think it."

Adele turned, brushing past Paige and exiting the nursery. Her head was beginning to pound, a slow headache coming on. There had to be a tie between the two victims. Unless… maybe it wasn't a serial murderer? Maybe just a coincidence?

Adele paused in the drive, facing the car, but then turning to glance back up at the old, looming stone mansion outlined against the lake.

She thought of the crime scene photos. The strange, beaded ligature marks…

No. Not a coincidence. Now, she'd simply have to prove it.

# CHAPTER TEN

Adele's eyes fluttered beneath the flickering light above the borrowed interrogation room's table. She winced as the two long cylindrical bulbs sputtered once more, eliciting a sound like popping bubble wrap. She glanced up and then looked away again, feeling another stab of a now familiar headache.

Now back in the precinct, she tried to find a comfortable position in the cold metal chair the locals had provided. Across from her, on the opposite side of a table scattered with folders and two borrowed laptops, Agent Paige had yet to sit.

She stalked from one side of the room to the other, taking a moment every so often to return to her borrowed laptop and scan the screen.

The last half hour she had made a big show of checking her watch. But Adele was too focused to acknowledge her. She scrolled through the files she'd been provided. Three of the manila folders were printouts of receipts and liquid assets. On her computer, she had bank transactions for Mrs. Churchville.

Her eyes felt dry, the poor lighting exacerbating her headache. But she couldn't give up, not now.

Even as she thought it, though, watched by the winking light and the unblinking glare of Agent Paige, Adele could feel sweat forming inside her palms. She could feel the quiet, building nausea from her headache, but also from something deeper.

She could feel the stage fright from earlier still lingering in the background.

"It's getting late," Agent Paige said, her voice betraying a flash of irritation.

Adele looked up, surprised. Paige was still pacing back and forth in the small room. Adele glanced down at the bottom right of her laptop screen.

"Oh," she said. "Nearly midnight."

"We haven't found anything," Paige replied, staring pointedly at the pile of folders next to Adele. "Best we can do is reconvene tomorrow."

"Don't wait up if you don't want to. I'm just going to go back through the financials one more time. Just in case."

"In case what?"

"In case I missed anything," Adele said. *In case I'm completely out of touch,* she thought quietly. *In case I failed this before it even started. In case I'm suffering some sort of mental breakdown.*

She tried to smile, to hide her thoughts and the racing pattern of their accusations, but it came out more like a grimace, which Paige returned.

"What are you trying to prove, Sharp?"

"Prove?"

"I get it, you work late. Now how about you come back with me so we don't have to bother the Brits to drive both of us to the hotel."

Adele hesitated, shaking her head. "I can call a taxi. It's fine."

"There's nothing there."

"I'd like to look one last time."

Agent Paige threw up her hands and snorted; she spun on her heel, shaking her head as she did. Without another word, bearing the air of someone simply dismissing her entirely, Agent Paige stalked back toward the door. She shot one more reproachful look toward Adele, then growling, barged her shoulder into the metal surface and left the interrogation room.

Just through the closing slit, Adele spotted a brightly lit hall, and the midnight precinct, without another soul in sight. She supposed bare bones would be working the night shift, which suited her just fine.

Fewer people to witness…

The door clicked shut. Sealing her in.

Witness what?

Her headache pulsed along with another sputter of the light bulbs. She felt carsick all at once, but refused to allow herself to feel pity. She returned her attention to the laptop, scrolling through once more, her eyes dry and strained.

She desperately wanted to go for a morning jog. Take a shower back at the hotel. But no, not now. She had to focus. She felt half the detective she'd ever been. Second-guessing herself, getting stage fright, feeling out of touch. She was alone, well and truly now.

In moments like these, in the past, she would take the opportunity to call Robert. He always knew what to do.

She allowed herself to close her eyes for a moment, but this was no better. She heard the sputter of the bulbs above. Across her mind flashed an image. A familiar image… *bleeding... bleeding, always bleeding.*

Not just her mother, though, no. But also Robert, beneath his red leather chair, tortured to death.

She remembered the small marble angel, the statue shoved in the mud. She remembered the way she entered the house, her voice calling in the dark mansion. The fear, and then the shout. And then she'd seen what the Spade Killer had done.

She hated him. Hated him with more than she had. And now, she feared him. Which was far worse. In the past, she had been too stupid to be afraid. Yes, that's what it was. Stupid. Stupid enough to get Robert murdered. Stupid enough to get others hurt too. Who else was going to suffer because of—

Her phone buzzed next to her.

Adele blinked, but then pushed the device away, refusing to glance down. Probably just Paige, goading her into quitting again. But Adele couldn't quit. She was losing her edge. And without that, all there was left was effort. Stark, naked, fervent effort.

She clenched her teeth now, scrolling once more through the finances. On one side of the screen she had Mrs. Churchville's information, and on the other Signora Calvetti's. "Come on," she murmured. "Something. Just give me something…"

Her eyes grew heavy, and the sputtering bulb above only irritated her further.

"Dammit," she cursed, as the lights flickered. In a fit of rage, she pushed from the desk, sending the chair scraping across the floor, and she lunged toward the light switch, flicking it off.

Now, in the dark interrogation room, her eyes strained toward the blue screen.

Her headache only worsened as she leaned in, scrolling through the finances. Her eyes like lead. Her eyelashes fluttering, drooping, and then…

***

Her head jolted off her folded arms.

Pitch-black.

For a moment, Adele panicked. Where was she?

Her hand lashed out, striking a pile of papers and sending them fluttering in the dark. Her knuckles brushed against the cold lid of the borrowed laptop. She calmed a bit, breathing heavily, focusing.

She was in the precinct. In the interrogation room. The laptop's screen had darkened to save battery. She blinked, clearing sleep from her eyes and groaning as she tapped the keyboard. The blue screen lit up, and she spotted the time. Two in the morning. She'd dozed off.

Adele cursed beneath her breath, shaking her head and feeling another bout of a headache.

How many people were still in the station?

She paused for a moment, both hands on the cold table, and her eyes darted to her phone, which had lit up with silent notifications. Frowning, she tapped the screen and winced. Two missed calls. One from Agent Renee, another from Agent Leoni. She shook her head, muttering to herself, and turned the phone over, facing the screen to the table.

Adele inhaled slowly, trying to focus. Financial records. That's what she'd been going through.

But nothing. No connection points. Nothing that stood out. The second victim divorced. The first victim inherited from her late husband.

Adele blinked.

Her late husband. Robert Churchville. What if all the assets hadn't been fully moved over just yet? What if she was looking under the wrong name?

Blinking to herself, Adele returned to the file and did a quick word search. *Robert.* He had died three years ago, leaving his fortune to his wife.

And suddenly, Adele froze, her eyes glued in the dark to the glowing screen.

Four lines on the spreadsheet. Four assets still in Robert Churchville's name, yet to be relinquished to his wife due to some sort of tax barrier. Adele hungrily scanned the listed items on the estate tax document. First off, some sort of Aston Martin. Another, an old trust fund. The third item on the list, though, caught Adele's attention.

A small summer country house in France.

She blinked, staring. She looked at the item, clicking, following the thread. And then she stopped. The country home resided in the Aquitaine region of France. The same region Signora Calvetti was said to have a summer home.

Adele's fingers trembled, but she clicked quickly over to the second victim's details. This time, instead of scrolling by purchase amounts and expected asset allocations, Adele simply searched for the word Aquitaine.

A second passed as the spreadsheet loaded…

Then….

A detailed description of a small country home in the heart of France. A vacation home.

Adele leaned back, the chair rigid against her spine. Her eyes wide.

"That's it," she muttered to herself. "Holy shit. That's it."

She blinked, shaking her head in equal parts relief and pending delirium. She winced against the headache, feeling her stomach twist.

Both victims had small country homes in the South of France. Both victims had summer homes near the other. A connection. Tentative, perhaps. But Adele knew Aquitaine. It wasn't a particularly large region. A coincidence?

Adele lowered the lid of the laptop, her fingers trembling again.

Couldn't be a coincidence. She had to sleep, and then talk to Paige. This had to be the break in the case they were looking for. The thread that would lead them to the killer before he murdered anyone else.

# CHAPTER ELEVEN

Elke Schmidt stepped down from the veranda, inhaling the morning air with a contented sigh. She walked barefoot around the marble circumference of her family swimming pool, pausing to make sure the children had turned the jets of the Jacuzzi off the night before. She glanced over her shoulder toward the enormous home they'd moved into five years ago, smiling and acknowledging the stone stucco and black shingle roofing. The house was perhaps a bit larger than they needed. But it allowed for the entertaining of guests and hosting of dinner parties. In fact, that very night they'd be hosting a get-together with some of their close family friends.

In one hand, she gripped the porcelain handle of a small coffee mug. A generic pink cartoon heart was painted on the side of the thing, and steam wafted up from the confines of the white cup. She inhaled the scent of the coffee and took a delicate sip, wincing against the sudden heat. She strolled across the edge of the pool, toward the black gate which led out onto their property. In the distance, she spotted the small barn for horses they had never bought. A pipe dream, her husband said. They didn't have enough time to take care of the horses. Still, hopefully one day.

Mrs. Schmidt didn't mind walking alone, along her property line, beneath the trees and toward the old barn. This was a safe neighborhood after all. A neighborhood for the wealthy and the well off. Few places in Germany were as safe as this one.

She felt the damp grass from the sprinklers beneath her toes, and she hummed softly to herself, reciting one of the piano pieces her daughter had been practicing the previous day. She took another steaming sip from her coffee mug as she strolled through the trees now, moving across the well-maintained yard and then past a small incline along the creek behind the house. Now, she could just make out the top of the roof, over the incline, and through the trees. It was harder to see the pool from this angle.

Mrs. Schmidt simply enjoyed the sensation of her toes pressing in the dirt, smiling to herself at the three-course meal she had planned for the party tonight. She would cater at least half of it, but still, she made a mean Sauerbraten.

That's when she spotted movement.

Elke frowned, staring up toward the old barn.

Something fluttered behind one of the trees ahead, and she heard the soft thump of footsteps, and then something moved past another tree and stopped.

Her breath came a bit quicker now and her eyes narrowed, fixated on the tree.

"Hello?" she said, softly, her voice extending over the grass.

She frowned.

One of the neighbor kids? A couple of times she'd been forced to speak with the Bauers next door about their children camping in the barn.

She sighed in an exasperated fashion and moved quickly toward the barn. Best to catch them red-handed.

"I see you there!" she called out. She had seen a flutter of motion, which had now gone still behind one of the larger oaks. Still, children couldn't often tell when adults were bluffing. "I see you there, come out!"

She quickened her pace, striding purposefully and frowning, some of the coffee sloshing over her knuckles with a steaming hiss. She winced and quickly sucked on the back of her hand, gently angling the mug so it didn't spill further.

"Come out," she demanded. "Peter, Luka? Is that you?"

She rounded the tree, all bluster and annoyance, still sucking at the back of her thumb.

And froze.

She stared for a moment and then yelped in surprise, the blood draining from her face as she dropped her coffee mug and it shattered against one of the protruding roots beneath her feet. She gasped, but the sound died as a hand suddenly lashed out at her.

Not a child at all. Not a neighbor. In fact, in a brief moment, she spotted a man with a mustache and dull, gray eyes. She had never seen the man before in her life.

"Miss me?" he growled as he lurched at her.

He was wearing a strange outfit. It took her a moment to realize it wasn't a bathrobe. In fact, it looked more like an old monk's habit. Something black dangled from his right hand, and swished about as he lunged at her.

Elke screamed and darted back. The man was fast, but she spent most mornings, after her walk and coffee, going for runs in the woods. She was quick too.

"Come here!" he snarled, missing, his hands groping toward her again.

She didn't wait to talk, and instead spun on her heel, sprinting back in the direction of the house.

But the man tackled her from behind, grabbing at her ankle, and they both collapsed with dull thuds to the dewy ground. She screamed again, her throat hoarse, fear flooding her. Her chest pounded a million miles an hour. Who was this? What did he want?

She tried to bite, to kick. She lashed out, her heel catching him on the bridge of his nose.

He yelped and released her ankle. Elke scrambled to her feet, dodging the other direction this time, and he missed another lunge. Now she was racing toward the barn, away from the house. A deadly mistake, but one that was hard to track amidst the chaos of the moment.

"Remember me?" he screamed out, rising from the mud.

She glanced back, but then looked forward again, breathing heavily as she sprinted around the barn, desperately looking for a discarded plank of wood, a rock, a rake. Anything to use as a weapon.

"You thought I was crazy," he screamed. "Didn't you, Mother?"

Mother? What was he talking about? Her heart raced and her throat prickled with terror.

"I've missed you too," he yelled.

She reached the barn, rounding it, and heard the sound of thumping footsteps. She looked frantically around. There, a stack of barrels. Could it serve as a hiding place?

She sprinted toward the trees, but heard more thumping footsteps. Had he doubled back? Was he trying to round the other way. She'd been stupid. She should've headed toward the house. Nothing for it now, though.

Hastily, she raced toward the barrels, her shoulder scraping on rough wood as she slid behind the wooden containers, crouched low near the earth, smelling mud and the damp mold at the base of the barn. She froze, on her haunches, breathing loudly.

The thumping footsteps followed, and she spotted a flash of movement between the gaps in the barrels toward the trees. She sat still, gasping far too loudly in her own ears, but there was nothing to do about that now.

She waited, her head resting against the wooden grain of the barrel.

And then, silence.

Her fear circled in spinning pulses, racing with the wild cadence of her thumping heart.

Had he gone the other way? She couldn't see any better, lodged behind the old barrels as she was. She couldn't stay here, though. She needed to get back to the house. Back to her family. Her phone had been left on the kitchen table.

Slowly, still breathing in shallow gasps, she began to inch around the barrel, toward the edge of the barn.

A shadow fell over her.

A single strand of black beads fell past the edge of one of the barrels, dangling down toward her nose, with an ebony cross at the very edge.

Two dull, gray eyes peered over the barrels now.

She screamed, and the barrel was thrown aside with a dull *thunk*.

She tried to scramble back, but this time he moved, anticipating the motion, and grabbed her, fingers tight around her throat, holding her still. He wrapped the black beads around her neck, and she gasped, spluttering, trying to kick.

And then he squeezed.

# CHAPTER TWELVE

Agent Paige paused near the hotel's small coffee maker on the second-floor landing. She poured herself a paper cup—black, no sugar. She paused, staring at the drink, reaching up and brushing a strand of hair behind her ear.

Adele had come back late the previous night. Paige had heard her enter the room next door sometime after three AM. Now, seven in the morning, Paige was going to meet the younger woman.

She glanced down at her phone for the second time, frowning at the text exchange:

*Where are you?* Paige had texted after visiting Adele's room and receiving no answer.

*Gym,* Adele had replied. *Second floor.*

Paige just shook her head, lowering the phone again. She had to hand it to Agent Sharp—the woman was a hard worker, no doubt. Impetuous, intrusive, and obnoxious, but still a hard worker. She'd stayed up until three on the case, and had woken up before Paige to go to the gym. A sustainable schedule? Absolutely not.

But still, credit had to be given, even if grudgingly. Perhaps Paige was being a bit hard on the younger agent.

She sighed to herself and reached for a second cup. For a moment, her fingers hovered over the paper container and then she grabbed the thing and poured a second cup of coffee, also black. If Adele wanted sugar, she'd have to work twice as hard. The coffee would have to be enough.

Grabbing both paper cups, Paige turned on her heel, stalking down the second floor's hall along a row of glass windows which revealed an old workout room. She passed a dance studio in the small London hotel, and then came to a halt outside an indoor track.

Adele was the only one inside, jogging around the red circle, sweat slicking her body, her eyes fixed ahead as she went around and around. No music, no earbuds, just a determined expression and a consistent pace. Paige watched, frowning as Adele circled the track, her legs stretching beneath her, the pace only picking up, it seemed. For a moment, it didn't even look like exercise. The intense stare, the wide-eyed look of focus—it almost felt like Adele was running away from some invisible ghost. Paige felt a soft shiver down her spine.

She pressed her shoulder against the glass, easing open the door and stepping into the stale gym. "Coffee!" she called.

Adele looked over, blinking suddenly and shifting the strange atmosphere over her workout. She paused next to a floor-to-ceiling window, panting briefly, and bent over for a second, checking her watch and then resting her hands on her knees and breathing at the floor, before straightening.

For a moment, she just looked at the second cup of coffee in Paige's hand as if the woman had sprouted a third arm. She stood on the opposite side of the room.

"Almost done," Adele called.

"We need to get going," Paige returned.

"I found a clue."

Paige blinked, then took a slow sip from one of the containers, long enough to process her reaction and then lowered it again. "Oh?" she said simply.

Adele bobbed her head, reaching up and wiping sweat from her forehead. "Both victims owned summer homes in Southern France."

Paige blinked, but didn't say anything.

"In the same region," Adele said, more insistently.

Paige shrugged slowly. "This is Europe. A lot of wealthy folk own homes in France."

"Yes… but that's a connection. It has to be." Adele looked off for a moment, blinking toward the window and wincing as if against a sudden headache. For a moment, it almost seemed like she'd forgotten Agent Paige was even there.

Sophie sighed, staring at the younger woman's sharp profile. She could see the exhaustion weighing on Adele. Could see the doubt in the woman's eyes, the frustration. Could see the need for some sort of approval in every askance glance and awkward gesture.

But what could Paige say? A second home in France was hardly significant. Besides, neither victim was even killed in France. The connection was spurious at best.

She opened her mouth to say as much, but then paused, staring at where Adele's sleep-deprived, sweaty form was outlined against the windows. Paige's gaze returned to the plastic cup of dark coffee.

Instead, she grunted and said, "Maybe. Here, coffee. Will help wake you if—"

At that moment, her phone began to buzz. At the same time, a ring tone began to twitter from a discarded sweater by the front doors. Adele frowned, jogging over toward the ringing phone buried in her clothes, as Paige also pulled her cell from her pocket.

She raised the phone, recognizing the number and feeling a cold chill down her back.

"Yes?" she answered, frowning.

"Sophie?"

"Foucault?"

The Executive cleared his throat on the other line. "Bad news, I'm afraid, Sophie. The killer got another. We have a third victim."

Paige felt her frustration spark, but she kept back the burst of emotion and simply said, "Where?"

Foucault cleared his throat, coughing briefly before saying, "Germany this time, Sophie. I need you both to head there straightaway."

***

Adele sat with one hand gripping the window seat's arm rests, and the other feverishly poking at her phone.

Out of the corner of her eye, she glanced at Agent Paige. "They haven't moved the body yet?"

Sophie leaned back in the airplane seat and shook her head a single time, staring ahead and frowning. She had an untouched cup of orange juice in front of her, her eyes fixed off in the distance. "Not yet," she murmured. "I hate these damn flights," she added, beneath her breath.

Adele raised an eyebrow, but didn't comment, instead searching for Foucault's number; she raised the phone, allowing it to ring for a second, and then a voice on the other end said, "Executive's office."

Adele swallowed, feeling a rising sense of anticipation. "Agent Adele Sharp. Could you please put me through."

The voice on the other end spoke without inflection. "He's not taking calls right now."

"Mary," Adele said, through gritted teeth. "I need you to put me through right now—it's important."

The Executive's assistant sighed on the other end, but then in that same dry voice, she replied, "Let me see if he's busy."

There was no dial tone, or music, but Adele could tell she'd been put on hold. She growled, clicking the phone to speaker mode, and looking to Agent Paige. "Did the Germans say anything about a summer home in France?"

The silver-haired agent continued staring off in the distance, swallowing once as the plane hit a small patch of turbulence, but then settled with a rattle of the cabin. "You're still obsessed with that?"

"It's the only connection we have. If this third victim has a summer home in—"

Before she could continue, though, a voice cleared on the other end, and she heard the rasping, throaty sound of the Executive trying to gain her attention.

"Sorry, sir," she said, quickly. "So sorry. Just, I wanted to ask if you knew anything about a vacation home in Southern France. I called ahead to the investigators in Germany, but I haven't heard back."

The Executive grunted then said, "Agent Sharp, I'm sure if they find anything they'll tell you. We have more important things to worry about than vacation homes."

"I... No sir, I don't think we do actually."

"Oh? What does a vacation home have to do with it?"

Adele leaned back, feeling a jolt of frustration. "It's like I told them, sir. The last two victims both had homes in the same area."

"And?"

"And, sir? It's a connection."

"Perhaps, but neither of the victims were killed in France. So I don't see how—"

"I know that, sir. But I was just thinking—"

"Don't interrupt me, Sharp. I need you and Paige to get to the crime scene. The body is still there, but I can't keep the coroner off for much longer. I've already arranged for your ride from the airport."

Adele tried not to let her frustration leak into her words. "Sir, I'm very confident that if we look into the vacation homes, we're going to find a connection."

For a moment, he paused and a soft static sound filled Adele's ear. He seemed to be considering his next words very carefully before saying, with the same lack of inflection as his assistant, "Is there a reason you're so focused on France right now?" His tone gave her pause, and it took her a moment to realize there was a pitying quality to it. She shivered, feeling unclean. She could have taken frustration, anger, impatience. Hell, she'd been given a master class in the cold shoulder from Agent Paige. But pity?

No, this emotion she couldn't stomach.

"Sir," she said, firmly, "this has nothing to do with my personal business. I checked; they both really do have homes in Southern France."

"I believe you. Just, are you feeling yourself?"

Adele frowned, glancing toward Paige. "Why? What have you been told?"

"Nothing. Should I have been told something?"

Adele wanted to press further on the vacation home line of questioning, but decided she was already skating on thin ice.

"Agent Sharp, if this is getting too much for you, and if you want to return to France—"

"No, sir. Sorry for interrupting. But no, that's not what this is at all. Oh, sorry, flight attendant. I have to go."

Adele hung up on the executive of the DGSI. She shivered, lowering her phone, doing her best not to glance in Agent Paige's direction, though she could tell the older woman was shooting sidelong glances.

The third victim had been killed only a couple of days after the second. The killer was escalating and as in the first two cases, he had scouted out the territory before, avoiding the blind spots in the security systems, targeting older, wealthy women.

The connection was in France. She was sure of it. And if they wouldn't listen to her, she'd have to figure it out on her own. For now, though, there was a body waiting in Germany.

# CHAPTER THIRTEEN

The trip from the airport passed in silence like the quiet hush before a funeral. It wasn't often that DGSI agents were able to reach a crime scene in another country before the body was carried away.

Again, perhaps predictably at this point, as they pulled into the German countryside driveway, through the arching golden gates flecked with paint and along the smooth red drive, Adele spotted a mansion in the distance. This time, the home looked old, and some of the walls were weather worn. Part of the roof was covered in plastic sheeting, suggesting reshingling. She spotted a blue pool beneath the patio as the car drew nearer.

They pulled to a halt at the smooth roundabout, and Agent Paige exited the vehicle first, moving toward a waiting police officer next to a row of trees outside a small black gate.

The moment she stepped out, Adele's senses were met by the odor of chlorine. She frowned, glancing from the pool to the still Jacuzzi. Her eyes traced the marble ground and the clear, slick blue porcelain slabs. Through the branches of the trees beyond, she spotted a small white and blue structure—a barn or maybe a garage.

Adele's attention was regained by Agent Paige, who was scowling at the officer by the trees and waving angrily at Adele, gesturing like a queen summoning a subject.

Reluctantly, Adele strolled over, quirking an inquisitive brow.

"What's he saying?" Paige demanded as Adele came close.

Adele hesitated, and then switching to German, said, "Excuse me?"

The officer in question was quite old with silver bangs poking out from beneath his hat, and a curling white mustache like a resting cloud. "I was saying the body is this way. The coroner is wondering when he can get to it."

Adele shook her head. "I can't be sure," she replied in perfect German. "Could you take us there, please?" Then, translating in French, she said to Paige, "He just wants to know when the coroner can get to the body."

Paige frowned, replying in French, "We haven't even seen it yet."

"That's what I told him."

"I see. Well, we don't have all day."

Adele decided not to translate this part, and instead fell into step behind their new German guide, moving along the row of trees in the direction of the waiting barn she'd spotted in the distance. There was no caution tape here, a sure sign this was private property.

As they neared the old barn, the white-mustached officer led them around the edge of the structure and toward a row of wooden barrels.

Here, Adele spotted three other police officers moving about the edge of the woods, or near the base of the barn itself. One of the officers wore gloves and was gently moving one of the barrels to the side, rolling it over and checking the bottom with close scrutiny.

As the barrel moved, though, Adele's eyes landed on the body. Pale flesh—cold and clammy from a night abandoned behind the small barn. The eyes closed, mercifully, both hands rigid against the corpse's sides, motionless.

Elke Schmidt, once upon a time. Now just a fleshy memory.

Adele blinked, feeling a sudden rushing headache. Other thoughts threatened to bob to the surface in her mind, but she staved them off with a growl and stepped forward, stooping low next to the body and frowning toward the victim's neck.

"Ligature marks?" Paige called, standing back and watching the scene with an unusual, nearly queasy expression. Paige didn't fare well on the flights, but this seemed different, somehow, than simple motion sickness.

Adele leaned in, eyes narrowed, breathing shallowly from her mouth. Experience taught her that inhaling through her nose within the vicinity of any corpse was an odoriferous venture in self-punishment. Even a corpse as fresh as this one.

A couple of the German officers were standing back now, still examining the barrel, but using this attention as cover to keep their eyes on her as well. Every so often they murmured to each other in low voices, likely thinking the DGSI agents couldn't understand them.

One was saying… "She's young to take a case like this…"

"Boss thinks it's a serial case," the other murmured in reply, rotating the barrel.

"Serial?" the first said.

"Yes. Apparently the younger woman is experienced catching serial killers."

The second officer muttered an expletive in disbelief.

Adele could feel the expectations settling on her shoulders now, and she shivered under the scrutiny. Her own gaze fixed on the corpse. Fingers probed out, not quite touching the body, but used like a magnifying lens to focus her attention. Her eyes narrowed as she stared at the angry red marks circling Mrs. Schmidt's neck. "Just like the others," she said, shaking her head. "The same odd markings. Like beads, or small bubbles."

Agent Paige shifted uncomfortably behind her, and the older agent said, "Strangulation?"

"Yes. As reported."

"So this is a serial killer," Paige replied.

Adele didn't look back, preferring to scan the body for further clues. No defensive marks that she could see. The woman hadn't been able to put up much of a fight. Judging by where she'd been found, behind the barrels, she'd been hiding. Which meant she'd seen the killer coming.

Adele straightened up, dusting off her pants.

"I don't think she knew the killer," Adele murmured.

Paige cleared her throat. "What makes you say that?"

"She was hiding back here. No defensive wounds, which means there was an initial attack." Adele turned now, her frame still facing the corpse, but her eyes now on Paige, who still maintained her distance, the queasy look across her features. "If she had known the killer, why would she have run, why would she have hidden?"

"Maybe he approached her threateningly. Maybe she had a bad feeling."

Adele nodded slowly, glancing back. "Maybe. But the killer has been careful up till now." Adele trailed off and glanced at the victim's feet, her eyes narrowed. "Barefoot," she said. "Scratch marks."

"She ran through the forest?"

Before Adele could reply, a voice called out from the trees around the barn.

All eyes swished in the direction, and Adele hurried around the wooden structure to see a German officer waving her fingers and pointing toward something in the grass amidst the row of trees.

Along with a grudging Paige, Adele hurried over, and went still.

"A mug," said the investigating officer. A pretty, red-haired woman with a smattering of brown freckles. "And look, the ground here is disheveled."

Adele nodded in gratitude and dropped to her haunches again, frowning toward the broken ceramic pieces. She looked back toward the barn and then swiveled, glancing in the direction of the large mansion looming behind the trees. It was barely visible from here.

"The husband, is he still up at the house?" Adele asked.

The red-haired officer who'd found the mug nodded once. "He took the news horribly. Hasn't left his room. His sister-in-law is on her way over, though. She might be able to provide more information."

Adele swallowed, tapping her fingers against her thigh. "It looks like Mrs. Schmidt was out for a morning walk. Carrying the coffee mug, and then the killer surprised her—she dropped it and ran, but he chased her down." Adele felt a shiver along her spine; she thought about being chased in the woods, no backup, no weapon. Nowhere to go. A familiar sensation of stage fright arose in her belly.

She clenched her teeth, pushing roughly back to her feet again, and turned toward Agent Paige. "She has a husband. That's different from the first two."

Paige nodded, frowning. "Perhaps that's why the killer waited to strike until she was away from the house."

Adele shook her head. "Which means he kept an eye on her too. To figure out her morning routine. He knew she'd come this way."

Paige gnawed on the corner of her lip, her back to the barn and the body, some of the queasiness having faded from her pale features. "She has to be in her fifties also," Paige said.

Adele glanced at her phone, scrolling to the file on Schmidt. "Fifty-five," she replied.

"Wealthy," Paige said, waving a hand in the direction of the mansion.

"Same as the first two. But not single."

"No, I suppose not. The husband isn't speaking?"

Adele shook her head, nodding toward the German officer. "Says he's too distraught by the death. Can't blame him. The sister-in-law is on her way…" At that moment, a sudden sound of voices and motion caught Adele's attention. She turned, frowning. "Speak of the devil," Adele said, trailing off.

Confronting the relatives of a murder victim was never fun to begin with. But from first impressions alone, this new arrival seemed the sort to make a difficult task nearly impossible.

# CHAPTER FOURTEEN

Adele watched as another police officer escorted a small, plump woman through the black gate surrounding the swimming pool. The woman looked to be in her sixties and walked with slow, shuffling steps, with one hand holding her large flowery hat in place, and the other carrying a small purse. The woman muttered darkly as she stepped daintily along the trail, trying not to sink into the soft grass and dirt with her high heel shoes. At last, she seemed to give up, and clicked her fingers toward the officer, as if demanding he take her arm. The German policeman looked mildly amused, but hid his smile while reaching out, aiding the older woman across the grass toward the barn.

Her cheeks were red, and she was huffing as she drew nearer, and Adele could hear her saying, "Don't rip my arm out, you big brute. Careful, careful."

The officer's amusement faded somewhat at the abuse, but he still helped steady the oddly dressed woman and guided her toward where Adele and Agent Paige waited next to the shattered mug.

"Well?" the approaching woman said, in a demanding voice. "Where is she? Where is my baby sister?"

Adele swallowed, feeling her stomach twist, but she held out a placating hand, and in German, replied, "I'm very sorry Mrs...." She trailed off, allowing the woman to fill in the blank.

"Schmidt. I'm also Schmidt."

Adele's brow furrowed in surprise.

The woman adjusted her purse, pushing back the brim of her hat. "My sister didn't take her husband's name. This isn't the dark ages anymore, young lady."

Adele blinked, but nodded slowly. The older Mrs. Schmidt glanced toward the snickering police officer behind Adele, and her red features turned even more crimson. "What are you gawking at? Go do something useful."

The officer behind Adele blinked in surprise, stuttering, but Agent Paige just waved at him, and the man turned, hurrying back behind the barn to rejoin the rest of the investigators.

"Well? Where is my sister?"

"You know why you were called here?" Adele said, hesitantly, and feeling a sudden surge of horror.

"Yes. She's dead. So I was told. Where?"

The woman was small, round, red-faced, and old, but she barked like a military sergeant. Adele had flashbacks of her own home in Germany, thinking of her father and his gruff nature. If he was a pit bull, this woman was a pit bull crossed with a Doberman. Her eyes were narrowed, and she looked ready to bite.

"Yes, of course," Adele said, quietly. "We'll take you to her. It's not a pleasant sight. But we do need help identifying the body."

"Identifying? You're telling me you don't even know it's my sister?"

Adele shook her head. "Your brother-in-law provided pictures. It's her. We just need someone in person to confirm. Protocol and all."

"Protocol?" The woman scoffed. "That's why I'm here?"

"We had hoped you would also be able to answer a couple of questions for us, Mrs. Schmidt."

"What sort of questions?"

"We're trying to find the man who did this."

"Man." She scoffed. "Of course it was a man."

"Do you mind answering some questions?"

"Well? What are they?"

Adele cleared her throat. "Did your sister have any enemies? Anyone who might want her—"

"Dead? Strangled to death? Violently? In her own backyard?"

"I suppose so, yes."

"No, my sister was a kind woman. Gentle. She was the nice one in the family."

Adele kept her expression placid.

For a moment, Mrs. Schmidt's eyes narrowed even more, if such a thing were possible, but then she shook her head at Adele. "No one hated my sister. No one. That husband of hers didn't have enemies either. He's as soft as a jelly doughnut. The perfect sort of man for my sister. He couldn't have strangled a pillow, no less Elke."

"All right. Do you have any idea who might've done this?"

"A sexual pervert."

Adele blinked.

The older Mrs. Schmidt bobbed her head, brimming with certainty.

"That's who it always is," she said, insistently. "Don't think I don't see the news. A man. Definitely a man. A sexual pervert. That's what they do. They like strangling women. Mark my words, it was a pervert."

"You know this?"

Mrs. Schmidt just shrugged. "Who else would it have been?"

Adele decided to change tack. "I had one other question. Your sister, was she religious in any way?"

"Bah. Nominally, maybe. Easters, sometimes. The Good Lord doesn't much like lukewarm believers. Is that what you're saying?" She scowled. "Do you think the Lord did this—because I'll tell you right now I've never heard such a stupid—"

"That's not what I'm saying at all. So you're saying she wasn't very religious."

"No, she wasn't. Neither was that doughboy of a husband. Weak, that's what he is."

Adele sighed, trailing off and fidgeting uncomfortably. She glanced toward Agent Paige, reflexively, and then looked back toward the victim's sister. "Final thing; did your sister own a second home in Southern France?"

She could practically hear Agent Paige's eyeballs scraping their sockets, likely catching the word for France and piecing it together.

But the rolling of her eyes went stiff as Mrs. Schmidt nodded her head bluntly. "Yes. A second house in France. They had one in Italy too. What of it?"

Adele shook her head quickly, feeling her pulse quicken and a slow prickle spread along her spine. She had known it. Another home in France.

"Do you know if the home was in the Aquitaine region?" she asked, her voice hoarse.

Mrs. Schmidt narrowed her eyes, frowning at Adele. "Yes," she said, slowly. "Is that important?"

Adele just waved a hand, trying to keep her own excitement in check. Nerves be damned, she still had it. The homes in France were the key. They had to be. The only connecting point. But how so? What did vacation homes in Southern France have to do with it?

She swallowed and gestured toward Agent Paige, saying, "We actually have to be going. The officers over there will help take you to your sister. Mrs. Schmidt, I'm very sorry for your loss."

The older woman just ignored Adele, grunting, as, in her high heels, trying to walk on mud and grass, she hobbled over toward the barn with the help of the officer who'd aided her through the gates.

Adele and Paige stood next to each other over the shattered fragments of the ceramic coffee mug, frowning in the direction of the stumbling older woman.

Agent Paige said, softly, "Coincidence, has to be."

"She had a vacation home in France. Just like the other two victims."

"That doesn't mean anything."

"Maybe. Or maybe it's the key to the case. What are the odds that all three—"

"I know what you're going to say. Low odds. But they're also wealthy. Wealthy people own many homes. It's not that unusual. Plus, Churchville also had a home in Italy and Germany. On top of this, the homes were nearly never used."

"Come on," Adele said, feeling her frustration rising now. She looked away from the barn, staring at Agent Paige.

"I know what you're thinking, but we can't keep hopping around Europe. There are no victims in France. How's that supposed to help us?"

Adele narrowed her eyes. "Paige, this is the best lead we have."

"And I say we should stay here, go through more financials. Maybe it really is a sexual pervert. We should talk to the neighbors."

Adele felt like yelling now. Briefly, she wondered if Paige was simply trying to avoid another plane flight. She supposed that accusing her partner of unprofessionalism wouldn't go far though. So instead, she just shrugged, turned, and began stalking back in the direction of the driveway and their waiting car. "You don't have to come if you don't want to," she said over her shoulder. "But I'm going. Alone if I have to."

She stalked through the trees, moving toward the gray asphalt drive. Behind her, coming from the victim's sister now, Adele could hear a series of curses, followed by a growl like from a wounded animal.

Adele could have stayed, perhaps, to try and comfort Mrs. Schmidt. She could have come alongside, helping her, trying to console her. But what was the point? Adele had seen what it was to shatter a soul. She didn't need to see it again. Mrs. Schmidt seemed tough. But even the toughest sorts had to face the mortality of those they loved. Adele was too tired, too exhausted, too preoccupied to witness another human's descent into grief. Such a strange pit, grief. So easy to enter, and so difficult to escape.

Adele could hear more cursing, and another sound like shouting.

Some people sobbed, or wept. Others just got angry. And still others became determined.

Adele quickened, marching now, striding between the trees toward the driveway and back to the waiting car. With Paige or without, she was heading to Southern France.

# CHAPTER FIFTEEN

His closest friend in the entire world was back in Germany. His friends had told him the beautiful, talented, wonderful agent Adele Sharp had returned.

The painter smiled, stroking the back of his knuckles and tracing them with a soft finger, circling, circling.

He reclined in the nude, his feet on the armrest of the long couch, his head not quite reaching the opposite armrest. He stared at the ceiling, still circling his finger over his knuckles.

He couldn't help but smile. The poetry of it all. The beauty. His naked flesh was speckled with greens and browns of acrylic paint.

He glanced over toward the large canvas, where he'd been working. Some of the paints had dried slower than he would've liked. And yet, despite the slightly oily and wet veneer, he had to say the scenic vista was one of his best works yet.

He always did his best work after a kill.

Robert Henry had been one of his masterpieces. He had shared it with his closest friend. She had been the first to find the work of art. Poetry in motion. Fate.

The painter smiled, shifting about and wiggling like a small puppy in the warm folds of a blanket.

Giddy, excited, delighted. She was in Germany. The beauty of it all, of course, was that was his next destination too.

His contacts with the German police hadn't realized just how valuable their information would prove. He still had his camera facing Adele's apartment, but she hadn't been there in a while. Which meant he needed more information. He had other plans, more delightful plans.

He got to his feet, pushing off the couch, struck by a sudden bout of inspiration. He tottered over to the canvas, stepping onto the plastic sheet. He looked toward his collection of paints, and then his eyes settled on the small glass jar. He dipped his brush in the jar, whistling to himself and still smiling, swaying with the soft music pulsing from his own lips. He danced slowly in front of the canvas, beneath the lights of the small studio. He poked with the paint brush toward the glass jar, flicking the last droplets off the end, and then added a streak of sheer red onto the canvas. A piece of Henry. A swirling, circling pattern, just over the painted trees and flowing river. He liked to include his friends in his paintings. He'd done so for the last twenty years. And soon, very soon, he felt near certain, his best friend in the world would help him paint the final masterpiece.

Not yet, though.

He frowned, reaching up and gently prodding at a slight streak, clearing it from the pale canvas. He lifted his finger to his lips, suckling on the digit and licking away the blood.

No, not yet. Adele would wait.

He already had his next masterpiece planned.

"A soldier is what I am," he whispered softly. "Look at my chest and look at it puff," he said, "look at me frown, and look at me growl." He giggled. "Look at how I am. So tough. So brave. They call him Joseph Sharp. They call him Joseph Sharp," he said, singing softly with the tune in his head.

He nodded slowly. Yes, Adele was back in Germany. And that was where he was heading next. Where his next masterpiece would take place. Adele's father would be a truly beautiful spectacle. First her mother, then her father, and eventually, his best friend in the world. Yes, it would be a trinity of masterpieces. The most beautiful craft imaginable.

"Because that is what I am," he sang softly. "That is what I am."

# CHAPTER SIXTEEN

It had felt like pulling teeth, but Agent Paige had finally relented. Now, Adele settled in the back of the taxi. Adele had taken the spot behind the driver and Paige sat front passenger side. They'd left the airport, and now were moving through the smaller side streets of the Aquitaine region in Southern France.

"Where is this damn house?" Paige snapped. "We've been driving for an hour."

Adele glanced at her watch, and then toward the small GPS with the thin purple line beneath the taxi driver's mirror. The man in front had learned not to answer Paige. Instead, he contented himself with staring out the window and leaning toward one of the vents.

For her part, Adele sighed, glancing at the passing trees of the French countryside and the distant gray and blue where the horizon met the ocean. The coastal portion of Aquitaine extended to meet the waters, witnessing the distant, expansive blue.

"Not much further," Adele said, softly, staring through the window and refusing to glance toward Paige. "The property manager's going to meet us there."

Agent Paige grunted. "Ah, the property manager. We've solved the case."

Adele refused to be goaded. They would be stopping at the first victim's vacation home, and Adele could only hope this would be the first domino to fall into place. For now, the killer still remained a step ahead. He'd been a step ahead the entire time. She shivered. That would change; it had to. Soon.

"Here," the driver declared suddenly, and Adele couldn't help but notice a slight tinge of relief to his tone.

Adele stared through the windshield as they trundled up a small road, toward the waiting beach house. It was much smaller than the mansions had been.

No hedges, or statuary here. Nor gates. Rather, the house seemed to be mostly wooden trim and stone arches. Bits and portions resembled a villa, but other parts seemed older, especially on the first floor. Adele frowned toward an archway, with slabs of gray stone circling the door.

"Think you can wait for us?" Adele said, softly, glancing toward the driver.

He looked at her in the mirror, his eyes narrowing. Adele sighed, pulling a fifty-euro note from her wallet and slipping it over the seat, patting her hand against the gearshift and then leaving the note wedged against the plastic. "Please?" she said, insistently.

The driver glanced at the fifty-euro note, glanced at Agent Paige, glanced back at the note. He looked in the mirror again, his eyes narrowing. Adele sighed, and pulled out another fifty-euro note. The last of her funds for the day. Out here, it would take some time to wait for another taxi. Time they simply couldn't afford.

She slid this next to the gearshift as well. The taxi driver flashed a smile now, all crooked teeth and cigarette-stained molars. "Happy to wait," he said, grinning in a way that wrinkled his face like a prune.

Adele nodded her gratitude, trying not to roll her eyes as she slid out of the taxi and followed Agent Paige out toward the waiting summerhouse facing the distant ocean.

The sun beamed down on them, and the late afternoon illumination dawned over the back of the home, casting its shadow across the sand in the backyard.

"We've solved it," Agent Paige declared, hands on her hip facing the house.

"We haven't even gotten inside yet," Adele said, testily. "We're here. How about we make the best of it."

As the two agents neared, the door opened suddenly, and a small woman with a bandana around her head waited for them, glancing suspiciously from one to the other.

"DGSI," Adele said. "Are you the property manager?"

"Sara Cote," the woman with the bandana said, crossing her arms over a blue maintenance uniform. A grease patch covered the sleeve, and she had a toolbelt around her hips, with a variety of hammers and screwdrivers and wrenches. She frowned from Adele to Agent Paige. "I got the call to meet you here. May I ask what this is about?"

"Investigation," Paige said, stiffly. "We just need you to let us in. It shouldn't take long." She frowned. "Shouldn't take long at all."

Adele followed the older woman through the door and into the summer home. As she did, she passed under another strange stone archway. Parts of the home look pristine and new. Varnished woods, and fresh beams with new coats of paint. Some parts, like the kitchen which she could see from the entryway, had modern marble counters, and cherry wood cabinets.

Other portions of the house, though, seemed out of place. The stone archway above was matched by the entryway itself—a strange patchwork of wooden tiles and slabs of stone. She frowned, stepping over the stoop and entering further into the house, flashing her credentials to the watchful eye of the property manager.

"When you called, I thought something might have happened to Mrs. Churchville."

Adele just shook her head. "We can't discuss an ongoing investigation."

Sophie Paige moved further into the house, glancing through the rooms.

"Is there anything?" Adele said, hesitantly, then trailed off. She thought for a moment, unsure where to start. She needed to know what to ask, to unlock the key to the investigation. But the clues wouldn't come. She didn't know where to start. All three of the victims had summer homes in Aquitaine. But what did that mean? She regarded the property manager. "Do you take care of any of the other homes in the area?" she said on a whim.

The manager shrugged. "Not really. Mostly I work for one of the local hotels. Why?"

Adele just shook her head. "Is there anything you can tell me about this place?"

"What would you like to know?"

*I don't know,* Adele thought to herself. Out loud, she said, "I'm not entirely sure. Just anything."

The property manager frowned, adjusting her bandana. "Anything? Well, I've been working here for about three years. The previous property manager was my uncle. He passed away a couple years ago."

"Sorry to hear that."

She shrugged. "He was old and happy. Surrounded by family when he went. Not much more you can ask. Do you want to know about the house itself? I'm afraid I don't know why you're here, Agent—"

"Sharp."

"Agent Sharp."

Adele sighed, wishing she could say more. But what else was there to add? She didn't know why she was here.

She was an investigator. Perhaps the questions were best left until after she did a little looking. And so she moved down the hall, after Paige. She turned to face a dining room with a large glass window looking out at the ocean. The table looked like it had been made in the shed, with plank wood screwed together haphazardly. A family project? A joke? The walls were painted green, and the floor, strangely, was tiled like the entryway. Strange slats of wood and old stone. Seemingly out of place compared to the rest of the modern architecture.

She frowned and moved to the next room, this time stepping in and pushing against the door. She was confronted by a small bathroom. A normal shower and sink, this time tiled with blue marble. But then her eyes darted toward a small window in the top right of the room. The window was off-center, as if wedged in the corner, and instead of glass, it reflected back reds and blues and greens.

Adele poked her head back out into the hall. "Is this a stained-glass window?"

The property manager frowned, approached, and glanced over Adele's shoulder toward the window. She shrugged. "Guess so. I don't really ask much about the homeowners' taste."

Adele stepped out of the bathroom now, crossing her arms and glancing toward the dining room and then again toward the bathroom. A strange array of modern architecture and what looked like old stone and windows. But what did that mean?

"Nothing," she murmured softly.

"Excuse me?"

"Look, is there anything else you can tell me about this place? Do you know when it was built?"

The manager shrugged apologetically, shaking her head and scratching at the back of her bandana. "I don't know. That's way before my time. But," she added, "I can probably find out. My uncle used to keep notes on these places. It was more of a hobby of his than anything." She shrugged. One hand tapped at her tool belt. "I just like fixing things, to be honest."

"Here's my card. If you find anything, please call…" Adele trailed off. "Is there a basement?"

The property manager shook her head. "No basements."

Adele began to move back toward the front of the house, frowning to herself. The rest of the home was small, with a few bedrooms, kitchen, and a lounging area. Again and again, she was confronted by the strange hybrid of modern architecture and old, historic hints. The fireplace looked like it was made of cobblestones. A couple more windows in the lounge reminded her of stained glass. Even one of the walls in the bedrooms was old stone. What did any of that mean?

And what did that have to do with the three murders?

Adele sighed, finally leaving down the hall again and rejoining Agent Paige on the doorstep. The property manager waited outside, tapping her foot impatiently, her arms crossed.

"Anything?" Paige asked, raising an inquisitive eyebrow.

Adele frowned. "Hold your horses. We still have to check out the second place."

"Because I didn't find anything," Paige said, innocently. "No death letters written in bottles. No confessions from murderers. No hidden weapons in the fireplace."

"Did you check?"

"I did, in fact. And there was nothing. Agent Sharp, I respect you thought this was a good lead. And I give you, it might not be a coincidence. But I think, at this point, we're just wasting precious time."

For a moment, Adele paused. Was Agent Paige right? Was she simply wasting time?

If Foucault heard about this, would he pull her from the case?

She was second-guessing herself again. She felt a flash of frustration—not at Paige, but at herself. She couldn't afford to think negatively. She had to focus, to double down. She had to trust her instincts.

*Robert is dead*, a soft voice whispered in her head. *Your instincts died with him.*

She gritted her teeth, one hand curling into a fist as she brushed past Agent Paige and marched down the steps toward the waiting taxi.

"Shut up," she said to herself. "Just shut up."

She could feel the curious glance of the property manager on her back, but she ignored it, moving toward the taxi.

The summer home of the second victim could have the clue she needed. She was right—about what, she wasn't sure. How it tied to the murders, again, uncertain. But still, she was right. She needed to be. There was no other option. She couldn't second-guess herself.

She flung open the front door this time, sliding in next to the taxi driver and ignoring Agent Paige's pointed look. This time, the older agent could sit in the back. She hadn't wanted to come here, after all. Besides, if the second house didn't turn up anything, Adele would have more than Paige to answer to.

# CHAPTER SEVENTEEN

As they pulled into the driveway of the second home, Adele's heart plummeted. She stared at the modern house, with white painted walls and ceramic shingles. Her eyes traced the wired fence and the vibrant, pink patio steps, seemingly cut from cotton candy.

She stared through the window of the taxi, blinking and trying to make sense of it. The house didn't resemble the first one at all.

"Is this what you wanted?" Agent Paige grumbled, staring through the windshield as well.

Adele took her phone from her pocket, quickly scrolling to the real estate listing as she pushed out of the back of the car. She stepped toward the summer home, facing the windows glinting in the late afternoon sun.

Nothing about it resembled the first house. This home was smaller, but closer to the ocean. Now, Adele could detect the salty, waterside air. Instead of sand, this house had stone slabs amidst grass, and a tasteful arrangement around the small Jacuzzi within the metal fence. She even spotted a mini fridge next to a garage, covered by an aluminum roof.

She approached the house, frowning as she did and taking the carved steps up to the patio. As she fiddled with her phone, she pulled up the website that had sold the home. *Not listed.* Below the warning, she spotted an estimate of the price and whistled. Even if she saved every penny she had for the next ten years, she wouldn't be able to afford it.

She scroll down, toward the title *year built.*

Only fifteen years ago. She frowned, scratching at her head and muttering to herself. What had she expected? What was the connection?

She strolled along the patio, the wood creaking beneath her footsteps as she moved toward the nearest window and peered into the house. Again, everything modern, everything as she might expect from a home built in the last couple of decades. No sign of old architecture or stone archways. No sign of stained glass.

She shook her head in rising frustration.

"Well?" Agent Paige called out from where she remained by the taxi.

Adele held up a finger, not daring to speak. She circled around the house, moving past the windows and the lower window wells. All three of the victims had homes in this area. The property managers were different, though. The owners were different. The real estate agents behind the sales also different. She'd double-checked that part.

The homes were all within a twenty-minute drive of each other. What was the connection, then?

She puffed a breath, closing her eyes as if against a sudden, surging headache.

What was she missing? Something obvious, no doubt. But what?

She wanted to yell at the sky, to shake her fist. She felt so close, but she had stumbled onto something. Like she had finally seized back some of her instincts. But again, it felt like she was butting against an immovable object with her skull.

Maybe Paige was right. Maybe the houses were just a coincidence.

"Come on," she murmured to herself. "Think. Think, dammit."

She strolled around the back of the house, noting no lights were on inside. Some of the windows were dusty, suggesting no one had lived in it for a while. She trailed her hand along the white siding, pausing for a moment to peer through a window into a bedroom. One of the curtains had been pulled completely shut, but the other left a gap for her to peer into a small, blue bedroom with a rocket ship bed frame.

Adele sighed. She'd missed it.

"Have we wasted enough time?" Paige called out behind her. Adele turned, frowning to acknowledge the glowering agent waiting impatiently by the gate, her arms crossed. Behind her, the taxi driver seemed relieved to have the car to himself again. His fingers rolled nervously on the steering wheel, waiting.

"I-I thought," Adele stammered, "I felt certain that…" she tried, trailing off.

"You tried and you missed," Agent Paige said with a sniff. She stared at Adele for a moment, and briefly, for an instant, it almost seemed like her eyes flashed with something akin to sympathy. She shook her head hesitantly and said, "It's been a rough month, I understand. But you're not going to help anyone this way. It's a dead end. We need to go back to the scene of the first crime and ask better questions."

"What questions? No one knows anything. The killer's been jumping from country to country, targeting wealthy women. There's no rhyme or reason. Two of them were irreligious, one of them a devout believer. Two of them were single, one of them married."

"All of them wealthy. All of them killed the same way."

"And," Adele said, insistently, more for her own benefit than Agent Paige's, "three of them owned homes in Aquitaine."

Sophie snorted, waving a hand toward the house. "All right, look, a summer home in France. We're here—so what? What's this doing for us? You read the same things I did. Different real estate agents. Different property owners. Different property managers. Different gardening services. Different housecleaning services. No common guests. No common family." Agent Paige listed off the information with a bite to her tone, her frown deepening with each second. As she spoke, Adele felt her stomach churn. Paige had always been the sort to catalog information quickly and meticulously. And now, as she revealed what she'd paid attention to, it felt like she was slapping Adele with each subsequent word.

"There are no connections. Houses don't murder people. Is that what you're thinking? Some sort of ghost? Some sort of evil house, hunting them down in other countries? I'm not sure how one of these structures would have gotten onto a plane. But then again," she waved a hand toward the ocean. "Maybe it swam."

"That's not what I'm saying. Obviously. There has to be something else. Something we're missing."

"You're impossible. You don't see sense. Just listen for a change. You've missed this one. There's no shame in it, and I don't blame you."

Adele blinked. From Agent Paige, these words were nearly akin to encouragement.

The older, silver-haired women crossed her arms, breathing slowly. "My oldest daughter, she's only a few years younger than you, you know?"

Adele winced. She knew that Agent Paige's daughter was a sore subject. After the incident ten years ago, when Adele had reported missing evidence, Agent Paige's daughter had given her mother the cold shoulder. Adele hadn't found out until Paige had told her the previous year, but it had caused no small amount of pain for the Paige family. Still, it didn't seem like Sophie was trying to press this point again. Instead, she said, "So I know how important it is to stick to what you believe. We live in a world where a young woman's opinion might not be minded. We have to be strong. I get it. I've done it myself. But there's also a strength in being able to say when you're wrong. Can you do that, Agent Sharp? Can you let it go?"

Adele swallowed, staring at Paige. For a moment, she wondered what it would have been like to have her own mother here, speaking to her. She wondered what it might have been like to have someone who understood, who could put themselves in Adele's shoes.

Her stomach twisted again, but also an ache formed in her chest. A longing, and a grief.

To her surprise, Adele found her eyes misting, and she glanced off angrily, trying not to let Paige see. She was too exhausted for all this. She needed sleep. She needed to regroup. Maybe Sophie was right. Maybe they needed to return to London and question witnesses more thoroughly. But maybe the real clue would be found in Germany. They'd never even spoken to the husband, and they hadn't gone through the financials. But what about Italy? The foul-mouthed board room member was worth another look as well, wasn't he?"

And yet, even as she contemplated these thoughts, Adele couldn't shake the small niggling worry in her gut. It was becoming more and more difficult to focus. More difficult to make a choice.

"Well?" Paige insisted, and her tone had softened somewhat. If anything, she seemed gentle. "Are you ready to let this go?"

Adele closed her eyes for a moment. Then she glanced back toward her phone, scrolling to the final address she'd been given. It was close. Only ten minutes away. Would it be worth it? Would it be worth risking Agent Paige's anger once more?

"I," Adele said, hesitantly, trailing off. "I guess maybe…" she began, but then biting back the words.

Paige just stood there, her arms crossed, her expression as severe as ever, but her eyes holding a strange, unusual compassion.

Adele didn't want to disappoint the older agent. The first home had been strange, but this one was normal, just another house. Yes, in the same region, but far enough away that did it even matter? Still, she glanced back down at her phone, at the third address. The final victim's house.

They'd come so far…

She nodded, convincing herself first, before, in a shaky tone, saying, "I'd like to look at the last place."

Paige went stiff, her eyes hardening like flint.

"It's only ten minutes away. I'd like to just check it out."

Paige breathed slowly through her nose, shaking her head.

"I know you think I'm wasting my time."

Paige growled, "No, I think you are wasting *our* time. More importantly, I think you're wasting the time of whoever the next victim will be. He's going to kill again. And we'll be over here, with our fingers up our noses, staring at houses."

Adele winced but pressed, "I just want to check it out."

"Adele, let me put it this way. You either come with me, return to the airport, or you go on your own. I'm done with this foolishness. I flew here with you, and you need to know when it's time to say quit."

Adele winced. Maybe she was being too stubborn. Maybe…

No. She couldn't back out now. She'd already made up her mind. Besides, Paige would never be her friend. She wasn't here to make connections. The less Paige liked her, the safer the older woman was. The fewer people who spent time with her, the safer they all were. The Spade Killer was looking for more victims, no doubt. The closer she got to people the more danger they were in.

So instead of protesting, Adele just shrugged. "Leave if you have to. But I'm going to check out the final house."

Paige snorted, staring at Adele one final time as if searching for a glimmer of doubt, but then grunting in disgust, turning on her heel and marching back toward the sidewalk. "I'll call my own taxi," she snapped. "This one smells like fish."

Adele felt a slight chill along her back, and with nerves still flitting about her stomach, like a rookie on the job, she turned around and began moving through the gate past the Jacuzzi and to the waiting taxi. The driver seemed relieved when Adele was the only one who slid into his car and gave instructions for the next house.

Paige stared through the tinted windows, glaring at both the occupants.

Adele refused to look back. She'd come too far to back out now. Undoubtedly, Paige would call Foucault to complain, to try and get Adele thrown from the case. The third house had to hold the answer for when that call inevitably came.

## CHAPTER EIGHTEEN

The trip to the final vacation home was a lonely one. Adele lodged in the backseat, and no sooner had the car scraped to a halt against the curb than she launched out the back, calling a quick, "I'll be right back," over her shoulder.

This final house was the largest of the three. The third victim had only passed away in the last thirty-six hours, and yet, as she approached the house, she spotted a man standing out front with a mallet and a yard sign.

The man was pounding the sign into the ground, whistling as he did.

Adele frowned in the direction of the fellow. Behind him, the house was the strangest of the three. It looked like the renovated portion of some castle. A courtyard angled off where a newer looking garage had been built, using a similar stonework to match the stony façade of the castle itself. Not a castle in size, so much as build. Stone turrets flanked either side of the main hub. Stone walls encircled thick windows. Most of the glass on the second floor was stained. The house seemed odd, archaic, like something off a postcard or out of a history book.

Adele's brow twisted, but she summoned her nerves and approached the man with the mallet.

"Excuse me," she said.

The man whirled around with a start, his eyes dancing from Adele to the waiting taxi in the back. He cleared his throat. "Who are you?"

The left side of the man's face was still, and didn't move with the rest of his expression. His eyes were half hooded, his mouth slightly downturned, suggesting, perhaps, the man had endured a stroke recently. His face was wider than his physique might have normally allowed, suggesting perhaps a man who had lost weight, but from his midsection first.

The man was shaking his head and saying, "I'm sorry, but this is private property."

"I don't mean to startle you. I'm Agent Sharp, with the DGSI."

The man fixed her with a stunned gaze. "Are you here about the owner?"

Adele glanced at the sign. A for sale sign. With *La Petite Realty.*

She pointed toward the sign and said, "You're selling the place?"

"Got a call this morning. They wanted it rushed. I only just got here. Sorry, but what is DGSI doing here?"

She ignored the question. "Who called you?"

The man shuffled uncomfortably, glancing back over his shoulder to Adele again. "A Mrs. Schmidt. The sister-in-law of the house owner."

Adele nodded slowly. This made sense. The husband of the third victim had been beside himself with grief. But the fiery, red-faced sister-in-law had seemed a commanding presence. Adele wouldn't have put it past her to put the house up for sale so quickly.

"Do you know why they're selling?"

"I don't. Just heard there was some bad business in Germany."

Adele combed a hand through her hair. Perhaps the husband didn't want the house without his wife. Perhaps the sister was getting ahead of herself and making a play for an inheritance payout. Whatever the case, Adele wasn't with financial crimes.

She said, "What do you know about this place?"

He glanced at the house and back at her. "Not much. It's in a good area. It didn't used to be, but things have looked up recently. Houses are going for three times what they were ten years ago."

"I see."

"Are you looking to buy?"

"No. Is there anything…" She trailed off, wrinkling her brow. "…strange about this place?"

"Strange in what way?"

"Any way."

The round-faced real estate agent scratched at his chin and untucked his collar, breathing slowly. "I mean it's old. But you can see that."

Adele sighed, shaking her head. Perhaps she should have gone with Agent Paige. Was she just fooling herself at this point?

"I don't mean to bother you, but there's a second house; 632 Route de Contis."

"What about it? Is it yours? We give very competitive rates if you're looking to sell."

"I'm just curious if you know who sold that home?"

The agent frowned a bit, leaning against the yard sign, and then said, slowly, "Funnily enough, I think I do. I try to keep track of most the competitors in the area. We're a small firm."

"So who sold that one?"

"It wasn't one of the big firms," said the real estate agent. "Which is why I remember it. Was a good deal from what I recall. You won't find the guy at an agency; he works out of a trailer."

Adele blinked in surprise. "A trailer? Where?"

"On an undeveloped lot on the other side of town, behind some of the eateries for the tourists."

"What's his name?"

"Etienne Durand."

"Do you have an address for Mr. Durand?"

"Look it up on your phone. He advertises. Say, are you sure you're not in the business for a house? Like I said, very competitive rates. This place, in fact, I'll knock a percent off the price, if you want to come in with a bid."

"No, that's quite all right. Thank you." Adele looked back toward the strange house. For a moment she considered going inside, but what would be the point?

She wasn't here because of the architecture. Odd though it was. She was here because this was a common point among all three victims. She just couldn't tell why. Why did it matter? The first building had strange architectural parts too. Some old columns, and the stained glass window in the bathroom. This third one looked practically like a miniature castle. But the second had seemed modern. So what was the connection?

Etienne Durand. The rogue real estate agent who worked out of a trailer on an undeveloped lot. Maybe he would have the answers she was looking for. And if not, she wasn't sure how she would be able to return and face Agent Paige or Foucault.

Especially not if another body dropped in the interim.

***

Adele stalked toward the small trailer, situated against the red brick wall of one of the eateries on the touristy boulevard. The windows were bright, orange light emanating out into the late afternoon. A large picture on the side of the RV displayed a grinning face, a little too exaggerated to be handsome, with a weak chin. The face was next to words that read, *Etienne Realty.*

Adele had found the address online and had read a few of the reviews for the place. Mostly satisfied customers, but a couple of one-star reviews had come from people who'd accused Mr. Durand of being shady with their money.

One had flat out accused him of stealing.

Adele rubbed her fingers against each other as she approached the door, and then rested her hand on her belt. She wrapped her fingers against the metal handle and called, "DGSI!"

A pause, then a sound like a small cough. "Customer or collector?" a voice called from inside.

She frowned. "DGSI," she repeated, louder now.

"What's that?" the voice replied.

"Police," she said.

The door suddenly swung open, nearly knocking into her. She took a quick step back, avoiding the swinging frame. A much smaller version of the man on the poster beneath the trailer windows blinked out at her.

The smile was almost to scale. It took up most of his face. Teeth nearly the size of thumbnails flashed out from stretched lips.

"Police?" he said, through his forced smile. "Well, I'm almost off work. Do you mind coming back later?"

The man had oily hair, slicked to one side, and his million-dollar smile seemed just a bit too white, suggesting whitening strips. His weak chin bristled with attempts of a beard to hide its structure, but the facial hair hadn't come in completely yet.

He wore a suit top, but his bottom half was clad only in boxers.

Adele glanced pointedly down at the man's underwear, and he followed her gaze.

"Whoops," he said, nonchalantly. "Sorry, I was working on the computer."

He made no move to return into the trailer and don some pants.

Adele sighed. "Are you Etienne Durand?"

"That's me. Who's asking?"

She crossed her arms now, placing one foot in front of the other. "Agent Sharp. I have a couple of questions for you."

His expression remained rather fixed. "Is this about that deal for the houseboat? It's not my fault they didn't have a permit. Besides, pending litigation, you're not supposed to harass me about that anymore."

Adele shook her head. "Boat? No, I'm not here about a boat. I'm here about a piece of property you sold nearly five years ago."

The man blinked, scratching at his chin. "Oh? Well, five years is long past any statute of limitations. My lawyer is on speed dial. He can be here in ten minutes."

"I'm not here with an accusation," she said, hurriedly, as he fished into nonexistent pants pockets for his phone, his hand moving instinctively. He peeled down the elastic of his boxers just a bit too far for her comfort. He quickly cursed and muttered, "Oh, sorry, there it is."

He spun around, reaching for his phone on his desk, which she could make out just inside the trailer's open door.

"Hang on," she said, quickly. "I mean it. I'm not here about the problem. I'm looking for information."

Etienne glanced over his shoulder, frowning. "What sort of information?"

"It's about a property you sold five years ago. 632 Route de Contis."

He wrinkled his nose, which gave his features a plastic, shiny look. "You have to give me a second. I sell a lot of property. One moment."

He slammed the door shut, leaving Adele outside, blinking.

For a moment, she considered knocking again, but then she heard movement about inside the trailer. A couple of curses, and then the clatter of a keyboard.

A second later, she heard a voice call out, "What was that address again?"

She hesitated, staring at the metal door, and glanced sheepishly over her shoulder at the taxi driver, who was watching her with an amused expression. She repeated the address, and heard more clacking on keys.

She straightened her suit, and, almost instinctively, double-checked to make sure she was still wearing her pants. Apparently, in this part of town, one could never be too careful.

Etienne reemerged after a couple of moments, slamming open the door again. This time she was prepared and kept her distance, lest she was sent flying.

"Yes," he said. "I sold it. So what?"

Adele felt a flicker of satisfaction. One step closer. One step at a time. "What do you remember about it?" she asked, keeping her tone even.

"Not much." He glanced back over his shoulder at a computer screen which she could see on the desk. "The parcel was owned by an old French firm," he said and tapped his nose. "About a decade ago I bought a few of those places from them. Cents on the euro."

Adele frowned. "So this is one of a few lots?"

"You're standing on another one, yes. All of them undeveloped in the same area. Ten years ago, this part of the region wasn't as expensive." He puffed his chest. "Independents like moi have helped develop this area."

Adele nodded, continuing. "All right, so before this housing boom, you bought up a bunch of the land. That particular parcel, do you remember anything about it?"

His stretched features now turned down in a sort of mouth shrug. "I remember that a house had recently been constructed on the land," he said. "The original owners left because the area was going downhill. The French firm who sold it to me gave me a good deal."

Adele remembered how the house back on the second victim's property had only been built fifteen years ago. Five years before Etienne had brought it and then sold it to Gianna Calvetti.

"The house," Adele said, "it's pretty modern."

"We didn't cut corners on it," he said quickly. "Well, at least the original builders didn't. Good materials. Is that what this is about?"

"No."

"You didn't find bodies on the property, did you?" he asked, his eyes widening.

Adele stared.

He shook his head. "Is that a yes?"

"Should I have found bodies?"

His eyes narrowed. "Did you?"

"No. Hang on a second, why did you think I might have found bodies?"

He wiggled his fingers. "I just looked you up. DGSI doesn't involve itself with minor property crime. So why are you asking about the place? No bodies I know of. Just guessing."

Adele exhaled slowly. Blinking a couple of times wondering if the word *bodies* had simply been a Freudian slip. Or an educated guess.

"This French firm you bought it from. Do you remember their name?"

"Of course. Look, the property wasn't that special. But I do remember one thing." He nodded slowly.

"Anything might help."

"Still not sure what I'm helping with, but all right. There was some old ruins on the ground. Some broken down building. It was cleared out, completely scrapped, they rebuilt on the same spot. Beyond that, I can't think of anything else you might be here about. This isn't some sort of historical site, is it? Because I don't own that property anymore. You'll have to take it up with the new owners. I can get you their address if you want."

His quick pace of words and his tone suggested he would do anything to get the federal officer off his door step.

Adele shook her head. "I have their address. But do you mind telling me what the name of that French firm was? The one who sold you the land?"

The independent real estate agent held up a finger, muttered to himself, and turned, heading back into the house. This time he didn't slam the door. She heard more clacking, the blue glow emanating past him as he bent over his computer. A second later, he turned back and said, "Becker and Associates. That's all I've got," he added.

Adele frowned, gnawing on the corner of her lip, trying to piece it all together. She still hadn't turned up anything. Cleared ruins on the second spot suggested maybe there had been an older building there as well. But she needed to find some connection. Anything at all. The families didn't know each other. Didn't go to church together. As Paige had said, didn't have similar real estate agents, nor guests or families. Which meant there had to be another connection; the properties themselves. Maybe the French firm would have it. At this point, she felt like she was grasping at straws.

And whatever the case, she couldn't keep going on like this. She nodded to herself as she turned without so much as a farewell; if she ended up another dead end, she would have to drop this thread. If she didn't reach a conclusion soon, and if this was all just a wild goose chase, her failing instincts, or failing investigative skills, were undoubtedly going to lead to another murder. And this time, it was all going to be her fault.

# CHAPTER NINETEEN

Compared to the small, makeshift office space out of the trailer in the abandoned lot, the French firm Becker and Associates was practically a cathedral.

Adele gazed up at the tall, arching stone entrances. Two steeples pointed at the sky, and her gaze drifted down the stone, toward a set of buzzers within an alcove next to stone slab steps.

She stepped off the sidewalk, a faint pounding in her chest at the odd arrangement of the firm's office space.

These were the folks who had sold the property to Etienne.

Something connected all three houses. Ruins. That's what Mr. Durand had said. The land had been cleared of ruins before building a house. Did the ruins matter?

Was it a coincidence? All of this seemed coincidental at this point. Why were the victims all in their fifties? Why were all of them wealthy? Why did they all own summer homes in southern France? Where was the killer? Did he live in the area? In France? Or was she just grasping at straws like Agent Paige insisted?

Adele felt a flicker of frustration. She wasn't sure where she had turned wrong. With a bounce in her step, coming more from frustration than eagerness, she took the stone slabs and pressed a finger, jamming into the buzzer and the small stony alcove beneath the arching doorway.

She waited a moment, standing outside the cathedral turned office building, tapping her foot impatiently on the stone steps. After a couple of moments, a voice croaked out over the intercom, "Becker and Associates. Second floor. Come in."

The doors buzzed, and Adele opened them, stepping in, reminded, briefly, of her days in a German school. She strode up a dark hall, which didn't look much like the external façade of the building. Inside, it more resembled an office space; an elevator occupied the far end of the hall. Adele ignored this, though, and the rows of doors with name plaques on them to her left, and instead made her way toward the stairwell to the right. Second floor.

She took the stairs, quickly, breathing slowly in and out, trying to focus and failing, but still trying to suppress the gnawing sense of unease in her stomach.

Adele hastened up the final few steps with rapid footfalls. She approached twin double doors at the end of the hall, next to where the elevator would have stopped. Golden letters against glass read the name of the French firm. Becker and Associates.

What was she hoping to find?

She wasn't sure. But for now, she was kicking over stones and seeing what the light revealed. And so, gritting her teeth, she pushed into the office, shouldering through the double doors.

Inside, the office was clean. The windows overlooking the street below were pristine, and the tables, with stacks of real estate magazines and legal brochures, were settled next to rows of comfortable leather chairs facing a small counter. Behind the counter, two women were chatting quietly to each other, and both of them paused, looking up at Adele as she entered.

One of the women, a very pretty, middle-aged lady, cleared her throat and folded her hands over the counter. "Can I help you?" she said.

"I'm here to speak with someone in charge."

"I see." The woman spoke like an impatient substitute teacher. She attempted a smile, but the look didn't suit her lips. "Do you have an appointment?" she said, with crisp, clear tones, enunciating the words as if afraid Adele might not be able to understand.

"I do not. My name is Agent Sharp, and I'm with DGSI." She flashed her credentials, and as she did, the demeanor of both the secretaries shifted.

The woman who'd been frowning now adopted a more pleasant, nervous expression. She cleared her throat, glancing every so often toward the door behind the counter. "I'm afraid Mr. Becker isn't entertaining guests right now."

"I'm not a guest. I'm here on an investigation. I'd like to speak with him."

"I'm not sure he's able. I believe he's in a meeting…"

Adele sighed. She'd been through the rigmarole before. Always the underlings preventing entry, and always the agent having to find a way to strong-arm or bluff their way through those doors.

It was a familiar dance, and a frustrating one. Already, she could feel the constraints of time coming in, like cold fingers wrapping around her neck. She didn't have time to dawdle, arguing with a secretary.

She didn't want to bully, nor did she want to bluff. So instead, she looked at the woman, then looked past her at the door, and shrugged. She moved around the counter and headed toward the door without another word.

"Excuse me, excuse me, you can't be back here!"

Adele ignored the protests, moving even more rapidly toward the door, her feet clicking against the varnished floorboards. "Mr. Becker," she said, raising her voice. "Police!"

She heard some more protests from the two ladies, and again, fully ignored the distraction. She'd come too far for that. She was a woman on a mission.

Adele tapped her fingers against the door, raising her voice even louder. Her eyes settled on a plaque, centering the oak frame in silver letters, which read *Mr. Pierre Becker*.

"Mr. Becker," she said, even louder now, "I need to speak with you, sir!"

"He's very busy," protested the voice behind her.

"Sir," Adele called, rapping her fingers against the frame again. "I'd like to speak with you about—"

The door opened slowly, with a creaking groan against hinges.

Even before the door had fully opened, she heard the patter of feet, of someone retreating back into the room, and then muttered conversation from the other end.

Adele waited as the door slowly sprung open, carried by momentum, and she spotted a man wearing slippers, his white hair jutting every which way, with an old, corded black phone pressed to his cheek. He was muttering quickly into the device and shaking his head every couple of moments, saying things like, "No, of course not. Double that. You have to double that. I won't sign. No, you're supposed to represent me. I mean it. All right, I'll see you at home for dinner. I love you too."

The man with the wild white hair clicked the old-fashioned phone back into its cradle.

He inhaled slowly, still facing an ornate desk, behind which an even more intricately carved chair had been pushed aside, facing one of the large windows. There was no computer in sight, nor cell phone.

The older gentleman finally inhaled, his shoulders rising and falling, and then he turned, slowly, raising a woolly eyebrow to examine where Adele stood in the door.

"Police you said?"

The man had more wrinkles than a Shar-Pei. His ears were drooping, and his nose quite long. His eyes seemed kind, but creased with sagging wrinkles, and more bags then a Parisian at a shopping center.

"Yes, sir. Are you Mr. Becker?"

"I try to be. What's this about?" He held up a finger and then added, "Actually, I'd like to see some identification first." He spoke softly, carefully, as if placing each word like a brick laying a foundation. He didn't raise his voice, rather allowing the silence to carry his intentions.

Adele stiffly removed her wallet and raised her credentials once more.

Instinctively, she began to lower the wallet again, but before she could, a hand reached out and held her, gently lifting her hand just a bit, and the older man leaned in, his eyes narrowed as he read slowly. He continued to read, taking in every inch and detail of the badge before at last lowering his own hand and nodding.

Hesitantly, Adele stowed her identification.

"I'm sorry, Mr. Becker!" a voice called from behind Adele. "I tried to stop her."

Adele kicked back with her heel, shutting the door with a *thunk*.

The older man didn't seem amused or worried, and instead zeroed his full attention on Adele. Next to him was a bookshelf with an entire row of what looked like encyclopedias, or maybe law journals. Whatever the case, there were many volume sets of green- and purple- and gold-bound books. Books, Adele was nearly certain, she'd never seen, much less read in her life.

"How can I help you, Agent Adele Sharp?" Still that soft, strolling tone of voice.

"I'm here about a property you sold to Mr. Etienne Durand," she said.

For the first time, a flash of emotion creased the older man's expression. He blinked and swallowed once. "If I remember correctly, Mr. Durand and I have not done business for nearly a decade. I wouldn't involve myself with that…" He trailed off, coughed once and shook his head. "That *man*, if you put a gun to my head. Are you here to broker a deal for him? Because I have to say the answer is no. An emphatic no."

"I'm not here for Mr. Durand. I'm here as an investigator, and I'm more concerned with one of the pieces of land you sold him."

The older gentleman crossed his arms. “Which one?”

Adele hesitated. “You need a computer? Do you have files?”

“We have files. But I don’t need them. Which parcel? We sold him six.”

Adele blinked. “You’re certain?”

“August second, a decade ago. Yes, I’m sure.” He tapped a finger against his forehead. “I keep most of my files up here. That technology,” he wiggled a hand toward her pocket. “It only makes the generation stupider.”

Adele couldn’t help but agree, but she didn’t particularly like having it pointed out. Still, she tried to stay on track. “All right,” she said, hurriedly. “So you remember all the properties. I’m specifically interested in 632 Route de Contis.”

The older man closed his eyes for a moment, the wrinkles around his lids smoothing just a bit and giving him a peaceful look as if he were sleeping. But then he dipped his head once and opened his eyes. “Yes, I remember it. Some old ruins were cleared out so we could renovate a new house. We sold it, but then the buyers backed out of the new construction. At the time, the area was having a recession.” He shook his head. “I thought I had bought some bad land. Sold it to Mr. Etienne, all six parcels as a bundle.” Here, Mr. Becker frowned even deeper. “He got it for a steal. Still bothers me.”

“Mr. Durand did say he got a very good deal for the property.”

“An extraordinarily good deal,” Mr. Becker said with a snort. “So what does that have to do with the DGSI?”

“I’m specifically interested in that property’s history. Is there anything else you can tell me? Who did you originally buy it from?”

The man paused, frowning for a moment, and then said, “Actually, I do remember that too.”

Adele stared, swallowing back a sudden surge of excitement.

“Who?”

He shrugged simply. “It was the church.” Mr. Becker nodded, putting both his hands in his baby blue suit pockets. “Yes, the church. In fact, they were selling off quite a bit of land which we bought up at the time.”

He knocked a hand against the desk and smiled. “Including this office space, in fact. They were allowing people to tear down old convents and cloisters. If I remember correctly that second location was bought from the church.”

Adele exhaled through her nose, thinking of the third location she’d visited—the miniature castle. "Do you know anything about 121 on the same street?"

The man wrinkled his nose. "I don't think I was involved in that sale. I do remember it, though. Yes, if I remember correctly I was outbid for that particular piece. Another steal of a sale. That one went a few years after the one I sold to Mr. Durand if I remember correctly."

Adele's mouth felt dry all of a sudden. "Also from the church?"

"I believe so, yes. It would have been at the same auction where I won the properties. Why do you ask, Agent Adele Sharp?"

Adele could feel her mind spinning, tracking the imparted information. Twice now, it had become clear the land was sold on the cheap. Her eyes narrowed and she glanced toward Mr. Becker… Could he have possibly been involved? Was that the connection? He'd owned the land the second home was built on, and he had a specific knowledge of the third, miniature castle-shaped, home.

What about the first, though? The one with the stained glass window in the bathroom?

Adele studied Mr. Becker a moment longer, doing her best not to betray her thoughts. Was this unassuming, elderly man somehow involved?

Could he be a suspect?

# CHAPTER TWENTY

She winced at the thought. He didn't seem particularly strong. His age alone precluded him from running down three victims, choking the life out of them.

Still… maybe he had an accomplice?

Delicately, Adele folded her arms and in a soft voice said, "If you don't mind me asking, sir, where have you been this last week?"

Becker acknowledged her with a frown, but then blinked and shook his head. "Excuse me?"

"Just a formality," she said, quickly. "Where have you been?"

"Here," Becker said, reflexively, his fluffy eyebrows dropping low. "Exactly here, every day. I don't take weekends either, Agent Adele Sharp." His face wrinkled a bit in a frown, and he waved a hand toward the door. "Ask Audrey—she's been here with me mostly." At this he coughed delicately and smoothed his sleeves, glancing off out the window once more.

Adele studied Mr. Becker's posture for a moment. He seemed mildly embarrassed, but not fearful. Perhaps a bit offended, but confident. The sort of confidence of a man whose alibi would check out.

Not that it much mattered. He didn't have the physique to be the killer. And the accomplice angle seemed a far stretch at this point. It wasn't like he'd managed to buy back the properties he'd lost on the cheap.

But if not him, then who?

At that moment, her phone began to ring. Adele held up a finger and turned, fishing the device from her pocket and answering. "Agent Sharp."

"Oh, ah, yes, hello," said a nervous voice on the other end. "This is Sara Cote."

Adele frowned in confusion for a moment, but then the name clicked and her eyebrows imitated Mr. Becker's, rising high. "The property manager?"

"Um, yes. Hello, you said I should call you if I found anything about the previous owners of the house."

Adele swallowed, finding her throat dry all of a sudden. "That's right. And?"

She pictured the small summer home on the beach, with the stained glass window in the bathroom.

"I found out who owned it."

"Yes?"

"It was the church," Ms. Cote said, her tone one of mild bemusement. "At least that's what I was told."

Adele didn't respond, the phone clutched in her hand now, staring sightless across the room while her mind spun a million miles a minute.

The church.

All three properties now had ties to the church.

She coughed delicately and said, "You're certain?"

"Yes. I spoke with one of their development offices directly." Sara Cote paused as if gathering her thoughts. She then, with renewed intensity, continued, "It sounds like a couple of decades ago they were selling old properties to migrate some of their churches and the like closer to the city."

"And this summer home," Adele pressed, quickly. "What about it?"

"A cloister," Ms. Cote's voice came, ushered by a burst of static which made Adele wince. "An old medieval cloister of all things. I suppose that explains some of the odd stone arches and the like. Well… is that helpful at all, Agent Sharp?"

Adele's mind whirred. She thought quickly to the third summer home, like the miniature castle… More a medieval building, though, surely… maintained, perhaps, but old and archaic. And as for the second property, with the modern home, hadn't she been told twice now that it had once been occupied by old ruins?

She lowered the phone slowly, pressing it to mute it against her collar. "Mr. Becker," she said, "your memory is quite impressive. Is there any way you know *what* exactly those ruins were on the property?"

He waved a hand, still frowning in her direction—no doubt miffed by the earlier line of questioning. For a moment, she worried he might hold out on her. But then he just shrugged his bony shoulders. "I told you—the church owned the land. The ruins were some sort of cloister. No choice but to knock it down and rebuild—it was in disrepair."

Adele could feel her heart hammering now, and she spun on her heel, hurrying toward the door. She lifted her phone again. "Thank you," she said, quickly. "If you find anything else, please call." Then she hung up, pushing through the door to Becker's office and back into the lobby.

She could feel her excitement mounting. The murder weapon—not beads, not pearls—a rosary. She'd had the thought herself. A theory at the time. Simply a theory.

But no longer.

Two of the summer homes had once been cloisters. The third, owned by the church, also—most likely—a similar history.

She kept her phone gripped in her fingers, ignoring the secretaries as she marched out of the small office space and into the hall once more, striding down the long, echoing corridor. She raised her phone now, calling Agent Paige.

She waited, feeling the tension in her chest rising, feeling fit to burst.

The phone continued to ring without answer and some of Adele's excitement was now replaced by frustration. At last, she was sent to voicemail.

Trying to keep her tone professional, Adele said, through half-gritted teeth, "Paige, the church owned all three properties. The killer is murdering wealthy women who own vacation homes in this region that were former cloisters and on church ground. It's a religious angle. He's going to keep at it! Call me!"

Adele hung up, jamming her phone back in her pocket as she hurried to the stairway. Everything was moving… nothing felt certain anymore. Her instincts were off. Maybe she didn't have it anymore. Had she totally lost it?

Her chest pounded, her eyes fixed on the smooth railing.

Motive was religious. MO obvious.

But this still wasn't enough to find the killer. Closer—closer than ever. But the murderer had proven himself more than resourceful, dancing around the continent as he had.

But what did it mean? Where was he headed to next?

She took the stairs two at a time, picking up her pace as she did.

Would he strike again in London? Germany?

Where would he kill? She had to beat him to it. It felt like she'd finally managed to pry open a door and get a peek inside the madhouse. Now she had to use this illumination to find the architect of these murders.

"I've got you," she muttered to herself, nodding firmly.

The only questions: Where would he strike next? And could she beat him to it?

## CHAPTER TWENTY ONE

Back in France—so lovely. Elke Schmidt breathed a soft sigh of satisfaction as he pedaled along on his borrowed bicycle. His habit was folded neat and tidy, stowed in the backpack slung over his shoulder.

Elke rolled his shoulders as he pedaled up the hill, wincing a bit against the still open wounds along his shoulders. The pain lanced sharp and sweet and he found his lips folding back, revealing teeth.

The man who now called himself Elke turned along a side street, glimpsing Bordeaux in the distance, his eyes tracing the outline of the city against the horizon, a welcoming embrace of stone and glass, witnessing the arrival of a tool of retribution.

He wheeled the bike into a side alley along cracked asphalt lined with dumpsters and the lingering odor of refuse and mildew. His nose twitched as he wheeled to a halt and stowed the bike behind one of the large green and blue trash cans.

He tested his movement gingerly, feeling the way his rough, burlap shirt rubbed against the open wounds. A car ride might have been more comfortable, more accommodating.

But Elke Schmidt didn't prefer vehicles. He practiced pain as a virtue.

A virtue *she* would share soon enough.

Breathing slowly in and out, Elke moved away from the stowed bicycle along the alley toward the mouth of the side path. He ignored the scent of the dumpsters, the trash and rot behind him, preferring to stare ahead, along the open road in the flank of France, his eyes inching up the large apartment building across the street.

His eyes flashed as he stared at the structure, glaring in the direction of the top floor apartment.

No movement discernible.

This particular judgment would be a difficult one. Harder to track the transgressor's movements—harder to detect her habits so high up.

His face twisted into a snarl and he pounded a fist *hard* into the stone wall next to him. He yelped in pain, feeling a knuckle crack from the force. He lifted his hand, his fingers trembling, staring at the back of his knuckles. A thick flap of skin had torn off on the cement. A moment later, blood suddenly pooled, pouring down his hand toward his wrist. Delicately, he pulled a handkerchief from his pocket, wrapping it around his knuckles where he stood in the alley.

The streets outside were mostly empty, save the occasional car skirting past. They were far enough outside the main hub of the busy city that they were allowed a modicum of privacy and respite.

Still, there was no rest for the wicked.

And the transgressor would face judgment soon enough.

Elke Schmidt folded his good hand over his injured knuckles, squeezing down, wincing and feeling tears of pain form in his eyes.

Three judgments already.

All of them successful.

He didn't need reconnaissance for this one. Perhaps her habits were unknown to him. Perhaps he couldn't perfectly track her schedule.

It didn't matter.

The Good Judge was on his side. Hadn't it been proven already? Wasn't it obvious?

He nodded, dipping his head once and then stalking across the street, sticking to the shadows, his head lowered.

A bit of homework never hurt. But he couldn't wait much longer. The vengeance was burbling in his chest.

"Remember me?" he whispered, glancing up toward the top floor as he walked. "Don't you remember me?" He remembered them. Remembered all of them.

The way they'd treated him as a child. The way they'd tried to beat it out of him.

They had called him the sinner—called him the fool. Now he had returned to share the truth.

A truth found only in pain and vengeance.

# CHAPTER TWENTY TWO

Adele leaned against the old cathedral wall outside the converted office complex, tapping her fingers against her arm, waiting impatiently.

She glanced down at her phone again, rereading the curt message.

*Fine. Omw.*

Adele rolled her eyes, looking up again, scanning from one side of the street to the other and feeling her frustration mounting. How far had Agent Paige gone? Surely she hadn't already gotten on a flight.

Already, Adele had waited nearly an hour outside the front doors of the office complex where Becker and Associates was located.

She could feel her anxiety returning, twisting in her stomach. She didn't like standing still, motionless, waiting helplessly for the cavalry to arrive.

As she waited, Adele could feel old emotions cycling wildly once more. Not only did her stomach twist and turn, but she could also glimpse flashes of memories.

Some conclusions were inevitable. She could feel the clock ticking in her mind. The killer was out there. *Other* killers were also out there. But this one in particular was biding his time, one step ahead, hunting his victims one by one. And Adele was only able to pick up the pieces in his wake.

"Come on," she muttered in frustration, glancing up and down the long street. She hastily pulled her phone out again, texting quickly: *Where are you?*

She waited, staring hopefully at the screen, but Agent Paige didn't reply.

It wasn't like she needed Paige, was it?

What was her next step?

She knew the killer was targeting people in this region, who had built homes on church land. She knew he was targeting them for religious reasons, that much seemed clear. He was resourceful, moving about the country and continent with impunity. Smart, strong, dangerous.

How would she find him, though?

Her stomach gave another twist, but just then a taxi appeared at the end of the road. Her heart skipped a beat and she stepped away from the wall, waving a hand.

The taxi pulled to a screeching halt next to the curb.

The vehicle moved with short, jolting motions, and the doors flung open, as if the taxi itself couldn't wait to be rid of its occupant.

Agent Paige stepped onto the curb without so much as a glance back at the driver, and then stalked toward Adele. The taxi didn't wait; no sooner had Agent Paige left than it squealed away, moving back up the streets.

"I'm here," Paige called out, likely replying to the hurriedly sent message. The silver-haired agent looked past Adele, eyeing the old cathedral turned office complex. She shook her head. "The church owns the land?"

"Religious motives," Adele said quickly. "It's like we thought." Part of her wanted to press, to make a deal out of it. Part of her wanted to simply yell *I told you so* and dance around, pointing a finger at Agent Paige.

Adele pictured the image in her mind and tried not to smile.

"All right, I'll bite, what next?" Paige snapped. It was testament to just how stubborn the woman was that she offered nothing like an apology nor an attempted justification. She simply looked at Adele with her piercing gaze, her face framed with silver hair, not a strand out of place.

Adele would have to wait for apologies. She had a killer to catch rather than an ego to assuage.

Her lips felt dry as she spoke quickly. "I made contact with the property owner who sold one of the parcels. He has an encyclopedic knowledge of land acquisition in the area. He doesn't like me much right now, as I may have hinted that I thought he was a suspect."

"Is he?"

"I can't be sure. He doesn't have the physique for the kills."

"Accomplice?" Agent Paige paused, but then answered her own question. "Nothing to suggest an accomplice."

"Exactly. But we can't rule it out either. Still, I need your help to get him to cooperate. We need to find any other tracts of land in the area that were sold. That's how were going to find the next victim."

Agent Paige nodded slowly, and if Adele hadn't been paying attention, she might have missed the note of admiration flicker across the older woman's eyes. Paige, not one to dawdle, brushed past Adele, moving toward the buzzers and pressing all of them at once. She waited impatiently, and a second later, the door buzzed. She shouldered into the old office complex, and, without waiting for Adele, marched up the stairs.

"Which one?" she called over her shoulder.

"Becker," Adele replied. She hastened over, catching up with Paige and returning up the stairs toward the doors at the top.

This time, Paige didn't knock, but simply barged in, coming to a halt in front of the desk, behind which the two secretaries were still seated.

By the looks of things, and their flustered conversations, they were still recovering from the last visit of the DGSI.

Now, though, they glanced nervously from Adele to Paige.

"We need to speak with Mr. Becker," Paige snapped.

Instead of waiting for a reply, she moved past them toward the door, which was still slightly ajar, and pushed it open with her elbow.

Adele, like a leaf caught up in a whirlwind, simply followed.

The two agents stood in the doorway again, both of them ignoring the protests behind them.

This time, Mr. Becker was sitting behind his desk. He had his old, corded phone in one hand, which he lowered slowly, whispering as his head dipped, "I'll call right back. I have clients." There was a soft ding as the phone pressed into its cradle, and the old owner of the firm glanced between the two agents.

"You're back," he said to Adele, betraying no emotion save in the tightening of his lips.

"We have some more questions," Adele said quickly.

Becker leaned back, folding his hands over his chest, resting the back of his head against the cold glass overlooking the small coastal town's streets. "This is beginning to border on harassment, Agent Adele Sharp. And you might be?" he said, turning to Agent Paige.

It was to Adele's absolute surprise that instead of a curt, biting answer, Paige simply dipped her head and in as polite a tone as had ever squeaked from those normally pursed lips, she said, "We don't mean to bother you, sir. My name is Sophie Paige, and we're here on government business, as my partner has informed you."

"Also with the DGSI?" he inquired.

"Yes, sir." Paige nodded once.

Adele tried not to stare in shock at the polite and respectful conduct of her normally acerbic partner. Was it simply a tactic to gain his trust?

Or a matter of the age difference? She'd always known Paige was somewhat old-fashioned.

The decorum wasn't lost on Becker, it seemed, who turned slightly in his chair, facing Agent Paige rather than Adele and addressing his follow-up to her. "Am I still a suspect, hmm? What is this, property crime?"

Paige shook her head quickly. "We're not here about you, sir. My partner here suggests you possess an encyclopedic knowledge of purchases and sales in the area."

"Damn right," Becker said, nodding once, some of his normally reserved demeanor cracking under the scrutiny. "I've been at this for nearly thirty years now. You're not questioning my recollection, are you?"

"No, of course not, sir. I know how it is to have youngsters come in and start kicking things around."

He snorted, but his eyes twinkled for a moment. "Tearing down fences they don't even know the purpose of."

"Exactly, sir."

Adele could have sworn that both Becker and Paige glanced in her direction discreetly, before returning their attention to each other. For a moment, she felt like a stick in the mud just standing there and wondered if perhaps she ought to just leave the room.

But then she reminded herself why she was there, cleared her throat, and glanced toward Paige.

Becker, noting the exchange, leaned forward again, his chair creaking as he settled his elbows on the table in front of him. As he hunched, he looked even smaller and older than he had before, like some crooked gargoyle angled off a stone turret, his features wise and weathered.

"How can I help you, Agents?"

Paige gave a surreptitious glance askance at Adele, much like the passing of a baton. Adele, mustering her courage, stepped forward and cleared her throat.

"Sir," she said, delicately, "I'm wondering if you know of any other property sales in the area, about the same time when you purchased the tract from the church."

"There were quite a few," the man said, nodding once. He slid his fingers up his face, pressing them against the bridge of his nose as if against a headache, his eyes narrowing as if he were focusing on something interesting etched into the wooden table." He coughed delicately. "I'll need you to be more specific, Agent Adele Sharp."

"Specifically," she said, "any sales from the church to local land owners. Especially sales with cloisters or old churches on the land. Within the same time frame. Do you think you can remember that far back?"

Again, she noted the old, corded phone, the complete lack of computer on his desk. She winced in consideration, wondering if this recollection routine was too much for the man. Clearly he had a photographic memory of some form. Her own gaze flicked to the many legal tomes lining his ornate bookshelf against the wall, then back to the man.

He was still staring, his brow creased in concentration.

Adele opened her mouth to speak again, but Agent Paige reached out, tapping—a bit *too* firmly in Adele's estimation—against the younger woman's wrist. She fell silent, simply watching, waiting.

The three figures in the small office room on the second floor, illuminated by the light through the open window, stood in momentary suspended silence, sharing an amalgam of concentration and suppressed unease.

If he couldn't remember, then Adele couldn't find the next potential victim. The killer had shown his hand. Perhaps he hadn't thought anyone would check vacation homes. Perhaps he hadn't considered someone might fly to France when the murders were in Italy, England, and Germany.

For the first time on this case, Adele felt like they were catching up. The killer hadn't seen them coming, and now it was entirely up to them to find his next step.

Which meant they needed targets.

She could still feel the pressure from Agent Paige's silencing hand, but Adele couldn't resist adding, like someone typing criteria into a search engine, "Specifically anyone who purchased from the church at that point, but who also is of a certain age," she said. "Married couples, or single women who would now be in their fifties. We can't discount male owners, if they've recently been married."

She winced now, feeling uneasy. Would he remember that far back? Her gaze surreptitiously scanned the walls for any file cabinets. Surely he didn't simply keep the information in his mind.

Even as the doubts began to creep in, Mr. Becker lowered a long finger, pressing it against his lips now, leaving a pale indentation and then looking between the two agents, blinking a few times as if suddenly exposed to sunlight.

"Twenty-three," he said firmly.

Adele blinked. "Excuse me?"

"Of the public sales reported in a five to ten year time frame purchased from the church for private ownership, there are twenty-three options."

Adele felt her heart clatter as if falling from a shelf and shattering on the floor. A jolt of horror filled her. "Twenty—twenty-three?" she said, her voice croaking. "Are you sure?"

He dipped his head a single time. "Very. I remember that sales period well. Was one of our best growth years, in fact."

"Twenty-tree is a lot of locations," Paige murmured next to Adele.

At the same time, the door behind them creaked open, and Adele heard the voice of one of the secretaries calling out, "Excuse me, Mr. Becker, you have another client. Is there anything I can get you?" She added this last part with an emphasis on the words.

Becker, though, held up a placating hand, watching the agents and waiting.

Adele, for her part, was shaking her head. "You're not mistaken?" she said.

Now Becker bristled, frowning. "No—I'm not. Not all of us require those infernal devices your generation substitutes for memory. Twenty-three *at least.* Those are of the ones publicly declared. Private sales also occur, of course. Sometimes through less than reputable agents hoping to offset transactional costs. Mr. Durand, for instance."

At least twenty-three sales from the church…

At least twenty-three potential victims.

Adele felt like she'd been walloped in the gut. All sense of momentum she'd been feeling now came to a screeching, painful halt.

There was no way they could track down that many potential victims. No way in that amount of time, especially given how many of them might live in other regions if not countries. It would take weeks, at best.

She felt her stomach twisting again, the nerves rising, her chest beginning to prickle in horror and frustration. For a moment, as she stared out the window, Adele felt like she couldn't breathe. She heard, as if echoing down a tunnel, the voice of the secretary again, trying to gain Mr. Becker's attention once more.

She heard, as well, the soft sound of another man—the aforementioned client, most likely—speaking with the second secretary in the lobby, murmuring the words, "How much longer for my appointment do you think?"

*Damn his appointment!* Adele thought to herself, feeling the rising wave of frustration washing over her now. So close, yet so far.

She thought they'd found a lead, but now she'd simply dove headfirst into a pile of hay, looking for a yellow-painted needle.

All the victims so far had been women in their fifties. But the property owners could just as easily be male with wives. Or, further, she couldn't simply assume the killer might not murder someone younger or older with *another* connection she hadn't spotted yet.

Too many variables.

Not enough time.

Despite herself, she found her chest heaving, hyperventilating. She could feel Agent Paige's gaze fixed on her now as Adele stood there, a culmination of nerves and frustration and anxiety and sleep-deprivation.

She was losing this race against time. And now, the flurry of emotions she'd endeavored to suppress, to subdue, came rushing back, rising like shadows against a cavern wall, cast wide and large by flames of opposition.

"Damn it," she muttered softly. "Damn it!" she repeated, a bit louder now.

"Agent Sharp," Paige said quickly, reaching out a steady hand and touching her elbow. "Perhaps we'd best consider things *outside*."

Adele could feel everyone's eyes on her now. Feel, even without looking, the secretary behind her, the new client waiting for his appointment, Mr. Becker in his chair, Agent Paige at her side. Could feel everyone watching, waiting.

She could feel, in addition, *other eyes.* Eyes not currently present.

But eyes just as searching and eager for her collapse.

*Bleeding... bleeding... always bleeding.*

A small sob crept from the twisting stage fright in her belly and escaped up her throat and out her lips.

Just then, her phone began to ring.

With trembling fingers, Adele reached down, pulling the device from her pocket, looking for a lifeline of some sort. Something to help the case. Some clue—something at all.

She glanced at the number.

John Renee.

Everything collapsed then. She wanted to answer, more than

anything… But she couldn't. He'd know what to say, he might be able to help. But she couldn't bring him into it. Not now. Not again.

*If you let them close, they'll all die!* the voice said in her mind.

"God damn it!" she screamed, flinging the phone suddenly away from her lest she give in to the temptation and answer. The device bounced off the large bookcase, ricocheting from the large tomes of green and purple with golden lettering.

The phone continued to buzz against the light carpet. Adele continued to gasp.

And she suddenly realized the scene she was causing.

She blinked, looking around slowly, breathing as if she'd just completed a marathon as her eyes grazed Mr. Becker's, darted to Paige, and then took in the two secretaries and new client staring open-mouthed at her through the doorway.

She closed her eyes, feeling on the verge of a mental breakdown.

"Sorry," she muttered. "Sorry," she repeated. "Sorry," she said a third time, now using it as a marching chant as she hastened across the room, ripped her phone from the ground and, eyes glued to the floor, marched past Paige, shouldered roughly through the gaggle in the doorway, and hurried out the front door.

Her phone continued to buzz beneath her numb fingers as she tried to escape the oppressive room and her equally oppressive thoughts.

# CHAPTER TWENTY THREE

John sighed, staring at the rejected call. He lowered his phone, closing his fist tight around it and leaning back in the recliner he'd managed to smuggle into his makeshift bachelor pad in the basement of the DGSI.

Across from him, his distillery bubbled and dripped, the beakers and glass tubing swirling with clear moonshine. The odor of the concoction wafted in the small room, carried by the air conditioning through the vents in the ceiling.

He glanced down at the cold glass in his hand, staring at the ice swishing around the clear liquid. On the floor, scattered across the ground—files. More files than John would ever admit to having studied. He had a reputation to maintain, after all. Some agents didn't think he could read.

But he'd done his homework, helping out the task force assigned to the murder of Robert Henry.

But still, everyone was turning up a blank. The Spade Killer, this man who styled himself some sort of sick artist—his name received from the park paths and gardens where he'd abandoned his victims—was still on the loose.

They even had a composite sketch now, thanks to John. But nothing.

No clues, no leads…

John had managed, even, to sneak into the room on the third floor, where the task force had been working. Their damn corkboard was practically blank. John had long suspected one could often tell the progress of an investigation by the number of items pinned to the inevitably available corkboard.

The one upstairs only held the faces of the victims, and a composite sketch.

No other details—no further substantiated clues.

John glanced at the damn phone again. She was ignoring him. Of course she was—he would have been surprised if she'd done it any other way. Adele was a bloodhound, but she wasn't a pack animal. No, she'd moved too much for that as a child. She was used to solving things on her own.

And now, she'd chosen to cut him out of the loop, along with everyone else. He never would have admitted it out loud, but the rejection hurt. More, perhaps, than he thought it would. He winced against the intruding thoughts. Quickly, he forced the emotions down, making a case for Adele, softening the pain.

It wasn't like he could blame her. No one else was even close to solving this thing. Not even after the murder of one of their own agents. Adele couldn't trust anyone—she wouldn't.

John hissed in frustration and then downed the rest of his glass in one quick gulp. He could feel his fingers trembling from frustration where they gripped the phone. He could feel a strange pulsing, twisting in his stomach… Pain? A bit of that.

But also guilt?

He frowned.

Why guilt?

Then he swallowed, realizing the obvious answer. He'd had the Spade Killer in reach. He'd nearly had the bastard, but had ended up letting the small man get away.

And then what? Then the killer had taken Robert, too.

"*Merde!*" John cursed, launching his empty glass across the room. It shattered against the door.

He stared at the reflective pieces of glass where they landed on the folders he'd been studying religiously. He'd hoped, perhaps, he could find something—anything—to help Adele. Then maybe she could have some peace. Maybe she'd answer his damn calls.

He felt like a little dog, scorned and whimpering, hoping to somehow please its human. Every cell in John, every prideful bone in his body, wanted to get up, stalk across the room, and forget the stupid folders, forget the phone…

But he couldn't forget Adele.

Which meant he couldn't forget any of it.

With a sigh, his eyes blinking blearily, he got slowly, wobbly, to his feet and moved back to the folders on the ground. Maybe he'd find something on another read-through. He'd just have to be more careful this time. Just a little bit more careful.

But he'd already been over the files five times by now. There was nothing. No clue. Nothing new.

Still, he had to try.

Not because he'd find anything.

But because he wasn't sure he'd be able to look Adele in the eye again if he didn't at least make the effort.

# CHAPTER TWENTY FOUR

Adele felt like her heart was trying to escape her chest. Her fingers trembled so badly she jammed them into her pockets as she marched away from the double doors to the real estate office, down the hall. As foul luck would have it, at that moment, a group of businesspeople from the office space across the hall suddenly emerged, stepping out into the corridor.

Again, it felt like everyone was watching her, and there was nothing she could do about it. Adele continued to move hurriedly, trying to outpace her thoughts, to outpace the nerves and anxiety swirling in her. Too many names. Too many potential victims. How could she possibly save them all? How could she stop it all?

She couldn't even stop Robert from dying.

She broke into a jog, ignoring the odd looks from the business folk in the hallway. She took the stairs three at a time and burst out the front of the office complex. She needed to move. To where, she didn't know. She just knew she couldn't stand still. Not now.

She broke into a jog, choosing a random direction and heading up the sidewalk, her eyes downcast. She needed to focus. But what was the point in focusing?

*Bleeding... bleeding... always bleeding.*

She shivered at the memory. Shivered at the thoughts of Robert, his blood staining the floor beneath his red leather chair. She shivered at the small marble angel, its eyes caked in mud, blind to what had occurred just within the house.

Adele felt like that statue. Blind, her face pressed to the dirt. Just as helpless, just as motionless.

A soft sob escaped her throat, and she growled, picking up her pace, running faster.

She didn't look ahead, keeping her gaze only ten feet in front of her. What was the sense in looking too far into the future? It only carried more pain.

*Focus,* she thought to herself. *You have to focus.*

Robert was dead. What was the point in focusing? All of his instincts, all of his training hadn't been able to save him. And more importantly, she hadn't been able to save him.

She continued to run, now sprinting, racing up the sidewalk outside the small coastal town. She passed by a couple of pedestrians carrying grocery bags, sidestepping just in time and nearly tripping over a fire hydrant. She managed to catch herself, ignoring the annoyed comments from the pedestrians, and slid into a side alley, gasping now, and slamming her back against the brick wall. She inhaled and exhaled deeply, smelling refuse and old moisture. She looked along the alley, toward the back, where a small lean-to of cardboard and old fabric had been set up. The makeshift home seemed empty for now.

"What now?" she murmured out loud.

Robert was dead. She had to face it. She had grieved him, hadn't she?

Then again, she hadn't allowed herself to cry at the funeral. Tears were no good. Tears wouldn't bring him back.

Nothing would.

But what about the victims now? What about those twenty-three potential victims? The killer would keep going, no doubt. Did they deserve to die just because she was going through a mental breakdown?

Was that what Robert would have wanted? What did it matter what a dead man wanted? The dead didn't want anything.

She found herself hyperventilating now, sliding down the alley wall, feeling the bricks rigid against her spine. She dropped into a crouch, her knees practically pressed against her, her arms dangling loosely over the top of her legs. She closed her eyes, focusing on breathing for a moment.

Her instincts had fled. She didn't even feel like an investigator anymore. She felt like a child, a child crying in the back of her apartment as the news came about her mother. A child forced to move across country back with her father, living in silence and fear. A child without friends, without help. A child alone. Robert had come along, after she graduated from university and was recruited by the French agency. He had seen something in her, or at least thought he had.

He'd been the father she'd never really had. Her own father was a harsh man, a taskmaster.

But with kindness and affection, Robert had taught her twice as much as the Sergeant ever had. Perhaps not a very fair or honoring comparison. Perhaps she ought to just be grateful she had a father, where so many didn't.

But Robert had been a father too. He'd been there for her and now he was gone. She hadn't been there to repay the favor. She hadn't been able to save him.

She began to shake, her shoulders trembling now. She wanted to cry, but what would that help?

And so she just sat there, cold, shaking, breathing heavily, her eyes sealed shut, refusing to look around, and refusing to acknowledge the alley she'd backed herself into.

Was this what Robert would have wanted?

She sat there for a few moments, trembling, and then she heard the click of shoes, the sound of a clearing throat. She felt, more than saw, a shadow fall across her, blocking out the heat of the sun.

She didn't want to open her eyes, she didn't want to acknowledge whoever was now watching her. She just wanted to be left alone.

"Agent Sharp," said Paige, her voice soft.

Adele continued to shake. This was the worst-case scenario. The last person she wanted there.

"Adele," the older woman's voice probed into the alley.

Adele looked up, slowly opening her eyes. She didn't want to, but sometimes, there was no choice. She beheld Agent Paige, watching her. "I'm sorry," she said simply. What else could she say?

"You did good," Paige said simply.

Adele blinked. Of all the comments she'd been expecting, this wasn't it.

Paige crossed her arms. "I didn't listen to you. But you're right. There was a connection between those three houses. I should've paid attention. We wouldn't have wasted time. That's on me."

Adele frowned now. It was a strange sort of commendation. Adele could feel some of the weight lifting from her shoulders, as if hefted by Paige, the burden carried in tandem.

"There's too many names," Adele said, quietly. "I don't even know where to start."

Paige pursed her lips, staring at Adele. Some of the usual edge returned to her tone. "You're not supposed to do this on your own," she said, sternly. "It's the reason they pair us, Adele. Do you know who knew that? Better than anyone?"

"Who?"

"Robert. I partnered with him once before, did you know that? This was earlier, before your time, when the agency was just a fledgling thing. They attracted a lot of recruits with Robert. He'd been a homicide detective with an incredible closure rate. A bit of celebrity in

Paris."

Adele sighed, nodding slowly. She had known this. She had known Robert was better at his job than she was.

"I can see how he's rubbed off on you," Paige continued. "I wasn't sure at first. But there's no denying that you're good at your job, Adele. And you're still young. Very young. You're what, thirty?"

"Thirty-four," she replied softly. For a second, the moment seemed to suspend. Was Paige *complimenting* her? Adele hadn't realized the woman knew how. And to compare her to Robert? Adele swallowed, feeling a sudden lump in her throat. Part of her wished it was true. Another part could scarcely believe it. Had Robert really rubbed off on her? She missed him so much.

Agent Paige watched Adele and murmured, "Thirty-four, is that it? You're still a baby, Adele. I can't imagine what sort of cases you will be solving when you get to my age." She shook her head, glancing off down the alley toward the makeshift house of cardboard and cloth, and wrinkling her nose in disgust.

She sniffed delicately and then glanced out across the street. Some of the sunlight swept in again, over the bridge of her nose, warming Adele's face.

"You're not supposed to do this alone. So don't try. I should've been here earlier, and I have myself to blame for that." It wasn't quite an apology, but it was damn close.

"I don't know what to do next," Adele said, with a sigh.

"This might help," Paige replied.

Her right hand had been against her thigh, but she lifted it now, and Adele realized she was holding a manila folder. She extended it toward Adele. "Looks like our photographic firm owner also has the sense to keep at least some printed records. His secretary got these for me."

With still trembling fingers, Adele took the folder and lowered it slowly to her lap, where she still sat in the alley. Paige leaned her shoulder against the alley wall, but then wrinkled her nose just as quickly and straightened again, dusting off her shirtsleeve.

Adele looked at the older woman. "You're not going to call Foucault?"

Paige watched Adele, tongue pressed inside her cheek. Then she simply shrugged. "Not yet. I've had worse partners…" Was that a note of sympathy? Perhaps even pity? Adele shivered. Paige continued, though, "Just tell me what you make of that."

Adele returned her attention to the file in hand. "What is it?" Even as she asked, Adele opened the folder, scanning the contents.

"Transaction history," Agent Paige said. "From all the sales in a ten-year period. Becker circled and highlighted the ones sold by the church."

Adele whistled, glancing along the three-page file. Tight, cramped cursive writing stacked in neat rows. Every few lines of text, one of the transactions was circled with a yellow highlighter.

"It was really quite impressive," Paige said, nodding in admiration. "Becker knew them from memory. But look, each of those was sold by the church, within the timeframe we're looking at. Each of them sold to private owners. But it also keeps track of everyone who bid on the properties. See there, in the column on the furthest right. Those were failed offers. All of them pending, and then turned down."

Adele tracked the folder and turned the page, scanning the document.

Perhaps Paige was right. Perhaps trying to do this alone had been her mistake. Perhaps thinking she could had been the error. Paige had procured the necessary piece of evidence when Adele had fallen to despair. Perhaps she shouldn't have counted Agent Paige out so quickly. Still, what would this do?

It was still more than twenty-three names. Still more than she could handle.

She tried to quiet herself, just scanning the folder, reading the transaction history. She looked from the purchase names to the pending sale information. She scanned through the list a second time, flipping through the three pages and squinting against the cramped, cursive handwriting.

Part of her wished Mr. Becker had heard of a computer or a spreadsheet, but another part of her was too focused to complain. Her eyes darted from each highlighted and circled transaction to the next.

"What's this right here?" she murmured softly. She tapped her finger against one of the pending sales that had fallen through.

Agent Paige nodded slowly. "Exactly," she said. "I asked him about that too."

Adele blinked, wondering just how long she'd sat in the alley.

"Lavigne Preservation," Adele murmured. "What is Lavigne Preservation?"

Paige murmured, "Flip the page, look at the next set of transactions."

Adele did. Under nearly every one of the transaction records, she spotted the same name. Lavigne Preservation. "A company?" she asked, wrinkling her nose. She flipped the page to the last one, and again, on nearly five of the church sales, in the pending column, with failed bids and lowball offers, she spotted Lavigne Preservation.

"Becker said it was a historian," replied Paige. "Said that fellow offered bids on nearly all of the church properties, making claims that they needed to preserve the historic sites rather than develop them."

Adele looked up staring at Agent Paige. "So you saw the connection too?"

Paige glared now. "You're good, but you're not the only one who knows how to do their job." She shook her head in disgust. "Some of you young ones, you really need to show a bit more respect, you know that?"

Adele held up a hand in apology and glanced back at the papers. "So he's a preservationist? A historian you say?"

"According to Becker he still lives in the area. Also according to Becker, he made some big stink about ten years ago when the final sales were completed. Protested outside a government building with some kooks and crazies, all of them frustrated that the land was sold for development or residential, as opposed to preserved for its historic significance."

Adele felt a flicker in her chest. Maybe she'd been thinking about this wrong. Maybe trying to track down the victims was a mistake. Maybe Paige was right. Maybe they'd found the killer instead.

"So some rabid preservationist went out of his way to lowball offers on all of these properties."

"Of course, Becker said he turned him down. Which, in Becker's own words," Paige said, pulling out her phone, pausing for a moment, then clicking the device, and a recorded voice suddenly spoke out:

*"...he went quite mad,"* the recording said, Becker's voice echoing through the speakers. *"Quite mad indeed. Furious I wouldn't sell to him. He kept saying I owed it to history. Owed it to faith. Said I owed it to God... Is that enough now? I really have to be going..."*

Agent Paige clicked off her phone.

Adele looked up, wide-eyed. "You recorded him?"

"He doesn't use technology himself, but he's not allergic to it." Agent Paige shrugged, placing her phone back in her pocket.

Adele's mind continued to churn. This was an important development. If this historian had gone so far to think he was entitled to the land, but unable to buy any of it, maybe he might go even further.

Slowly, Adele slid back up the dusty alley wall, her mind racing.

She swallowed slowly, muttering, "We have a criminal record on the guy?"

"I haven't called it in yet," Paige said. "I just got out of talking with Becker."

Adele nodded quickly, dusting off her pants and closing her eyes for a moment to think.

"A historian. Not enough money to make a dent on the properties. But enough zeal and frustration to organize protests outside government buildings. Invoking God and morality as entitlement to those properties. Do you think it fits the MO?"

"Look at Mrs. Churchville's property, Signora Calvetti's, and Mrs. Schmidt's," Agent Paige said, softly.

Adele quickly flicked back through, moving from each of the addresses they'd already visited of the summer homes. She read the pending sale column on each and looked up, eyes wide. "He made offers on all those houses," she said quickly.

"Exactly."

"We need to find out what we can about Lavigne Enterprises. Find out about this historian. Especially check to see if he has any criminal complaints."

Agent Paige studied Adele for a moment, standing out in the sunlight, looking at where Adele stood in the alley. For a moment, she just watched the younger woman, and then her eyes seemed to flash with something akin to a smile, though it didn't reach her lips. She nodded once as if in satisfaction, and then turned, her shoes clicking as she began to move back up the sidewalk. "I already called a cab," she said, over her shoulder. "You can call the police. Get the information yourself."

Adele hefted the folder and then hurried after Paige, fishing her own phone out quickly, feeling some of the nerves, the anxiety, subsiding once more.

She knew she couldn't keep on going like this, not without addressing the underlying issue. Then again, if she did address it, she wasn't sure there would ever be any going back.

Perhaps, at least for now, some skeletons were best left buried in the closet.

If it saved lives, she supposed she could wait a moment.

Perhaps she was losing her instincts as an investigator. Perhaps she never had them. Agent Paige seemed to think she was at least somewhat good at her job. But Robert was dead. Her mother was dead. And for now, the killer had escaped custody. If she didn't hurry, she'd receive the ultimate proof she had never known what she was doing to begin with.

She simply couldn't let that happen.

# CHAPTER TWENTY FIVE

Adele watched their third taxi driver in the same day shoot uncomfortable glances toward Agent Paige. The older detective had her sidearm resting in her lap while examining the device.

Despite the obvious discomfort of their chauffeur, Agent Paige remained on task, saying, "Repeat that for me; are you sure?"

Adele, sitting in the backseat, lowered her phone, her cheek prickling from where the device had been pressed moments before. She swallowed, saying, "He has a record. Hassling some of the property owners, even stooping to vandalism."

Agent Paige glanced back, mercifully tucking her gun back into the holster. "Violent?"

Adele shrugged. "It sounds like Mr. Gregor Lavigne snuck into the basement of one of the new constructions and set fire to the place. According to him, he'd been told the building was slated for demolition anyway."

Agent Paige whistled softly, and then, her eyes darting, she snapped, "Keep your eyes on the road." She tapped the GPS with a firm finger, "Get us there, fast." The driver snapped to attention, his fingers gripping the steering wheel. Paige returned her attention to Adele as if nothing had happened. "So he tried to burn down the house?"

"According to the police report, which is from seven years ago, he was just trying to send a message. To his credit, no one was living in the house at the time."

"Still, arson, harassment, vandalism." Paige nodded, returning her attention through the windshield to the road as they moved quickly through the coastal region. The address for Gregor Lavigne led to a less reputable, more run down part of the town. Adele could feel her heart hammering as they moved quickly. She checked her phone again as it buzzed, sliding to the file sent to her by the local police. Again, she scanned through the contents, reading the police reports with quick, skimming bursts in between glances out the window.

She could feel her heart quickening, her eyes fixed through the windshield ahead.

Adele said, quickly, "Is the address right?"

The taxi driver cleared his throat. "Number fifteen," he said, "yes?"

Adele nodded, pressing back now and lowering her phone. Her own hand strayed to her firearm at her hip. She pressed her fingers to the holster, closing her eyes for a moment and feeling a strange reassurance.

There were closing in. Gregor Lavigne, of Lavigne Preservation, had a history with the victims, trying to get their properties with lowball offers. He'd been proven to have a temper according to Mr. Becker, citing God and his faith as entitlements to these properties. And now it had become clear he had a rap sheet as well. Arson, vandalism, harassment. Could he have escalated?

She leaned forward now, peering past the taxi driver's shoulder, her eyes fixed ahead. The driver was slowing, rolling past some of the more run-down, single-story houses lining either side of the street. A couple of duplexes, and even some townhouses at the edge of a cul-de-sac were also worn, with old coats of paint, and yards given to neglect.

Adele scanned the peeling numbers on one of the houses… 12.

"We're getting close," she said.

At that moment, she heard the rumble of an engine. She looked ahead, brow furrowing, as an old gray sedan with a duct-taped window began to back out of a communal driveway.

They continued to trundle forward along the curb, the tires scraping against the cement. Adele's eyes landed on the two digits of the house outside the shared driveway.

15.

"That's it," she said, suddenly pointing.

Agent Paige leaned forward, looking through the windshield at the car backing out. "Is that him? Is that him?" she repeated, urgently.

Adele rolled down her own window, trying to get a good look. For a moment, as the car backed out, she glimpsed a swarthy face with a thick, bushy beard.

The beard was more wild than it had been in the photo the police had provided her, but the man's squinting eyes and comb-over were unmistakable.

"It's him, it's him!" Adele said.

Agent Paige yelled out of the front of the car. "Stop!"

This didn't work. The car backing out of the drive continued to pick up pace.

"Block him off," Agent Paige said hurriedly.

Instead, the taxi driver froze, instinctively slamming on the brakes to avoid hitting the car.

"Dammit," Paige screamed.

Ahead, through the windshield, Adele thought she spotted Mr. Lavigne glance into the rearview mirror. His squinting eyes widened in his fuzzy face, and for a moment, their eyes locked.

Adele breathed heavily, willing the man to put his car in park, to stop.

And for a moment, it seemed like that was exactly what he might do.

Adele watched with bated breath, waiting as the car paused at the edge of the driveway, its red brake lights flashing, one of them dimmer than the other. For a moment, everything seemed frozen in time.

And then Mr. Lavigne's car screeched, jerking backward and pulling sharply away, picking up speed as it began to move down the road, back toward the highway.

"Dammit," Agent Paige repeated. "Get out now, get out, you imbecile!" She shoved sharply at the taxi driver, who tried to protest, but Agent Paige said, "Government necessity. Get out."

The taxi driver seemed ready to protest further, but as Agent Paige shoved at his shoulder, her clothing shifted, revealing her holster once more, and trembling and cursing, the driver quickly slid out of the front seat, moving onto the sidewalk.

"He's getting away," Adele shouted.

Agent Paige was already sliding in the driver's seat, not bothering to buckle, before putting the car in drive and with an equally loud screech, tearing away from the curb and spinning the car, leaving rubber on the ground as she aimed for the fleeing jalopy.

Adele could hear the protests and shouts of the taxi driver behind them, feeling a jolt of sympathy and making a mental note to make sure the man was compensated for any damage or wasted time. But for now, Mr. Lavigne was getting further away.

She watched as the duct-taped window turned, along with the rest of the jalopy, moving on to the larger road leading away from the side street.

"Go, go!" Adele shouted.

Agent Paige didn't need a second invitation. Still unbuckled, she slammed her foot into the gas, and the car screeched again, fully turned now, skidding out of the cul-de-sac and up the street.

The taxi shuddered and rattled with the rapid acceleration, and Adele gripped the backrest of Paige's seat, her wide eyes fixed on the car ahead.

The old car was turning again, moving toward the highway now.

"Hurry, before he gets away!"

Paige growled and spun the wheel again, this time tearing out onto the larger road and moving across three lanes of traffic. Luckily, only a couple of cars were on the roads, and only one of them honked as she flew up the street, following Mr. Lavigne's vehicle.

Agent Paige leaned on the horn, but this only seemed to increase the car's speed in front of them.

"He's running," Paige snapped.

"He doesn't know we're police," Adele retorted, feeling her heart hammer. "We're in a taxi. We have to cut him off! He's not going to pull over."

Agent Paige gunned the engine, speeding now, catching up to the car as they both pulled out onto the highway, merging into a fast lane of traffic.

A large truck merged into the same lane as they did, and Agent Paige had to skip onto the shoulder for a second, to avoid a collision. The truck behind them leaned on its horn, and Adele's heart jolted.

That was close. Still, she could see Mr. Lavigne now moving into the left lane, heading toward one of the ramps.

"Go!" Adele said quickly. "We have to cut him off. Get him to pull onto the shoulder!"

"Call backup," Paige snapped. "He's running."

Adele wasn't so sure, though. The eccentric and entitled preservationist had seen them pull up, no doubt, but there was nothing about them to suggest they were law enforcement. For all he knew, he was being chased down by two crazies. Still, she fished her phone out, preparing to call but keeping her eyes on the road ahead as Agent Paige moved in and out of traffic, trying to catch up with the surprisingly quick jalopy.

Their taxi continued to grumble and shake as they raced forward.

"He's going to take the exit!" Adele shouted, her phone forgotten for the moment. "Get in front of him, get in front!"

Agent Paige gritted her teeth, jolting the wheel to avoid an SUV moving too slowly in the left lane. She veered in front of another truck, passed the SUV, and now came directly behind the jalopy.

They were so close they were practically bumper-to-bumper.

Adele could see the widened eyes reflected in the mirror ahead of them again.

She glimpsed Mr. Lavigne flash a middle finger in the mirror and then quickly merge, moving off the highway to the exit.

"Before he turns!" Adele said quickly.

At the same time she glanced up at the large signs over the road. A small white etching of a plane indicated this was an exit that led to the airport.

Paige remained focused, still bumper-to-bumper with the fleeing jalopy. Mr. Lavigne picked up speed as well, trying to distance himself from what he likely assumed was a crazed taxi.

Paige continued to lean on the horn, and now Mr. Lavigne returned it, blaring back at them.

"Careful," Adele shouted.

Paige slammed on the brakes just as Lavigne did too.

She nearly slammed into the back of the car, but then the jalopy sped forward again, leaving them stalled behind.

Paige growled, and floored the gas again.

"Hang on tight," she insisted. And then Agent Paige quickly veered onto the shoulder, slamming along the security rail and scraping the side of the taxi against the gray metal. Adele winced, but at the same time, Agent Paige, with this same maneuver, pulled sharply in front of the fleeing vehicle. Apparently the taxi at maximum speed was a bit faster than the preservationist's old, worn out car.

Adele heard the sound of squeaking tires, slamming brakes, and screeching horns. At the same time, Agent Paige brought their car to a full halt, guiding the jalopy off the edge of the road.

Luckily, Mr. Lavigne had slammed on the brakes as well. His vehicle screeched, and with a scraping protest, crunched against the metal barrier on the opposite side of the road. Adele heard something shatter, likely a headlight, and she heard more blaring horns, this time coming from behind the stalled cars.

But she was already throwing open her door, gun in her hand, shouting, "DGSI, hands where I can see them!"

The moment the gun appeared, the honking behind them faded. A truck and two SUVs were trying to get past, but now, at the sight of Agent Paige and Adele, both armed, they began to back up quickly. One of the SUVs even pulled off the shoulder, wheeling back and nearly slamming into the cement divider.

"Out," Adele screamed. "Out with your hands up!"

The bearded man in the front shouted incoherently. His window rolled down, though, but both of his hands were still out of sight.

"Show me your hands!" Adele screamed.

"Are you insane?" a voice was yelling from within the car. "Idiots!"

"DGSI," Adele shouted. "Show me your hands!"

With his window down, at this declaration, Mr. Lavigne froze, looking sharply up at her. His squinting eyes peered out from a bearded face. His comb-over was slick with sweat, likely from the excitement of the chase.

Agent Paige was circling the other side of the car, her own gun pointed toward the window. She slid past the window covered in duct tape, growling loud enough for him to hear, "If I don't see your hands in the next five seconds…"

Mr. Lavigne's hands were still beneath the steering wheel. For a moment, he seemed caught in a decision, but then, as the two agents circled toward the front of his stalled car, and Adele spotted the smashed headlight, fragments of glass scattered across the highway, he finally raised his hands slowly, placing them on the steering wheel.

"All right, turn off your car," Agent Paige snapped.

"You want to see my hands or have me turn off the car?" Mr. Lavigne snapped back.

Instead of answering, Adele jolted forward, reaching through the open window and pulling the keys.

She stepped back just as quickly, snapping her weapon to attention. She gripped the keys, staring at the stalled car, breathing heavily.

"Get out slowly," Paige growled.

Mr. Lavigne was breathing heavily, shaking his head quickly, "What is this about?" he demanded. "You have no right."

"We can talk after you get out of your car," Adele shouted.

Reluctantly, Mr. Lavigne reached toward the door, putting his hand outside to use the external handle, making sure his fingers were still in full view. He gave a sarcastic roll of his eyes, and then slowly opened the door, sliding out the front seat. "You're gonna hear from my lawyers," he scoffed. "You better believe the city's going to pay. Oh yes, they're going to pay. You two idiots have just made my life. I don't know how stupid you can be. You could've killed me." He reached up, rubbing at his neck and wincing. "In fact, I think I'm injured. Yeah, ouch. That hurts."

Adele kept her weapon raised. Agent Paige was glaring, saying, "I'll show you what hurts if you don't shut up. Keep your hands up. Interlock them behind your neck."

At the same time, Paige glanced over the car in Adele's direction, and gave a significant nod toward the waiting vehicle.

Adele returned the look, and, allowing Paige to keep Mr. Lavigne secure, Adele quickly holstered her weapon and moved around to the back of the car. She peered through the windows and spotted a black duffel bag.

She opened the back door, ignoring Mr. Lavigne's protests, and reached for the duffel bag. She unzipped it quickly, glancing inside, but only found folded shirts and clothing.

She shook her head. "Come on, come on," she muttered to herself, her voice muffled by the steel frame of the vehicle. She bent over the luggage, then paused, her fingers grazing a paper protrusion out of the side pocket. Frowning to herself, she pulled the item completely free of the pocket, examining it.

A plane ticket.

Her heart jumped. She stared at the plane ticket, blinking in surprise. She turned it over quickly, examining the date.

"I have a ticket here!" she called out into the air.

"Where to?" Paige responded.

"Spain," replied Mr. Lavigne, the fury still audible in his tone. "So what. It's not illegal to fly to Spain. What are you doing—you can't go through my stuff!"

Paige growled. "There are two possible targets in Spain, Adele," she called out.

"Targets?" Lavigne said, swallowing. "What are you talking about?"

Adele ignored this and lowered the ticket, glancing back into the duffel bag.

"You fly frequently?" Agent Paige was saying, her voice muffled from outside the car. "I bet you do, don't you. Been to Germany recently?"

Mr. Lavigne retorted, "I travel a lot for my job."

For her part, Adele's eyes were caught by something wedged in the side of the duffel bag. She reached out, pulling a Bible from the side. But what had caught her attention was the glinting, ebony carving dangling over the edge of the Bible. She pulled, and realized she was now holding a rosary.

Her heart skipped a beat.

She lowered the Bible carefully, respectfully, placing it back on the clothing, but then held the rosary, lifting it up and over the roof of the car, showing it in Agent Paige's direction.

The response was instant.

"Turn around," Agent Paige snapped. "Mr. Lavigne, you're under arrest!"

# CHAPTER TWENTY SIX

Adele stood shoulder to shoulder with Agent Paige, standing beneath the winking red light from the recording camera behind them over the one-way window. The blaring white lights from the fluorescent bulbs above the interrogation table beat down mercilessly.

Mr. Lavigne blinked in the light, his hands cuffed in front of him, the chain looped through a metal bracket protruding from the steel surface. His eyes stared straight ahead, fixated on the one-way glass mirror, the rest of him rigid and stern as if sealed to the chair itself.

Adele risked a quick glance at her watch, swallowing as she did.

Five minutes without response to any of their questions.

Five minutes of complete silence.

"We know it was you," Agent Paige said, trying a new angle as she stepped around the table and banged an open hand against the metal surface. "No use denying it. You killed them, why?"

The preservationist didn't blink, didn't move. He remained rooted in place.

"You can't expect to get away with it," Paige pressed, leaning in now, her shadow swelling across his cautious form. "Why not just come clean. Tell us why you did it. Then you can speak with anyone you want. Do you have family, Gregor? Anyone who misses you, waiting to see you? We can bring this to a quick close if you just speak honestly with us. Well? How about it?"

Adele had to hand it to Paige. The way she moved her whole body while interrogating the suspect suggested years of practice. She transitioned seamlessly from overbearing and firm to accommodating and considerate. She used the light shining above her like a sort of spotlight, moving her body nearly imperceptibly to allow more or less light past her shoulders as she pressed for information.

The whole effect was dramatic.

And yet, Gregor Lavigne remained silent, staring stonily ahead.

Paige glanced up at Adele in exasperation, shrugging nearly imperceptibly. Adele swallowed, stepping in now, trying not to betray her emotions. One hand emerged from her pocket, carrying Mr. Lavigne's rosary, dangling the beads in front of his nose and allowing the small wooden cross to shift back and forth.

"Is this what the Lord would have wanted?" Adele said.

Perhaps a low blow, to go after a man based on his faith. But wasn't that exactly what the killer had been doing? Besides, her intent wasn't to disrespect the cross, but to jar Mr. Lavigne out of his seeming vow of silence.

And… as the rosary dangled before his nose, the tactic seemed to work.

He blinked briefly, his eyes darting to the side for a moment, before returning to attention, staring straight ahead. He swallowed softly and gave a quick shake of his head. "That's mine," he said.

"Ah, our little fox can speak," declared Agent Paige, slapping a hand on the table again. "I wasn't sure. Well, little fox, can you tell us why it is you were heading to Spain?"

"Lawyer," Mr. Lavigne said firmly.

"He's on his way. Now you answer one of my questions."

"Lawyer."

"Is that really how you want to play it?" Adele asked, still holding the rosary in front of the man's nose. "Are you truly the sort to protect buildings, old structures, instead of people? To prey on the helpless?"

He glanced at her, eyes narrowed. "Lawyer."

Adele felt a flutter of frustration, but forced herself to keep her cool. If Agent Paige could keep from flying off the handle, then so could Adele. Still, Mr. Lavigne had more patience than she would have liked. Then again, after reading his file she supposed this made sense.

Once, on a trespassing rap, he'd chained himself to an old building ready for demolition. He'd stayed that way for three days and nights, peeing into bottles and refusing to eat or drink anything. He'd only left after falling unconscious from sunstroke and being cut free by local police and taken to the hospital.

Mr. Lavigne clearly was determined in his cause. Fanatical, some might say. Though Adele would be lying if she didn't say she respected him at least a little. Few people were as disciplined or focused when it came to the things they claimed to care about.

Now, though, had that fanaticism, that dedication, turned into something… more violent? She still couldn't be sure. He hadn't admitted anything, nor had he denied it. He'd simply clammed up, demanding his lawyer.

She continued dangling the rosary in front of him, staring at the cross and giving it a little shake. "Does your faith approve of murdering old women? Is that the God you serve?"

Her words had their intended effect. His eyes widened and he turned on her sharply, gritting his teeth. "You don't know what you're talking about."

"Well, help me understand then."

"Lawyer!"

"Mr. Lavigne, surely you can see—"

"Lawyer!"

"Why did you kill them, Mr. Lavigne? They didn't do anything to you! What was their crime, hmm? Protecting land—was that it? Some sort of sick retribution? Is that why you strangled them with *this*." She gave the rosary another little shake.

At this final declaration, though, Mr. Lavigne seemed genuinely taken aback. "Law—hang on, what? Don't be insane. That's for prayer."

"Not for everyone. Not for the man killing women who live on land you tried to buy."

"Lawyer!"

At just that moment, there came a knock on the door.

Three sets of eyes spun around, witnessed by the blinking red camera over the mirror, and the vibrant fluorescent lights spanning the room.

A man in a police uniform poked around the edge of the steel door, wincing apologetically. "Sorry, Agent Paige," he said, quickly. "Just popping in as you requested. Mr. Lavigne's lawyer is running late. Caught in traffic. Should be another hour or so."

Paige flashed a thumbs-up and a quick wink, which Adele briefly noticed. She frowned. Paige had been the one who said Lavigne's lawyer was on the way. Had she delayed calling the man, though?

Adele felt a flicker of unease. She supposed the less she knew, the better. Lives were on the line…

Then again, isn't that what everyone said to justify breaking the rules?

She sighed, returning her attention to Mr. Lavigne, whose expression had turned sour at the news. He continued staring stonily at the mirror again, it seemed, settling into a quiet stupor.

Adele sighed, letting the rosary fall from her hand and piling with quiet *plinking* sounds against the metal table. She lifted her hand then, shaking a finger slowly.

"Three murders in such short time," she said. "And we have the proof it was you. Why not save us the trouble?"

Mr. Lavigne stared at her. His eyes flicked to the door for a moment, then darted down to the rosary between his chained hands. He coughed briefly, clearing his throat, and said, "You and I both know this is simply harassment. Who put you up to it, hmm? Mr. Durand? Mr. Becker? One of the other soulless firms? Isn't it enough you had me fired last year?"

"I thought you were traveling for work," Adele murmured.

He snorted. "New job. Selling damn insurance. First my job, now you have to come after my freedom too? Is it because you know you're doing wrong? You know you're turning sacred land for coin?" He shook his head in disgust, sneering in a very Paigesque fashion.

Adele blinked against this sudden tirade. It hadn't been in his nature to speak up until now. As he did, though, she felt a flicker of uncertainty bolt across her stomach.

"What do you mean?" she pressed. "We're not here for anyone but ourselves. We're investigating a serial murderer."

"So you said," he scoffed. "I know a set-up when I see it." He stared straight at the blinking camera above Adele now. "Hear me?" he called, raising his voice. "Whoever is trying to railroad me—I'll fight. Don't think I won't. The truth will set me free. You will one day face the Lord—don't doubt it! Liars never prosper!" He shook his head angrily, spitting out these last words, droplets of saliva arching beneath the bright lights and scattering across the metal table. He shifted, his cuffed hands dragging the chain through the loop of metal with a scraping sound as he pressed his shoulders back against the chair.

"That's what you think is happening?" Adele said. "You think we're trying to set you up?"

"He's acting," Paige snapped. "Don't believe a thing this killer says. I see right through you, Gregor. Don't think I don't."

He sniffed, shaking his head now. The knowledge his lawyer was tardy seemed to have loosened his lips a bit. He swallowed and muttered a couple of times before turning to Adele and saying, firmly, "I've never killed *anyone.* If you're being honest—if you really think I had something to do with a crime, just know wherever you got your information is false. Mr. Becker, Mr. Durand, Ms. Reber… Any of them? They all would love to see me come crashing down. One of them accused me, yes? Without a shred of proof, no doubt."

Adele swallowed, trying to track the conversation. Clearly, Mr. Lavigne was furious. At first, she'd taken the anger directed at her for some sort of shtick. Now, though, she was beginning to wonder. What was making him so furious?

"You think this is a set-up, then? Are you denying the murders?"

"I just did, didn't I? I've never killed anyone. This is all about money. That's what it is. They know that I'm petitioning the government about that cathedral they've turned into an office complex. Just like the Lord driving out the money changers and lenders, so I will bring this to every government and authority until we have that space cleared out. As God is my witness, we will." The bearded man bobbed his head quickly, the visible portion of his scalp beneath his comb-over flashing sweaty beneath the bright lights.

"You flew to Bristol a week ago," Agent Paige said, firmly, lifting her phone and studying the information they'd been provided. "You then took a flight to Italy. You could easily have driven to Germany from there, couldn't you have?"

"Germany?" He blinked. "I was in Germany recently, so what? I fly for work."

"Work?" Paige snorted. "Is that what you call it?"

Her words were riling him up again, but once more Adele saw the sense in it. Mr. Lavigne was beginning to lose his cool, and the more angry he got, the more he seemed willing to talk.

"Yes," he snapped. "I'm a historian. I work as a preservationist for landmarks, land, and monuments. Specifically related to the church. I don't just care about French history, but European history. So yes, I travel sometimes."

"You only just got back two days ago."

He shrugged. "Like I said, I travel a lot. Can you think of anything… Oh, I don't know, particularly religious that might be in Italy? Any guesses?"

"Don't get lippy," Agent Paige snapped.

Adele watched the exchange, trying to make sense of it. They'd gone through Mr. Lavigne's flight records. It was true, he'd traveled a lot in this last month. The first murder had been in London, about the same time he'd flown into Bristol. He could have easily driven the distance, hoping to throw police of his tracks. Granted, he hadn't flown to Germany, but driving from Italy seemed the most likely solution.

Adele didn't blink, staring at the side of the bearded, self-proclaimed historian's face. He was full of bluster and rage, but that didn't make him a killer.

"Give me your word," Adele said suddenly, staring from the rosary to Mr. Lavigne. “Swear on your faith that you didn’t kill anyone.”

# CHAPTER TWENTY SEVEN

The moment she said it she blinked, surprised at the words. The flashing camera light above her seemed conspicuous all of a sudden, but she let the words linger, allowing them to fill the strained gap of silence now extending over the room.

Mr. Lavigne blinked, glaring at her now and turning from Paige. Adele didn't look away. She held his gaze, her own expression just as sincere.

As they exchanged furious looks, Mr. Lavigne's expression began to shift. Some of the fury fled his eyes, and his eyebrows began to twitch up ever so slightly. He swallowed once, frowning in confusion now. It was an odd thing to see a man's emotions switch so completely.

A second longer passed and he glanced from Adele to the rosary and back. Suddenly, his twitching eyebrows rose completely, and his mouth formed a small circle.

"Dear Lord," he murmured… "Wait, are you serious? Hang on—this isn't… You're not just here because…" He coughed. He turned frantically now, glancing from Paige to Adele, blinking as he did as if suddenly waking from a dream.

At the same time, blood seemed to flee his cheeks. His expression paled completely and he began to stammer, muttering as he did. "Wait—wait, h-hang on. Hold on one moment. You're actually with DGSI?"

Adele stared in confusion. "Yes. What did you think we were?"

"I… I thought you were…" He trailed off, shaking his head. Now his features were completely pale. "All that stuff…about murders? You're serious?" He strained this last word, his tonal inflection rising an octave.

"As the grave," Paige snapped.

Adele watched as pieces fell into place across Mr. Lavigne's countenance. He was a paranoid man, no doubt. Odd and unusual. She supposed one would have to be to choose his thankless line of work. She didn't doubt there had been run-ins with powerful real estate developers or financial firms in the past. By the sound of things he'd had more than one altercation.

Had he really mistaken this interview as some sort of strong-arming tactic? Coming after him because of his work?

Adele had faced paranoid killers before…

But just as possible: paranoid and innocent.

She tapped a finger against the metal table, causing the beads of the rosary to rattle. "This is no joke, Mr. Lavigne. We've had murders in the same countries you've visited these last two weeks. The timeline of your travels perfectly matches the itinerary of our killer. The victims in question all live in a twenty-mile radius of your home—or at least own property. You've had altercations with them before and have proven to stoop as low as arson."

He snorted. "That old thing from seven years ago? I told them then—I was told the building was slated for destruction that week. A lie by Etienne Durand to try to get me thrown in jail. Do you know the man?"

Adele shook her head. "It's not relevant if I know him. I don't care about the arson per se. What I care about is that." She pointed at his rosary. "The murder weapon."

He slumped now in his chair, his hands flat on the table all of a sudden, his knuckles as pale as his cheeks. "I—I can't believe this," he muttered. "You—you can't possibly believe—you don't really think—"

"How about you tell us your version of events," Agent Paige said quickly. "What were you in Bristol for? Why did you then fly to Italy?"

"Business!" he exclaimed, his voice like the yowl of a cat whose tail has been stepped on. "All of it business! I have the itinerary in my phone. Meetings—all meetings. Once with a historian's guild, another time with a group of young preservationists. All above board. I have itineraries, phone calls, and names. Tons of names who can vouch for me!" He nodded quickly, wagging his head. "You have to believe me!"

"What times?" Paige pressed.

"Oh… I—let's see." He glanced off now, closing his eyes in thought. Words were coming quickly. His demeanor having shifted entirely. Another ploy? More acting? Or a paranoid man reaching an obvious explanation?

He coughed and said… "Bristol, probably from ten in the morning until nearly ninc at night!" He said this as if he were declaring a victor in some race. "And… and Italy… I was north of the Vatican. Not far, mind you. Near Rome at times. But mostly taxi drives from one site to another. I have receipts too!"

"What times?" Adele pressed.

"At least until ten at night," he said quickly, wagging his head and breathing slowly in relief. "Yes, at least until ten. Nine and ten both places at the latest."

Adele considered Germany for a moment, but set it aside instead to think. She considered the details of the case, studied Mr. Lavigne. He seemed sincere. But sincerity wasn't exculpatory. Liars were often sincere.

Plus… though he provided promises of an alibi of receipts of witnesses of meetings…

The alibi was for the exact wrong time frame.

"The murders happened late at night," Adele said, quietly. "One after midnight, another just before… You would still have had plenty of time, Mr. Lavigne."

He paled at these words, gasping now. "I—I didn't do it."

"We don't believe you," Agent Paige snapped. "If you have no alibi, no witnesses at that time of night…"

"My hotel…" he said, trailing off. "Well… at least, I'm sure they would have seen me. I—well, I did get back late one of the nights. But that was just from the drive. I stopped for food. I—I have receipts for that too, I'm sure." He seemed to be panicking, stuttering and shaking his head now, his eyes wide. "Please, you have to believe me. I didn't kill anyone. I never have. I—I swear! I swear!"

Adele shared a long look with Agent Paige across Mr. Lavigne's head, their eyes meeting. Adele quirked an eyebrow and Paige glanced toward the video camera above the table, giving the faintest shakes of her head.

Adele sighed but nodded once. She turned on her heel and began to move toward the door, closing her eyes to think.

Just another move, another attempt to jar him, to loosen his lips. Now fear had given way to panic. Panicked people spoke. Often more than they should. Adele still wasn't certain if Mr. Lavigne's lawyer had been delayed, or intentionally waylaid. Now, her only focus was on stopping another murder.

If they had the right guy, then this was already over…

*What if you don't?* a voice murmured in her mind. Adele winced, pausing now by the door, giving Mr. Lavigne a moment to witness her retreat, to raise fear in his chest.

She paused long enough to hear him blurt out, "I swear it on my faith! That's what you wanted, no? I didn't kill anyone! I swear it on the Lord himself. I never killed anyone! I didn't!"

Adele froze, glancing back at Agent Paige now, twisting and fixing her eyes on the older agent.

Paige gave another small shake of her head and Adele sighed softly, closing her eyes. She turned completely, rotating in the doorway. "You wouldn't lie to the Lord, would you?" Adele asked, frowning. "Would you?"

Mr. Lavigne was sputtering now, shaking his head wildly, blinking as if caught in truck headlights on a rainy highway. His beard puffed out as he wagged his chin. "No—I'm not lying. Please. Please—you have to believe me!"

Adele waited now, standing in the doorway. What more was there to say? It was his word against the evidence.

"Do you have any alibi for after eleven?" Adele said, her voice softening a bit despite herself. She found her tone was almost pleading. "Give me a reason to believe you," she said. "Something besides your say-so."

Mr. Lavigne shivered, shaking his head still and murmuring, "I—I don't know what you want. I didn't kill anyone. I swear I didn't. *I didn't.*"

"Any alibi? Any at all?" Paige murmured, lowering her cheek next to his and whispering in his ear.

Mr. Lavigne clenched his teeth, still shaking his head, murmuring a sudden prayer beneath his breath.

"Mr. Lavigne," Adele said. "You need to give us *something*."

He stared across his rosary beads, his eyes now fixed on his reflection in the mirror. Something about what he saw must have startled him as his eyes suddenly widened and he began to breath heavily. He blinked a few times, shaking his head. He glanced at Agent Paige, as if seeing her in a new light. "You're playing me," he murmured. "You're lying. You have to be."

"Lying about what, Mr. Lavigne?" Paige said, sternly.

But he set his teeth now, his chin jutting out in defiance. Some of the red returned to his cheeks as anger swelled once more in his chest. He glared stonily at the mirror again and, in a low growl of a voice, nodding his head as if in a sudden decision, he snapped, "Lawyer. Lawyer now."

"Mr. Lavigne—"

"Lawyer!" he screamed. And then he dropped his head, pressing his forehead against his chained arms. His shoulders shaking.

Agent Paige tried another couple of queries, but he continued ignoring her. Adele watched the whole scene with equal parts disturbance and pity.

Was he faking? Acting?

She'd seen killers play emotions before…

He had no alibi. He was at the murder locations. He had altercations with victims before. He'd made offers on all their properties. And, on top of it, he had a rosary in his luggage while trying to fly to Spain where at least two other property owners were located. His flight had been to a city just next to a potential victim's home town.

No alibi…

Adele sighed slowly, watching Paige stand outlined by the fluorescent lights.

"Well?" Adele mouthed toward Paige.

The older woman glanced from Mr. Lavigne's shaking shoulders over to Adele.

"Mr. Lavigne," she tried one last time.

But before she could say anything else, he simply gasped out. "Lawyer!" And then fell completely silent, his shoulders still trembling, his head bowed against the cuffs.

# CHAPTER TWENTY EIGHT

Paige shook her head, breathing slowly and then turning and approaching Adele.

There was a sudden knock on the door and it cracked open. The same police officer from earlier glanced in, his eyes darting for a moment to Mr. Lavigne where they lingered and then turning to Agent Paige. "Should I call that lawyer now?" the officer asked in a whisper.

Adele glanced sharply at Paige, who didn't return the look. Instead, the older woman nodded once. "Might as well. Tell him his client is being uncooperative. That'll make sure he makes double time."

The officer nodded quickly, hurrying away to make the call. Agent Paige held a hand against the door, stepping into the hallway outside with a sigh before glancing back where Adele still stood in the threshold of the door, her back to Mr. Lavigne's shaking form.

"You didn't call the lawyer?" Adele asked, slowly.

Agent Paige quirked an eyebrow. "Calling him now," she said.

"I—are you—what if—"

Paige rolled her eyes, placing a hand on her hip where she stood in the small coastal town's police station hallway. "We delayed a call for five minutes, and we now know he has no alibi. Do you think we would have gotten that with his lawyer?"

"Yes…but… but…"

"This isn't America, Adele. His lawyer is coming. There's no problem here, is there?" Her tone took on a bit of an edge.

Adele remembered how Agent Paige had hidden evidence ten years ago to protect her husband. She remembered how Foucault had covered for her. Remembered the fallout from it all. She swallowed, glancing back over her shoulder toward Mr. Lavigne's shaking form. Then she sighed, stepping out into the hall and allowing the door to swing shut behind her.

"No problem," she murmured.

Paige nodded once, reaching up a perfectly manicured hand to pat Adele on the cheek. "Good." Then she turned on her heel, beginning to move up the hall toward the break room.

Adele followed quickly, her stomach twisting and turning in

perpetual motion as it had done for nearly two weeks now. Perhaps longer. Ever since…

*Bleeding… bleeding… always bleeding.*

She briefly closed her eyes, her feet tapping on the polished floors as she caught up with the shorter agent. Playing fast and loose with honesty around calling a suspect's lawyer was one thing… Lying to a suspect another.

But imprisoning an innocent man? A completely different venture.

And Adele still wasn't certain of Gregor Lavigne's guilt. The self-proclaimed historian and preservationist was an odd, paranoid duck to be sure. But that didn't make him a killer.

Who wasn't odd in their own way?

She winced, picturing the way she'd flung her phone across Mr. Becker's office space after receiving a call from John.

No… she couldn't just ignore her gut. Something still didn't sit right.

Just a feeling, perhaps…

Agent Paige had paused and was looking at her now. "What?" she said, frowning in the hall, framed in the break room door. "What is it? You look constipated."

Adele swallowed, hesitant.

Did she dare voice it?

Her instincts had betrayed her before. Should she allow them to do so again? Was she playing too close to the sun once more? Her instincts had brought them to Mr. Lavigne. Did she really want to admit she might have missed it?

Could she refuse to follow her gut, though? Wasn't that what Robert had always said? Trust your instincts…

Did she dare?

Her instincts had led to Robert's death. Her mother's death.

Did she dare trust them?

She paused, her jaw unhinged like some rusty door in the back of a house. She hesitated, swallowing, and then, in a creaking, hesitant tone, unsure what she was going to say before she spoke, Adele eked out, "I'm—I'm not sure he's our guy."

Agent Paige frowned for a moment, studying Adele.

Adele felt her whole world closing in. She wondered how angry Paige might be. Already, she'd jerked the older agent around the country, around the continent. This was her fault after all, wasn't it? She'd been the one who insisted they come to Aquitaine. And now they had a perfectly good suspect with no alibi.

So why did she think he might be innocent?

"If… if it's not him," she said, her voice hoarse and scratchy in her own mind. "If it isn't," she coughed, "then we're going to wake up to another murder. If the killer is still out there…" She trailed off.

Agent Paige continued to frown, studying Adele. At last, her thin line of a mouth parted slightly. She breathed, exhaling for a moment as if trying to summon a tiring patience.

But then, to Adele's absolute astonishment, the older agent said, "I think you might be right."

Adele blinked. "You do?"

"I'm not sure it's him…" Agent Paige shrugged. "Not sure at all."

Then she turned toward the break room, walking just as stiffly as she had down the hall. Though the room was empty, Paige passed the nearest table, moving toward the coffee pot along the wall.

Adele stared after her partner, stunned.

If Paige agreed with her on this… then maybe Adele's instincts weren't so fried after all.

But on the other hand… if Paige agreed with her on this, and they were *both right…*

"What now, then?" Adele asked, swallowing.

Paige glanced back, pouring herself a cup of steaming coffee—pure black. "We keep looking into it," she said, simply. "Let the police continue the interrogation. Lawyer will show up soon enough anyway."

Adele breathed a soft sigh.

Agent Paige was right. The lawyer would arrive soon, undoubtedly. The killer, if he was still out there, would strike again, soon. Which meant they were running out of time. But where else could they look? What else could they do?

As if sensing her thoughts, Agent Paige raised her phone and gave it a little wiggle. "I took pictures of that folder from Mr. Becker. Makes it easier to compare the pages side by side. I can send you a copy if you like."

"The potential victims?"

"That's right."

"There are dozens."

"Twenty-three."

Adele winced. "Too many. We'll never find the correct victim in time."

"Maybe not. But if we're right about being wrong…" Paige sipped the steaming cup of black coffee and tipped her head down the hall toward the interrogation room, "then we better start somewhere."

Adele sighed, but then nodded once, slowly sliding into one of the break room seats and pulling out her own phone. "Can you send me those pictures?"

"Yes. Coffee?"

"Sure, thanks."

Agent Paige paused for a moment, and then said, "Sugar?"

"Sure. Thanks."

In Paige's words, if they were right about being wrong, then the killer was still on the move. Time was almost up. They had to hurry… no time for despair now. Adele had to find *something*.

## CHAPTER TWENTY NINE

"Just admit it, damn it! So we can all go home!"

The voice echoed down the hall from the break room and Adele winced. The lawyer had arrived nearly an hour ago, and still, the locals were interrogating Mr. Lavigne.

Evening stretched across the break room, peeking through the windows across the long hall of the small-town police station. Adele could hear, through the break room glass, more shouting from the interrogation room.

She returned her attention to her phone, her eyes aching from the strain of staring at the screen.

For nearly two hours now, she'd gone through the three pictures of Mr. Becker's cursive notes. Not quite a spreadsheet, but readable enough.

Adele's left hand steadied her phone, while her right hand gripped a pencil, pressed to a yellow legal pad. She frowned as she flipped to the third and final page. "Emma Martin," she murmured, softly… "Did they get back on her yet?" she called across the room.

Agent Paige, who was already on her third cup of coffee, held up a silencing finger, frowning a shade to match the contents of her cup. She scrolled through her phone and in an annoyed tone asked, "Who?"

"Emma Martin," Adele returned. "Bought the property September twenty-third. The original offer was—"

"Yes," Paige snapped, impatiently. "Yes, they got back. She's still alive, still living in Cheshire."

Adele blinked. "Cheshire. That's near London, isn't it?"

Paige shrugged. "Do you have Emile Schroeder? Just came in."

Adele glanced at her legal pad, scrolling through the finely detailed information. She paused, then tapped against the sheet. "Yes," she said, quickly. "Germany, right?"

Agent Paige wrinkled her nose. "How about Steven Everett?"

Adele sighed, glancing at the sheet again. Then she shook her head. "Which page?"

"Third, bottom name," Paige returned, taking another long sip from her coffee mug. "I swear, I don't know what we pay these desk jockeys for," she muttered darkly. "Get paid just as much as me to sit on their fat asses by their computers and it takes them a year to get me some simple information." She downed her cup and pushed away from the table, turning to pour herself a fourth cup. She cursed, though, finding the pot was empty.

Adele looked away, glancing back at the legal pad.

For her part, she didn't blame the folks back at the DGSI. They'd provided information on all twenty-three of Becker's highlighted names. Locations, ages, and names…

A bit of a picture was beginning to form on the legal pad. Now, Adele had almost fifteen of the spots filled in. She sighed softly, glancing at the list again, her eyes glazed and trailing over the notes she'd taken.

For a moment, she lowered her phone, trying to focus.

What did it all mean anyway?

The locations were important; not just of the summer homes or the church properties but of the potential victims. Why they were important, Adele didn't know.

The killer had skipped from country to country.

First, he'd killed in London. Then he'd gone to Italy. Then Germany.

Who knew where he'd hit next…

She placed a hand over the glowing screen of her phone, if only for a respite from the glare. She blinked a few times, massaging the bridge of her nose briefly before returning her attention to the yellow legal pad. She tapped the rubber end of her pencil against the paper, thinking to herself, trying to piece it together.

"Emma Martin and Steven Everett…" she murmured softly. "Steven's married," she called out, raising her voice.

"So?" Paige snapped back, fiddling with the coffee pot.

Adele blinked. So? A good question. So what? Steven was married. "Means he has a wife. She's about in her fifties too," Adele said, consulting her yellow legal pad. "Both still live in England. Not far from London, actually."

Paige turned now, crossing her arms, gripping an empty Styrofoam cup that she'd crushed beyond use. "And?" she said.

"And…" Adele paused. "Why didn't he just kill all three of them while there?"

The moment she said it, she felt a tug in her stomach. Instinct. The sort of instinct calling for her to pay attention, to follow the lead. A bloodhound with a scent. A bloodhound with a bad cold, trying to catch a scent. And yet, she felt like she was on to something.

Paige said, "What's your point?"

"My point," Adele said, slowly, tracing the other names on the yellow legal pad. "Look at these names. A good few of them live in France, to be sure. But… look, these two in the UK. These two in Germany. *Three* in Italy. Why did he only kill one in each place, moving from country to country?" The more she spoke, the more she felt her pulse quickening. "It doesn't actually make sense, does it?" she pressed. "If the killing is simply about the land, why not bump them off as quickly as possible? Take out three in the London area before moving to Germany then doing the same."

"I don't know why psychos do what they do, Adele."

"No—I get that. But people who murder aren't random. They have reasons, usually. At least this sort of killer does. He's flying around the continent for *specific* victims."

"We're still not sure it isn't Mr. Lavigne."

Adele sighed. "I know… but… You have reservations too."

Paige stared forlornly at her crushed cup. "I'm beginning to lose those."

Adele shook her head, glancing from the legal pad to the screenshot of Becker's highlighted names. "For some reason, the killer isn't *solely* interested in old church properties. Something else is going on here… Something…"

She trailed off, frowning in consideration.

"What is it?" Paige said after a moment, watching Adele. "What's the matter?"

Adele breathed a soft sigh, her breath shuddering with the exhalation. And then she pushed to her feet, nearly toppling the chair as she did. She snatched the yellow legal pad, jammed her phone into her pocket, and spun about, marching out of the break room and down the hall.

"Adele!" Agent Paige called after her. "Agent Sharp, where are you going?"

"To get answers," Adele replied.

# CHAPTER THIRTY

Adele marched directly toward the interrogation room door, gripping the metal handle and feeling the cool surface against her fingers. Maybe she'd been considering this wrong. Maybe instead of seeing Lavigne as a potential suspect or victim of overreach, maybe she needed to think laterally.

Maybe Lavigne was an asset…

What sort of asset?

She supposed she was about to find out. She flung open the interrogation room door, clearing her throat as she entered.

Four people crowded around the table.

All four figures turned sharply as the door shut behind Adele with a *thump* and a loud *click.*

"Can I help you, Agent Sharp?" said one of the police officers on one side of the metal table. It was the same man who'd been complicit in the late phone call with Agent Paige. Now, the subject of the ruse, the lawyer, was sitting on the opposite side of the table, next to Mr. Lavigne. The lawyer was a very small man, both in stature and girth. He had wild, jutting hair, sticking up in the back and smooth in the front. He couldn't have been much taller than a child, and he wore an immaculate brown suit. The lawyer's briefcase was on the table, and already he had pulled out a couple of forms, which it looked like he was sifting through and showing his client. For his part, the suspect, Gregor, was eyeing Adele with the severest of distrust.

She felt her stomach twist, but glanced at the two police officers on one side of the table, and said, "I need to speak to Mr. Lavigne alone."

The police officers hesitated, and one of them cleared his throat. "Are you sure?"

"Quickly, if you please," she said, insistently.

The officers glanced at each other, but then shrugged and moved away from the table, passing by her on opposite sides. Another dull *thud* and a *click* suggested they'd left the room.

Adele's neck prickled. She clutched the yellow legal pad in her right hand. She waved the papers toward the lawyer. "He doesn't need to be here for this either," she said to Mr. Lavigne.

The lawyer began to protest, but before he could, Gregor said, "Why? Do you believe me?"

Adele glanced uncertainly around the room. She took three quick steps over toward the blinking red lights of the camera above the mirror. She reached up, clicking it off. Then she returned her attention to Gregor.

The lawyer began to sputter in protest again, jabbing a small finger toward the camera.

But Lavigne cleared his throat and reached out with a cuffed hands to steady his representative.

"What do you want, Agent?"

Adele shifted uncomfortably from one foot to the other, and then, slowly, she sighed. "I need your help," she said. "If you're telling the truth, and if you had nothing to do with it, I need your help. It will go a long way to clear your name."

The lawyer was speaking quickly now, muttering beneath his breath. "Don't listen to her, Gregor, you can't trust them. You need me here, and Agent," he said, raising his voice, "all of this is highly irregular. Is it true you questioned my client before I arrived?"

Adele ignored him, her gaze fixated on Mr. Lavigne. "You're a historian, yes?"

At the word, the man perked up a bit. He coughed delicately. "I know my area," he said. "Architecture of religious persuasion in the eighteenth and nineteenth centuries," he said. "Parts of my interest branch into the twentieth century as well." Was it her imagination, or had his chest puffed a bit as he said this?

Adele swallowed, shaking her head. "I need your help then. I need you to help me find out where the killer is going to hit next."

"Agent," the lawyer began to speak, "this is all on the record. I hope you know, just by turning off the camera, it doesn't mean—"

"You can leave," Gregor said quickly.

Adele blinked in surprise. The lawyer looked like he'd been shot. He turned sharply. "Gregor," he said, quietly, "listen to me. You can't trust them."

But Mr. Lavigne shrugged one shoulder. His chains rattled. "Is it important he isn't here?" he asked to Adele.

She cleared her throat, glanced at the yellow legal pad, then back at Mr. Lavigne. "I just need your help," she said, simply.

Gregor Lavigne studied her for a moment.

"Your historical expertise," she pressed.

He frowned. "Don't flatter me."

She winced, but nodded apologetically.

Gregor made a shooing motion with his cuffed hands. "I'm fine, Arthur. I'm going to be okay. Just stand outside, I'll call if I need you."

The small, diminutive lawyer seemed to want to protest further, but then, at an iron look in his client's gaze, he sighed, shrugged, and slowly got to his feet, shaking his head. His wild, jutting hair was dark beneath the lights. He hefted his briefcase, and, muttering, brushed past Adele, moving out into the hall. Another *thud*, and a *click*.

Cameras still off.

They were alone.

For a moment, Adele and the suspected killer just studied each other across the table.

"You had nothing to do with this?" she asked, softly, staring at him. "Is that your story?"

"You have my word," he said. "As a devout Catholic."

Adele considered this. Her father took his faith seriously. Swearing on the Bible was just as close to swearing on his own mother. Most religious people, at least to the degree Mr. Lavigne was religious, took their faith seriously. An oath on it wasn't taken lightly. But that didn't mean he couldn't be lying through his teeth, playing her emotions and instincts. And yet, somehow, she shared the same sense as Agent Paige. They had missed a step. Mr. Lavigne wasn't the killer. Which meant she had to find out who was.

Now, standing alone in the room with the suspect, she nodded resolutely, making up her mind, and she marched across the line of sight of the deadened camera.

"All right, here," she said, stiffly. "You know about those properties from ten years ago, the ones sold by the church. Is that right?"

"The ones Becker was after? So he *is* the one who put you on me?"

"Just answer the question. You know about the church properties?"

"You already know I do. We bid on them."

"You lowballed."

"Is there something I can help you with, Agent? I can just call the lawyer back in if you want."

"No, I'm sorry. Look, I need you to tell me about these addresses." Adele pulled her phone out, scrolling to Becker's cursive handwriting and placing the device in front of Mr. Lavigne. She waited, smelling sweat, and feeling her own legs beginning to ache from her rigid posture. She shifted back and forth, waiting, watching.

"All of them?" he muttered. She flicked to the next screen, and then to the third page. She zoomed in on the highlighted names, allowing Mr. Lavigne to read the addresses.

"What about them?" He looked up at last, frowning. "The church properties. Right? Is that what you're curious about?"

"I already knew they were church properties. I'm specifically wondering what sorts of church properties?"

"That's all? Easy. Cloisters and convents mostly. A church or two thrown in there."

Adele frowned. Cloisters and convents? This lined up with what she'd learned at Becker's. "So refuges? For nuns and the like?"

"Exactly. Well, for the most part."

"What you mean for the *most* part?"

"I—now mind you, I have done my research. Most of them were your usual run-of-the-mill cloisters. Most of them were staffed by perfectly respectable and lovely women of God. You have to understand this."

"Why do I sense a *but* coming?"

"I'm not sure I like your tone. You come in here with my rosary, dangling it about as if it didn't matter. Using my faith in a way to leverage me." Mr. Lavigne was shaking his head, clearly frustrated. "I wish you would judge my faith by its claims and content, rather than its abusers. Anyone can wear a title."

"Claims and content aren't my area. I'm specifically looking for a murderer. He's killed three women already."

"I just want you to understand, most of these convents, these cloisters, were run by good people with good intentions." He paused and glanced off, his expression carrying a glint of shame. "Not all of them though," he said, softly.

For a moment, Adele forgot to breathe. "What do you mean?"

He winced, shaking his head. "I actually don't know if I remember the exact one. It's on that list, I think it was an early listing. But," he coughed delicately, "there were stories, rumors making the rounds. It was an older convent, but a special place."

Adele's eyes flicked back to her phone. "What about it?"

"It was where they would send special cases," he murmured softly. He looked up now. "I'll admit, even in the twentieth century, their methods were archaic."

Adele shivered. "Methods for what?"

"Like I said, not all of it is salvageable history. I have a couple of diary entries back home, in fact. Pictures of the place that would help me remember exactly what street it was on. But, vaguely, I do remember this particular cloister was run by folk intent on curing demonic oppression."

"Come again?"

"Demons, Agent Sharp. Many have them. For some, they're simply memories. For others," he said, shaking his head, "they're darker, and more real. Many in my church certainly believe there are spirits out there. Forces for evil."

Adele didn't blink. "I've seen evil. What does that have to do with this particular cloister?"

"Troubled youth were sent there. They were considered demon possessed. Modern science might suggest they were more mentally ill than anything. Medicine hadn't been developed at the time, though. Some of them, even to this day, wouldn't have benefited. Hard cases, tough cases. Some of them insurmountable."

"They were sent to this particular convent you're talking of?"

"Like I said, most of them were harmless. But this one, they didn't know what to do with these children. And so from what I remember, they would send the most troubled, the most difficult, the most," he paused and trailed off, "*possessed*, to this convent. And so it was staffed by some of the harsher, harder women. The ones who could deal with such traumatized cases. Children. Their methods," he winced, shaking his head, "weren't very kind."

Adele shivered, staring at the side of Mr. Lavigne's face. "And this convent, you say you have diary entries?"

"Maybe, somewhere. I think so. But I do have a picture, I know that. It came out when I was researching some of these properties to make my case to the government."

"The case to prevent their sale?"

"My case to enable their preservation," he returned. He shivered now, looking off again.

Adele's mouth felt dry and her fingers cold. She spoke softly, but sincerely. "Mr. Lavigne, if you're innocent, we have a killer out there. What I need to know is how I catch this particular predator."

He shrugged. "For me to help you further, I need my books and collections. I have them back at my house; other than that, there's not much I can tell you."

"And you have a picture of the people who ran this convent? You'll be able to tell me exactly which address it was?"

Mr. Lavigne looked at her, and he dipped his head slowly once and said, "Yes. I could help if you let me."

She stood slowly, shifting back and forth. "Could you tell me where this information is?"

He looked at her, and his eyes narrowed, "I can't say I remember that either."

So that's how it was going to be. She was cornered, and Mr. Lavigne seemed to know it. Could she trust the guy? Obviously not. He was still a suspect. A very likely suspect, despite all the acting, and emotions, and posturing. The cameras off, the lawyer was gone, the police officers left too. The decision was now Adele's.

"Will you help me?" she murmured.

"Will you help *me*?"

It weighed heavy on her; one way or another, she was taking a risk. She closed her eyes for a second, ignoring the speculation, the scrutiny across the table. Ignoring the bright lights above her. What would Robert have done?

Perhaps, more importantly, what would he have told her to do?

*Trust your instincts,* a soft voice whispered in her mind.

Courage didn't always require storming a gunman's position. It didn't always require battling a serial killer over a discarded knife. Sometimes, courage was simple, found in the smallest choices.

*Trust your instincts.*

She sat there, feeling the swirling anxiety in her stomach. No part of her wanted to trust her instincts. No part of her wanted to shoulder this weight again. She didn't want the blame for another death. Someone else could take the lead. Someone else could make the fatal decision.

But no decision was just as good as the wrong one. By not trying at all, she failed by default. Another little thing Robert often said.

*Trust your instincts.*

"Dammit," she growled. "Fine, you're coming with me." She reached into her pocket, pulling out the handcuff keys and moving toward Mr. Lavigne.

# CHAPTER THIRTY ONE

Adele could feel eyes burning through her shoulders as police officers in the precinct watched her march Mr. Lavigne down the marble stairs and out the front of the sliding glass doors.

"Adele," Agent Paige was insisting beneath her breath at her side, skipping to keep up, "what are you doing? Agent Sharp. Adele!"

But Adele kept her eyes fixed ahead, one hand on Mr. Lavigne's shoulder, guiding him toward the unmarked SUV Paige had managed to borrow from the locals. Her other hand clutched the keys as if they were a life line tossed into choppy waters.

This had to work.

Either her instincts were on the verge of altering the case… or they were about to get her killed and help a killer go free.

"Adele," Agent Paige snapped as Adele clicked the locks and then opened the back door, gesturing at Mr. Lavigne to enter ahead of her.

"After you," she muttered.

"*Merci*," he returned somewhat chagrined, rubbing at his wrists. Mr. Lavigne's diminutive lawyer was standing on the top step outside the precinct recording everything with his cell phone.

But the historian didn't hesitate in sliding into the back of the SUV. Adele moved hurriedly around the front toward the driver's side and waited impatiently as Agent Paige, still blustering and protesting, entered the vehicle as well.

"Adele!" Paige was still saying. "Have you gone mad? Why isn't he in handcuffs?"

Adele started the engine, again weathering the storm of the directed attention. She cleared her throat delicately, glancing in the rearview mirror and holding Mr. Lavigne's steady gaze.

"To your home?" she said, softly.

"That's where my collection is," he replied, equally calm. He kept glancing between Paige and Adele like a spectator witnessing a tennis match.

Adele nodded, gunned the engine, and began maneuvering out of the police parking lot, still enduring Paige's protests without comment. It wasn't until she'd guided onto the side street, leading back toward the rundown neighborhood where they'd first sniffed Mr. Lavigne, that she finally glanced toward Paige and gently but firmly said, "I know what I'm doing."

Paige blinked, caught mid-protest. She swallowed, leaning back, still unbuckled in her seat. She had twisted in such a way that it allowed her to keep one eye on Adele and one eye on Gregor. "Do you?" she said at last. "Truly? Because it looks like we're taking a suspected serial killer for a joy ride without cuffs or backup in a civilian vehicle."

"I know. But I don't think he did it," Adele said, simply. "He has information. I think it's going to help."

"Help what?"

"Actually solve this. Hold on—I'm going fast."

She floored the pedal, tearing up the street and ripping down the long road, moving by memory through the small coastal town toward the westernmost section.

She glanced in mild recognition as she passed the old trailer where Mr. Durand worked, his smiling face beaming out from the placard on the side of the mobile home in the abandoned lot. As they passed, Mr. Lavigne uttered a quiet series of expletives.

Agent Paige kept her gaze fixed firmly on the side of Adele's face, but still spared a scathing glance every couple of seconds for the back seat.

"If he's the killer," Paige whispered, her voice as low as she could manage, barely audible over the sound of the engine, "this could all be a trick. We're following him into his *lair.*"

"His home," Adele said.

"Home turf advantage."

"A calculated risk."

"Adele!"

"No—look, too late—we're here now!"

She pulled up to the small, squat single-story home with the peeling number 15 etched into the faux brickwork on the side. A jutting piece of wood had been snapped off, suggesting a mailbox had once occupied the space but no longer.

Overgrown weeds poked through cracks in an already broken pavement, leading to the house with greasy windows and dusty porch steps.

Adele parked with one wheel on the curb and, without readjusting, hopped out of the car, circling to the back and throwing open the door.

"Well, Mr. Lavigne, we're here. Lead the way, sir."

The bearded man with the squinting eyes combed fingers through the thinning top of his hair. He coughed delicately, glancing nervously from Adele to Agent Paige and then, with slow, careful movements, he slid out of the car onto the cracked sidewalk.

"It's—ah, just the front door is locked. We'll have to go around the back."

"Adele!" Paige insisted.

"Fine," Adele said. "Around the back it is. Lead the way."

Gregor nodded quickly, moving slower than might have been warranted, but, likely in his mind, providing Agent Paige with no excuse to draw her weapon.

Adele's fingers buzzed with excitement, her chest hammering. Her eyes fixed on Gregor's form as he moved through a small, white gate past a large, gnarled tree jutting between the driveway and the house in the small, cramped space allowed for it. Adele followed along with Agent Paige and as they moved along the side of the house, Gregor called over his shoulder, "Any idea when I can get my car back?"

"After impound," Adele replied reflexively. "I'm sure we can figure out a way to cover costs. Please just focus for now, sir."

Gregor sighed but then moved around into an overgrown backyard, more weeds and thorns than grass. A small shed, not much larger than a doghouse, occupied a back portion of the equally tiny lot. He stepped over a discarded pile of tires and past a row of small shingles which had been laid neatly out as if to dry in the sun.

"What are those?" Adele asked, frowning at the shingles and glancing at the roof of the house. They didn't match.

"Nineteenth-century brickwork," he said, a note of excitement creeping into his tone. "I managed to get them from a demolition site." The excitement vanished just as quickly to be replaced by scorn at this last phrase.

He stepped toward a door two stairs down into the foundation. Adele glanced uneasily at Paige, whose hand rested firmly on her holster. Both of them exchanged long looks and waited as Gregor fiddled with a combination pad. His fingers trembled badly though, and after a moment, a soft beep left him cursing.

"Sorry," he said, "forgot I changed it. One sec."

He tried another combination and then another beep and the pad flashed red.

"Damn it," he said. "Hang on… Yeah, there we go." A third time, another beep, but longer this time, and a soft click. Gregor fished a small silver key from a tray inside the keypad's receptacle and used it to open the low door in the base of the home.

A sheet of dust dislodged from the top of the frame, falling across his shoulders and swirling about in the failing light outside his house. He coughed, waving a hand around his face, and then with a look over his shoulder, he stepped into the darkness, swallowed by the house.

"Adele," Paige said quickly, her voice warning.

Adele stepped forward, down the two cement steps. She frowned at the still swirling dust. Didn't seem like a well-used entry at all. Had he been lying all along? Was she walking into a trap after all?

She pictured Robert, how she'd found him. *Trust your instincts.*

She swallowed, shaking her head, but then stepped into the darkness after Mr. Lavigne. As she entered the gloomy basement, a light clicked on and suddenly warm, yellow tones illuminated the room. Mr. Lavigne stood on the opposite side of the lower level, a single, naked support beam between them. For a moment, they just watched each other. His eyes were wide, unblinking. He tugged at the edge of his beard with sweaty fingertips and then, in a croaking voice, he said, "Here—this is my office."

He turned away from a light switch and stepped into a small room at the back of the dusty, naked hall.

Adele shivered, listening as Agent Paige finally joined her in the bare basement.

Paige muttered, "He's probably killed people down here too."

"Don't be dramatic," Adele muttered. "He's just not much of a decorator."

"He decorated his patio with old broken pieces of clay."

"Yes, well, I never said he wasn't eccentric."

Adele shivered and then approached the single, small room in the back of the basement.

As she drew nearer, she heard a strange, melodious sound… humming… Mr. Lavigne was humming to himself. She drew nearer, entering the small self-proclaimed office and glancing around.

She blinked in surprise.

Compared to the rest of the house, this room was practically a penthouse.

Everything clean, clear. Even the small window in the top part of the wall was pristine, and dressed with a neat little curtain with polka-dots. The walls themselves were *plastered* in perfectly arranged and sequenced rows of old artifacts and pictures. She spotted crucifixes made of wood, or stone, and—in one case—what looked like bone. She spotted an old nun's robes and a monk's habit. She spotted rosaries next to old chalices and wine glasses. She spotted a row of neatly arranged bricks, each of them a different color and hue, with white labels and clear printed writing with dates like 1923, or 1862. She spotted hundreds of black-and-white pictures assorted in binders and folders in a small bookcase beneath the window. The items in the binders were obvious as two of them were already open on the desk in front of Mr. Lavigne where he was quickly sifting through, muttering to himself, clicking his fingers next to his ear and wagging his head as if agreeing with some unheard proclamation.

"Gregor?" Adele ventured, softly. "Find what you're looking for?"

He murmured some more, still clicking his fingers strangely next to his ear as if somehow he found the sound soothing. His hands didn't tremble as much now that he was down in this room and when he replied, his tone was brighter, more energetic than it had been in any other setting, even when being chased by Agent Paige's ramrod driving style.

"Yes, yes, here—here it is." He nodded quickly and then tapped a finger to one of the open folders. "I knew I had it. Here. See? 632 Route de Contis. I knew it was here."

Adele blinked. 632 Route de Contis. The same address she'd asked Mr. Durand about. The home which had been knocked down and the rubble cleared—built up again. She shivered. What were the odds of that?

"That's where this convent was built?" she asked, slowly. "632 Route de Contis?"

Gregor nodded quickly, still tapping a finger rhythmically into his binder. "There, there, see? The address. Written right there."

Adele leaned in now, brushing nearer to Mr. Lavigne. Again, she smelled sweat, but also dust and something strange and sweet which seemed to be coming from a small row of jars against one side of the wall. She frowned, staring at the jars. "Is that…"

"Urine," he said quickly. "Don't worry, it's my own."

"That worries me."

"It helps keep the brass clear. I tinge it with honey, an old trick. Sweetens the fragrance. Those buttons were from an old cardinal's uniform, you know."

Adele stared at the brass buttons suspended in human urine and grimaced, glancing back at the binder now. She could hear Agent Paige moving surreptitiously behind her. Adele could practically hear Paige's thoughts. If Mr. Lavigne wanted to strike, to attack, now would be the time to do so. With her so close, in cramped quarters, out of sight from anyone else.

But he still leaned over the folder, pointing at an old black-and-white Polaroid taped to the page. Adele surreptitiously glanced at his hands—no concealed weapon she could determine.

Trust your instincts.

So she brushed past him now, shoulder to shoulder, staring down at the indicated picture.

In the cramped frame, she spotted an old, wooden and stone building with a circular window centering a crowned doorway. She hesitated, glancing from the photo to the white writing above the frame.

632 Route de Contis.

The photo itself displayed what looked to be a small and *old* building.

"That's the cloister I was speaking of," he murmured. "That's it. The one where they sent…" His voice went softly hoarse, "the demon-possessed children."

"The mentally ill children," Adele replied.

"Perhaps both." He shrugged, his shoulder rubbing against hers.

Again, she glanced toward the jar of urine-soaked buttons and grimaced.

"All right… So that's what we're dealing with. You mentioned you might have a picture of the nuns who ran this particular cloister. Do you?"

"Yes—yes, of course. Here. Look." He flipped the folder to a second dividing page, muttered to himself, scanned and then flipped the page again. "Damn it," he said. "I know it's here some—there!" he suddenly declared, jabbing an excited finger toward a picture pressed to the middle of the divider, surrounded by other old black-and-whites.

This picture, though, deserved its centered location of honor.

Five women in the frame, standing in front of the familiar building now. One of them, in the middle, stood in just such a way that the round window of the old 632 Route de Contis building served as a sort of halo behind her head.

The other woman all stood angled toward this middle-most person.

All of them wore tight gray hair in buns, their eyes severe and certain, their postures docile but hinting at a hidden will of iron. Their hands were folded in front of themselves, their dresses low, past their ankles, brushing the ground, their shoulders back in perfect postures.

Each of them looked near carbon copies of each other.

Adele leaned in staring, stunned. She felt her heart flutter.

They also looked similar to others…

"Paige, look at this," she said sharply.

"I'm fine back here," Paige returned. "Describe it to me."

"No—seriously, come look."

Paige sighed in frustration, but then, with the sound of slow, cautious footsteps, she began to approach from behind, muttering darkly to herself. She circled around Gregor, preferring to press in on Adele's other side, her one hand still fixed to her holster, which, Adele noticed, was unbuttoned.

"Look," Adele said, quickly, jabbing a finger toward the indicated picture again. "See that? Anything unusual about them?"

Paige frowned, leaning in, staring at the picture of the five women. "No," she said, softly. She shrugged. "They look the same. Old and gray." Paige reached up with one hand, brushing her hair behind one ear and scowling at the picture.

"Exactly—they look… Healthy, though, yes? Powerful. All of them in their fifties. All of them sharing a certain… bearing, yes? A proud bearing."

Paige blinked, staring at the photo. "And?"

"If any of our victims were somehow taken back through time, dressed a certain way, would they stand out at *all* in that photo?" Adele asked, feeling her heart flutter in excitement, her mouth dry with anticipation. Her eyes itched from not blinking, but she kept her gaze fixated on the centered picture. "It's uncanny. They would fit right in. All of our victims would, wouldn't they?"

"I—I suppose so. You think he's going after a certain type because of this photo?"

"I think… Yes."

"We already knew he had a hard-on for old ladies with money and pride. So what? How does that help us narrow anything."

This time, Adele glanced toward Mr. Lavigne. "Well?" she said, softly. "Anything that might—"

"Before she'd even finished, he flipped over the photo and tapped a finger. "Their names," he said, quietly.

Adele blinked, staring now at the five names scribbled on the back of the Polaroid.

As she did, her mouth slowly fell open and a prickle sped up her spine and along the back of her arms. "Holy shit," she said.

"Careful," Gregor snapped, crossing himself.

"Sorry," she murmured, leaning in now and rereading the names.

"Ella," she said, softly. "Aileen."

"Gina," Agent Paige completed, also leaning in now, a stunned note to her tone. "The names," she said. "They're…"

"Practically the same as our victims'," Adele said, shivering. "Obviously, Elke Schmidt is closer to Ella. Gina to Gianna Calvetti and…" Adele felt prickles across her face. "Aileen to Alaina Churchville. But still, a letter here, or there… That's it. That's why he's targeting them. That's the narrowing focus." She tapped her finger insistently just beneath the photo but stopped when Mr. Lavigne growled.

She raised her hand in a placating gesture, but then read the last two names. "Jacqueline. And Candela…"

"The remaining two names," whispered Agent Paige. "Think that's who he's targeting next?"

Adele's eyes shone as she stared at the picture, feeling an old sense of excitement settling across her. A sensation she hadn't experienced in a while. "Jacqueline and Candela," Adele said. "That's going to help us narrow down the list of twenty-three. It has to. Shared names—close names. Those are going to be the targets!"

Paige muttered softly in disbelief, but then turned and began to move out of the room, fishing her phone from her pocket as she did. She stood in the doorway now and Adele glanced back to watch as Paige cycled through the pictures she'd taken of Mr. Becker's highlighted documents with potential victims.

For her part, Adele glanced at Mr. Lavigne, who still stood docile by the table, his eyes darting between the two agents. "So," he murmured, "have I been helpful?"

"Very," Adele said. "Yes."

"Am I free to go?"

"No, but you're free to stay. A police car will be by, watching your home for the next few days, no doubt. Don't leave town."

"I travel for work," he insisted.

"I'm sorry, sir. It's the best I can do."

Adele glanced over her shoulder once more, her eyes fixed on the severe-faced women outside the old cloister, now turned new home.

She didn't believe in cursed land… At least, she didn't think so.

Demons were now explained by science.

At least, so she thought.

Somehow, though, standing in that basement, shivering in the cool draft of the old home, surrounded by odd artifacts and brass buttons and old photos of a bygone era, she felt a slow trickling sense of anxiety rising that had nothing to do with Robert, nothing to do with her skills as an investigator.

Real or not, she felt now they were on the very edge, poised to catch a demon before it struck again.

She felt another chill at the thought and shivered, glancing around the room. Perhaps a premonition, or simple instinct, but Adele felt near certain, whatever the case, they were almost out of time.

"We need to check the names," Adele said quickly. "And any translations of those names or nicknames. Especially if found on official documents. I don't know how he's getting access to the names… but he is somehow, that's how he's finding his victims."

"Most sales with the church were public record," Mr. Lavigne called out from behind her.

Adele began marching toward the door, toward where Agent Paige was still flicking through her phone, her face glowing blue in the light of the phone.

"Come on," Adele murmured, quietly. "We need to move. We can check as we go."

# CHAPTER THIRTY TWO

"Jackie Eymard and Candace Danis," Adele said, urgently, hissing through her teeth.

"You're sure?" Agent Paige snapped, now sitting in the driver's side, steering the vehicle up the road, away from Mr. Lavigne's home. It seemed like all worries about releasing the killer had faded now in the face of this new information.

"Yes," Adele insisted. "Jackie lives in Spain."

Agent Paige glanced sharply over. "Spain?" The car practically stalled, as she began to apply the brakes and twist the wheel.

"I still don't think it's him," Adele retorted. "A coincidence."

Agent Paige growled, readjusting the wheel and pressing the gas once more. "He had a ticket to Spain, Adele," she said, insistently.

"I know. But why would he lead us to those pictures? The killer is out there. He has to be."

Adele turned her attention to her phone, cycling through the pictures of Mr. Becker's list. She scrolled through the names again, glancing at the yellow legal pad where she had written down the additional information, double-checking.

She shook her head, "Candace Danis and Jackie Eymard. The only two names that are close matches to our Jacqueline and Candela."

Paige drummed her fingers against the steering wheel. "Let's say it was just a coincidence he had a ticket to Spain. Where's our other possible victim?"

Adele winced, reading. She cursed and muttered, "She's one of the ones I couldn't pin down. At least two locations I could find. She travels for work."

"You have a phone number?" Paige said, insistently.

"I'm sure I can get one."

"All right, well, I'm heading toward the police station, just in case. I'll call ahead to Spanish authorities, and get them posted out at Jackie Eymard's place. Protective custody."

Adele nodded quickly, as Agent Paige kept one hand on the steering wheel, and the other fished into her pocket for her phone again. She raised it, already dialing the number for the DGSI operatives in Spain.

For her part, Adele glanced at the final name. If Mrs. Eymard was safe, that meant the only remaining target would be Candace Danis. But where was Mrs. Danis? At least two locations. One of them in Italy, but the other was the summer home in France.

She shivered, lifting her phone to make a call of her own.

She could hear Agent Paige rattling off information, already communicating with the Spanish authorities. Adele felt a slow, cresting sense of relief. At least Mrs. Eymard would be safe.

But Mrs. Danis was in the wind. The killer was on the hunt.

Adele quickly scrolled through her notes on the yellow legal pad a second time. She glanced down at Mr. Becker's list, cycling over to the furthest column.

She froze. There had been no phone number for Mrs. Danis herself, but there, written in the margins, was a number for someone else. She leaned in, squinting, trying to read the cramped number.

It was listed under an insurance column. But it didn't have the same code as the other French insurance agencies. So who did the number belong to?

It was worth a shot. Adele quickly dialed, raising her phone, feeling the car increase speed as Paige took them back toward the precinct. Adele could feel the vehicle shake from the strain as Paige put it through its paces. She could hear Paige now raising her voice, yelling at someone on the other end of the line. Jackie was in safe hands in Spain. Mrs. Danis, though, needed help.

To her relief, someone picked up after the third ring. "Candace Danis?" Adele said, quickly.

A voice cleared on the other end, and hesitantly replied, "Excuse me? Who is this?"

Adele's heart plummeted, sinking somewhere in the vicinity of her toes. The voice was male. "I'm trying to reach Candace," Adele said, quickly. "My name is Adele Sharp, I'm an agent with the DGSI. Who am I speaking to?"

There was a pause, then a frustrated clearing of the throat. "Is this a joke?"

The person spoke perfect French. Adele tried not to let her frustration show, as she insisted, "No, I'm not joking. Please, this is important, who is this?"

"Gabriel Danis. Candace is my wife," said the voice testily. "Is she okay? I was supposed to see her tonight. What's going on?"

"You're not with her?"

"My wife travels for work. Who did you say this was?"

"Agent Adele Sharp. I'm with DGSI. The agency works on crimes that—"

"I know what DGSI is. What's the matter with my wife?" The voice on the other end cracked now with anxiety, some of the frustration replaced by fear. "What happened? Is she okay?"

"Sir, as far as I'm aware, your wife is fine. But we have to find her. I can't repeat how important that is. We have to find her *now*. Where is she?"

A swallow. "I'm not sure where she is. She likes to stop by the apartment after work but is supposed to meet me in Aquitaine tonight," the man said, hyperventilating now on the other end. "I'm already on my way. I was at the airport. Look, where is she? What happened?"

Adele paused. This was the worst part. The uncertainty of it all. Still, she had to keep focused. "Nothing has happened yet, sir. Please remain calm. We're contacting your wife. Do you have a phone number for her?"

"Yes, of course."

"Could you please text it to this number, right now. The same number I'm calling you on."

Adele heard muttered curses, but the voice faded, suggesting the phone had been taken away from the man's ear as he complied with the request. Adele waited patiently, allowing the man a moment, likely with trembling hands from adrenaline and fear, to type out the information.

A few seconds passed, and then her phone buzzed.

Adele glanced at the number, exhaling slowly. "Sir, everything is going to be okay. Please, just remain calm."

"This isn't a joke?"

"No, I'm sorry. Look, you have an apartment in France?"

"It's just outside of Bordeaux."

Adele shivered. "Outside of Bordeaux? How far?"

"We have a summer home in Aquitaine too. It's about an hour drive."

Adele gritted her teeth. An hour was a long time. "Please, sir, can you give me the address. Text it to me as well."

"Hang on, wait. Is everything okay?"

"It's fine, sir. Please don't call her. We're going to have someone with the police do that, to make sure she's safe."

"Safe? She works in finance. What couldn't be safe?"

"We have reason to believe she's in danger. But it's all going to be okay." As she said it, Adele felt a jolt of guilt. *Would* it all be okay? Did she dare promise something she didn't have control over?

She could feel the fear emanating on the other line. And so she doubled down, staving off her own sense of guilt. "It's going to be okay. I promise. Just calm down. Your wife is going to be fine. I'm sorry for scaring you, sir. But we need to reach her. Text me that address. Now."

The man cursed some more, but then another buzz suggested he'd sent the message.

"Look, can you just tell me—"

"I have to go, sir. Sorry. Everything is going to work out." She hung up, feeling another jolt of unease and frustration. No time for emotions now, though—now she had to act.

Ahead, she spotted the small precinct through the windshield. Agent Paige had brought them back to the station. The silver-haired agent was holding her own phone, staring at it and muttering to herself.

"Is everything okay in Spain?" Adele said, switching her attention and trying to calm her rising sense of nerves. She'd made a promise, one she couldn't keep if she didn't play this perfectly. There was no time for wasted energy on doubt or fear now. All that remained was action.

"The Spanish are on their way. Jackie Eymard should be safe," Paige said, firmly. "What about you?"

Adele glanced at the address that had been sent, clicked it, and it displayed a location outside Bordeaux. She shook her head slowly, plotting the route on her phone. "Far. Two locations. About an hour separating them. The summer home is one, and another apartment near Bordeaux."

Paige huffed in frustration, shaking her head. "We have to split up. I'll take the summer home."

"Her husband seems to think she's at the apartment, but is going to be meeting him here. So she might be in transit right now."

Paige shook her head, pushing out of the car and swinging the door open all the way, steadying herself against the frame. "All right, then you go to the apartment. I'll take a couple of police to stake out the house on the coast. You call if you need anything. I'll arrange a police presence at the apartment."

Adele felt a flicker of anxiety. Would the police be able to stop this killer? He'd already avoided three security systems, traveled past port authorities, and made a fool of the locals… Adele felt a shiver of fear at the thought. Police presence or not, she had to be there herself. "Can you get a ride?" she said, urgently.

Agent Paige nodded, turning to glance toward the precinct and then back at Adele, "You better hurry. He's been out there for a while, and it's getting late. He likes to kill at night."

Adele glanced at her phone, realizing it was now reaching evening. She had time, didn't she? She had to have time.

As she thought it, though, she considered the third murder. He hadn't attacked at night then. He'd been lying in wait during the day, attacking Elke Schmidt outside her barn while she had been walking with her coffee. No guarantee he'd wait to strike again.

Muttering darkly, she slid across the car into the driver's seat Paige had abandoned, slamming the door shut and nodding quickly. "Stake the summer home, bring backup. I'll contact you if I need anything."

Paige gave a single, severe nod. "Hurry," she said.

Adele was already putting the car in gear, tearing out of the parking lot, the tires screeching as she pulled onto the street, glancing at the GPS on her lap and placing her phone in the seat next to her, turning the volume hastily to maximum.

She felt her heart hammering, feeling her own words catching up with her. How dare she promise everything was going to be okay? What if it wasn't? What if she had just given false hope?

What if they were *already* too late?

Would Mrs. Danis be in the city? In their apartment? Would she already be on the move? Or worse, had she already reached the summer home? And had the killer been lying in wait?

This flurry of thoughts roused an indignant snarl, and she floored the pedal, ripping through the streets and breezing through a red light, ignoring the horns behind her.

She sped onto the highway, pushing the speedometer and moving through traffic even faster than Agent Paige had when pursuing Mr. Lavigne.

Adele could feel that same sense of premonition she had back in that creepy basement. The same sense of fear cycling through her veins.

They were out of time. Already, she could feel it, like a dark presence clouding her mind. Already, the forces of evil had closed in…

They were too late. Too late by far. Just like with her mother… like with Robert…

But there was nothing else to do but try. Now pushing nearly a hundred, Adele ripped through traffic, ignoring horns, ignoring flashing lights. She tore through the highway, heading toward Bordeaux, following the GPS chirping on her phone.

As she did, hastily, she reached for her device, realizing she'd forgotten to text the phone number to Agent Paige. Someone had to warn Mrs. Danis.

# CHAPTER THIRTY THREE

Her keys clinked in the porcelain dish by the front door, and Candace sighed softly, shutting the door and locking it behind her. She pressed her shoulders against the wood, staring at the ceiling and breathing slowly. She had left the fan on earlier. Already, the heat was growing oppressive. The air-conditioning had been broken for nearly two weeks in the spacious apartment. She wasn't sure what the point of having another home in the city was if it only made her sweat like a pig. The meetings she took couldn't be entered without preparation. And now, as she stood, glancing up at the rotating fan above, she wished she had prepared a bit more for this last venture in capitalism.

She adjusted her sleeves and pushed away from the door and the porcelain dish.

It was a large apartment, on the higher end, just outside Bordeaux.

She massaged the back of her neck, wincing. Two days ago, she had taken a flight from Italy, their other home in the area. Sometimes, vaguely, she wondered if all this hopping around was worth it.

She was due to meet her husband at their home in Aquitaine in the next couple of hours. Then she hoped there would be some relaxing.

There was nothing like the French countryside, especially near the coast, to help put effort in perspective.

"Go to business school," she muttered to herself, "it will all be worth it," she said. "Got to love golden handcuffs." She shook her head, moving across the small space now and toward the bathroom.

A shower would be nice, some cool water in the hot apartment. Maybe a little bit of music, then, and a book. She could get a couple of chapters in before having to head out to meet Gabriel.

For a moment she closed her eyes, pausing, beneath the fan, feeling the wind across her skin. It would be nice, one day, to simply retire in the countryside. To put the rest of this away. Maybe they could even sell their home in Italy. Maybe even this apartment. They could use the money to get a boat, or a luxury mobile home. See the sights, spend some time together. They never had children. Which suited both of them just fine. They'd always been each other's adventuring duo.

She smiled now, feeling the wind from the fan against her face.

It wasn't all so bad. It wasn't like this life they'd managed to carve out for themselves would have been possible without all the effort. Still, sometimes it was nice to dream.

She placed her phone on the small counter next to the microwave and plugged it into the charger, turning it on and pausing a second while it booted.

No sooner had the phone roused than it began to ring.

She glanced down and blinked in surprise. Three missed calls. All of them from her husband. She felt a flicker of worry. She hoped he wasn't postponing the trip to the countryside. It would be just like him to try to get in a couple of extra days of work.

This new call, though, was from a new number.

Sighing, she lifted her phone and answered, "Yes?"

"Mrs. Danis?" Came a crisp, clear voice on the other end. "My name is Agent Paige, with the DGSI. Are you alone?"

Candace blinked, trying to track the words. As she did, a slow prickle began to creep up her spine. She shivered where she stood, shaking her head slowly. "Excuse me?"

"Are you alone?"

"Who is this?"

"Agent Sophie Paige. I'm with the police. We think you're in danger."

At this, Candace laughed softly. "I think you might have the wrong number, madame."

"You're in an apartment outside Bordeaux, yes? You're going to meet your husband at your summer home in Aquitaine in the next hour, right?"

The smile died on her lips. She felt a chill, completely out of place in the warm apartment. "How do you know that?"

"Like I said, I'm with DGSI. You need to tell me right now, are you alone?"

Her eyes darted around the room, and she breathed softly. "Yes, yes, I'm alone. Are you sure you have the right person?" she said, shaking her head and trailing off.

"Look, I need you to stay on the line. We're sending a police presence over now. They'll be at your apartment soon. We have an agent coming too. She should be there within the hour. Please, stay where you are, lock your doors, and whatever you do, don't let anyone in unless they're police. Can you do that?"

Candace shivered at the tone in the woman's voice. For a brief moment, she half expected the woman on the other end to break into laughter, bringing her in on the sick joke. But the expected chortle never came. Instead, the self-proclaimed agent repeated, "Understand?"

Candace shivered now, glancing around her apartment and toward the locked door.

No motion, no movement. She was alone, surely. Who would want to kill her anyway? It didn't make any sense.

"Agent Paige, is that your name, I think you're probably overreacting. I don't know what this is about. I work in finance."

"Just stay put and don't let anyone in."

Another set of shivers crept up her spine, and she glanced over her shoulder down the hall in the direction of the shower, and toward the shut door of her bedroom. She swallowed. "All right. Is my husband all right?"

"He's fine. He's been informed and we're trying to do the best we can. Police are on their way, and my partner will get there as soon as she can. Stay put."

***

He could hear the soft murmur of a voice outside the bedroom door.

He sat on the bed, his head bowed in silence and prayer and contemplation.

The blankets were stained in blood. His own, of course. His whip lay draped over the headboard.

He would have to clean up the bed, maybe burn it. No sense leaving DNA evidence lying around.

He closed his eyes, smiling to himself. The pain throbbed in his back from where he had scourged himself. His hands were also bloodied. He didn't always strike his palms or fingers, but sometimes, on special occasions, it felt like the right thing to do.

He remained sitting on the bed, facing the door, head still bowed. She had arrived only a couple of minutes ago.

Candela. Oh how he'd missed her.

"Did you miss me too?" he whispered softly.

He could hear the voice now, drawing nearer. Could hear a slight edge to the tone all of a sudden, and he frowned. It was an edge he recognized. Fear.

Why was she afraid now? She shouldn't be afraid. Not yet.

He stood slowly to his feet, blood dripping down his back, staining the comforter, and then pattering to the floor. He winced against the pain across his shoulders, and approached the door, pressing his ear to the wood.

"DGSI?" a voice was saying quickly. "I'm not sure I know exactly what you do. Who is out to kill me?"

The voice became muffled again, as if the mouth had turned away.

His own heart was hammering now. Someone was telling her. Tattletales. There had always been tattletales.

He clenched teeth, biting his tongue hard until it bled.

He remembered that time he had snuck out to watch the moon and say his prayers outside of the small, locked basement.

The others had tattled on him.

He winced, glancing down at his thumb. One of the knuckles was missing.

He growled to himself, reaching into his pocket and pulling out the rosary. His monk habit lay draped across the floor, and he dangled the rosary over his fingers, staring at the beads outlined against the brown mesh of the robes.

The mothers at the cloister had not been kind to him.

"Oh worthy Judge," he murmured softly to himself, "as your eyes trace this world and settle on only the upright, pay mind to your servant," he whispered. "Witness your hand in motion. Witness the retribution of the saints."

As he spoke, tears began to form in his eyes.

He could hear the voice on the other end, still speaking. Police, most likely. Heathen gods themselves.

He had no respect for the police. None at all.

This was not their world. This was not their claim.

He tensed, murmuring a soft chant beneath his voice. "Bless my hands," he said. "Give me victory over my enemies."

If they were warning Mother Candela, that meant they would likely be warning others. Did they know about Spain?

No doubt. He would have to be extra careful after this, to be able to achieve his final end. To bring complete justice. And then after that, what lovely plans he had. Plans that would rock the world itself.

But first things first.

He felt a righteous indignation rising in his chest. They thought they could corner him. They thought by warning the lamb to be slaughtered they could forestall judgment. But they were always wrong.

A lesser vessel might have ran. Might have tried to save his own skin.

He smiled now, feeling the agony lancing up his back. He had never been much for preserving his own skin.

He'd come here for a reason. And he would see it through. He would be patient, though. He would stay, and once she entered the room, then he would strike. Just as he planned. He'd been meticulous before, and there was no sense allowing fear to hamper him now. Besides, by the sound of things, she had locked the door. She was going to stay put. Perfect.

A second later, the voice had stopped. He heard the sound of the shower now being run, the creak of the shower door. He closed his eyes, sitting back on the bed, still bleeding. He glanced at his missing knuckle on his thumb; slowly, he began to shift through the rosary, flicking the beads one at a time, murmuring prayers softly beneath his breath as he waited.

He would allow the sacrificial lamb to cleanse herself first…

And then the fury.

# CHAPTER THIRTY FOUR

Adele made the hour trip in thirty-five minutes, breaking every speed limit there was and blowing multiple red lights. Now she hopped the curb, the tires skidding as she flung herself from the vehicle, already running as her feet hit the sidewalk.

Ahead, she spotted two uniformed police officers standing idly by the door, muttering to each other beneath their breaths, their arms crossed. As the men spotted her, their hands darted to their weapons. One of them raised a hand, calling out, "Stop!"

But Adele was already fishing her wallet out, flashing her credentials as she hurried forward. "DGSI!" she snapped, "Get out of my way."

But the officers blocked her entry into the apartment lobby. One of them, a muscular man with a handlebar mustache shook his head quickly, saying, "Sorry, mademoiselle. Orders are no one enters."

"I'm DGSI!" she snapped. "My partner is the one who gave you your orders."

She had come to a halt now, poised to try and burst between the officers, her chest pounding. Her instincts were screaming, and her eyes darted up, scanning the building, her gaze jumping from one window to the next, trying to locate… locate what? Movement? Reflections?

She breathed heavily, panting at the ground and feeling a cold numbness spread along her spine. She could feel the clock ticking in her mind, feel it pressing in around her. *I'm out of time,* she thought to herself.

*Trust your instincts.*

She closed her eyes trying to focus, allowing the officers blocking the entrance to get a longer look at her identification. One of them reached up to his radio, muttering into it, "I have an Agent Adele Sharp here. Hold for badge number."

She glanced at the first officer with the handlebar mustache. "See anyone come by?" she demanded. "Has anyone entered the building?"

"No," the man said. "Not since we arrived." He glanced at her ID again and seemed to relax a bit.

Adele could feel her heartbeat pounding, and her pulse raced. "Out of my way," she snapped. "*Now!*"

The officer who had radioed in gave his partner a quick nod. Both of them stepped aside, but the first one said, "No one's gone inside. Everything's all right."

"I'd like to see for myself," she muttered, shouldering past them and hastening toward the two sliding doors. Channeling her inner Agent Paige, she ran her finger down all the buzzers, waiting. The intercom crackled, and a second later, the door buzzed open. She ignored the static voice from the intercom saying, "Who is it?" And instead, she hurried into the lobby.

It was nice. To the left, through the large floor-to-ceiling window, she spotted a glimpse of a belowground pool. Potted plants and tasteful artwork adorned the walls. Two such plants framed the elevator doors next to the stairs.

She passed the elevator, hurrying to the stairwell and taking them three at a time, sprinting. She glanced back down at her phone as she did, fumbling with the device and clicking it on, scanning toward where she'd been texted the address.

Third floor. 3G.

She picked up the pace, swirling around one banister, taking the steps rapidly, up the next. And finally, she reached the third floor, slamming her shoulder into the door and bursting out into the hall. This hallway was also tastefully decorated. More plants, more paintings, and the faint scent of caramel on the air. She spotted a couple of candles with sputtering wood wicks in alcoves of the concrete walls. Green paint gave way to blue wallpaper, again giving an assuaging, calming feel.

Adele felt anything but calm.

She raced toward the third door on the left. 3G. She stared at the lettering, and gasping, reached out, knocking hard. She shouted. "DGSI! Mrs. Danis, are you all right!"

She waited, listening. Somewhere down the hall, she heard a neighbor's door open with a click.

"Stay inside," she shouted over her shoulder. She slammed her fist against 3G again. "DGSI!" she yelled.

No answer. She stared at the door, pondering. No way she could just kick it in. Something was wrong.

She raised her gun, pointing it at the door handle. "Stand back!" she shouted.

She fired twice, angling her body so the bullets wouldn't ricochet.

The door handle snapped, and the door clicked. She reached toward the shattered handle, and this time kicking out hard, sending the door careening inward.

She stood, framed in the doorway, and it took her vision a moment to adjust on the horrifying scene within.

An older woman, with a towel wrapped around her, was lying on the floor in the hall, struggling and gasping.

A man wearing a monk's habit stooped over her, snarling, his features stretched in preposterous ways. His hands wrapped around her throat, and beads pressed to her neck, choking the life out of her.

The woman strangled a gasp for air, reaching a hand toward Adele, one hand trying to push back the man choking her.

"You remember me?" the man was saying, his eyes fixed on his victim. "Did you miss me?"

"Get off!" Adele screamed, finding her voice with a swallow, her gun raised.

If the killer heard her, he gave no indication. He hunched like a gargoyle over his victim, his arms strained beneath his monk's habit, spittle flying from his lips as he muttered quiet musings.

The woman's face was turning blue. She was no longer choking or struggling as much. Adele breathed heavily, aiming now, her finger squeezing the trigger.

But at that moment, the killer seemed to notice her and continued strangling, but ducked low, pressing his cheek against the victim's, whispering, "Did you miss me, Mother Candela?"

Adele noticed one of his hands was missing part of its thumb where it gripped the rosary wrapped around the older woman's neck. Adele hesitated for a brief moment, gun raised. She didn't have a clear shot. She refused to be responsible for someone else dying.

With a snarl, Adele sprinted forward, racing along the hall and jamming her gun into her holster.

She charged the killer, leaping through the air before she'd covered half the distance. The killer, though, finally reacted. He spun *over* the choking woman, trying to distance himself from Adele. She hurtled past, tripping over his form where he remained hunched, throttling.

"Get away!" he screamed. "Get away! You dare interfere! Go!"

"It's not her!" Adele screamed, reaching down and grabbing the man by the neck now, trying to yank him free. "It's not Candela! It isn't!"

"How do you know about her!" he screamed, and then tried to add something else but now Adele's arm had gripped his throat tightly.

He choked and spluttered and one of his hands released the rosary, stretching back and groping toward her to try and rip her off.

Adele held on for dear life, choking the strangler, trying to keep him from moving. His other hand released now, and his would-be victim let out a sudden, moaning gasp, accompanied by a pitiful whimper.

The killer went for Adele's fingers now, trying to crack a pinkie back. She yelled, releasing her grip and jerking her hand away. At the same time, the killer spun around, lashing out at her with untrained but wild abandon.

"Get back!" he screamed. "You don't know what you're doing!"

Adele didn't hesitate. She darted forward and tackled the bastard off the victim. Shoulder hit chin. Face hit carpet. Pain. A loud *thud.*

Both of them crashed backward into a door, sending it jarring into the bedroom.

For a brief moment, Adele spotted blood-spattered blankets and droplets of crimson on the floor. But then, just as quickly, the man struggled, pushing at her. He shifted and kicked, his features stretched in horror and fury, his eyes wide, mouth gaping. "Get off me!" he screamed. "Get off!"

"Stay still," she gasped, trying to hold on. But he was strong, very strong.

With a shout, then a scream, the man flung her bodily with almost unnatural strength. She slammed back into the wall, stumbling over the gasping form of Mrs. Danis.

Adele tripped and got to her feet again, circling, trying to reach for her gun. But the killer lashed out, slamming his fist into her wrist. For a brief moment, his stretched, leering features settled into a furious glare.

He had a thin mustache, and wild, bugging eyes. He was breathing heavily, with a chin that seemed equal parts masculine and rigid, as if perhaps he might have lockjaw.

He had scars all along his cheeks, down his neck, over every visible portion of his body that she could see. His hands were laced with scars and cuts, some of them still fresh.

Adele gasped silently, struggling for control of her weapon. If he grabbed it, it would all be over.

The man screamed and huffed, snarling like a wounded animal. She kicked out once, twice, trying to slam her heel into his shin. He howled in pain.

Adele stumbled back, tripping over the fallen form of Mrs. Danis.

The woman groaned—still alive. Still holding on.

Adele again fumbled for her weapon, free once more with space between them.

The killer glared at her, gasping, watching as her gun began to raise, and he cursed, shoving toward her, *fast.*

Adele felt his oppressive weight land on top of her, sending her reeling back. His fingers scrambled for her neck. She yelled, trying to bite at his hand, her teeth grazing flesh. Blood now poured down the man's arms from his back, speckling her and landing on the ground around her with quiet taps.

For a moment she just struggled under his oppressive weight, kicking. As he drew nearer, she saw the lines in his skin, not just scars, but wrinkles. She felt a flash of realization. He was strong for his age, but still old.

She lashed out, trying to kick.

Her foot caught him in the fork of his legs, and he howled in pain, loosening his grip for just a moment.

She went for her gun a third time, but again with a snarl, he grabbed his rosary from where it lay discarded, draped across Mrs. Danis's neck, and this time lashed out at her with it.

He slammed the beads against her throat, his other hand arcing in as well. With his knee, he pinned her wrist to the floor, crushing her knuckles and preventing her from reaching her firearm.

"You don't know what you're meddling with," he whispered. "Do you think she missed me? Are you going to tattle? I don't like tattletales."

"Get off me, that's not Candela!" Adele yelled.

But her words fell mute as the rosary pressed to her neck.

Something that gave hope for so many was now being utilized to choke the life out of her. The beads pressed to her neck, hard, shoved against her throat. She let out a strangled gasp, trying to shake her head, to jar the beads loose. She swallowed, but it felt like she was scraping sand down her throat.

She kicked again, catching him once more. He yelled in pain and scrambled back.

She took the opportunity to finally pull her gun free and aim, but he kicked, sending the gun clattering beneath a small table.

This motion, though, distracted him, and Adele reached up, ripping hard at the rosary.

Her fingers burned, the sudden cuts laced across her knuckles. But at the same time, with a yell, she ripped the rosary.

Beads suddenly scattered everywhere, just like the droplets of blood from the man's back, where she could now see stains throughout his monk's habit.

The killer howled in fury as the beads clattered around him

He scrambled with his fingers, trying to scoop some up. Now, his weight lifted, and Adele shoved with her hips, throwing him off.

She lunged for her gun, but felt a hand grab her ankle.

The killer screamed, "You're preventing the Judge's work! Don't you understand!"

His voice echoed with pain, sadness, grief, and rage all at once.

The sheer howl like a banshee's call reverberated in Adele's chest, piercing her and for a moment she felt an odd sense of pain.

But then Mrs. Danis let out another gasp, fighting to keep breathing, and Adele focused once more.

"You don't know what you're doing," he spat.

Adele was done talking, and her gun began to rise. But just as quickly, the killer seemed to reach a decision.

"Not that way," he spat. "Vengeance is mine. Failure must be punished."

As the gun rose, he turned, sprinting toward the nearest window, screaming as he did.

"Don't!" Adele shouted.

At the same time as she began to fire, the killer slammed into the window, the glass shattering amidst blood and spit and sweat as flesh swept out in one giant heave, and the killer tumbled, dipping out of sight.

Adele sat, gasping, breathing heavily. For a moment, she just stared at the smashed window, not quite believing her eyes. But then she heard soft sounds next to her and Adele turned away from the window. She reached out with trembling fingers toward Mrs. Danis.

"Are you okay?" Adele gasped, still breathing heavily. "Are you all right?"

The woman groaned more, moving, but then croaked out in a weak voice, "Help, please help."

Adele got to her feet shakily, still breathing heavily and wincing where her shoulders had slammed into the wall.

She blinked, dazed, trying to clear her vision and murmuring, "Stay still. Help is on the way."

She fished her phone out with trembling fingers, her gun still gripped in her other hand, the cold metal rigid against her skin.

"You're going to be okay," she said, breathing slowly, feeling a sudden burst of relief. For the first time, she felt like she was telling the truth. "You're going to be all right."

Hastily, still hyperventilating, she raised her phone to call for an ambulance.

## CHAPTER THIRTY FIVE

Adele sat on the hood of the sedan, staring up at the hospital. The vehicle was still running, but making a strange screeching sound every couple of seconds. She supposed the loaner hadn't been intended for breakneck speeding through the streets of France.

She crossed her arms, sighing softly as she stared at the hospital, waiting… waiting for the news…

She couldn't enter. Not now.

The last time she'd visited someone in the hospital, they'd ended up dead months later.

She shivered, closing her eyes and staving off a headache accompanied by a procession of accusing images.

No… She couldn't enter, and so she waited.

Agent Paige emerged through the sliding doors of the glass and white stone hospital. Adele perked up, staring as Paige approached, walking along the sidewalk and drawing nearer. She waited, trying to read the senior agent's features, trying to discern her thoughts even from a distance.

Paige's hands were folded daintily in front of her, her eyes fixed on Adele as she approached.

"Well?" Adele asked, staring. "Did they make it?"

Paige shook her head. "Not both of them. The victim did though. Mrs. Danis is going to be all right. Some scarring, no doubt, but she should be fine."

Adele exhaled slowly, feeling like she was releasing an elephant from her shoulders. For a moment, she felt weightless, sitting on her car, staring at Agent Paige. A silly grin began to spread across her features and she shook her head side to side in disbelief.

"She made it… I don't believe it. She survived…"

"Good job," Paige said, simply, nodding once.

And for the first time, it felt there wasn't anything biting or hostile about the other woman's praise. She approached the car and turned to face the hospital as well. She paused as if considering whether she ought to sit on the hood of the vehicle. But then, wrinkling her nose in disgust, she remained standing, arms crossed.

"Excellently done. She's alive because of you."

Adele swallowed. She closed her eyes. *Trust your instincts.* That's what Robert had told her all those times.

She nearly had missed it. She'd nearly failed…

She only just arrived barely in time to save Mrs. Danis.

She swallowed. "Him?" she asked.

"Jonah Baresi," Paige murmured. "Dead the moment he hit the ground. They had fingerprints from a small-time robbery nearly six years ago. He was nearly in his sixties now."

Adele shivered, folding her arms together and hugging them against her chest. "He was strong… Very strong."

"Yes. Also schizophrenic, according to his medical records."

Adele glanced at Paige, wincing. "So was he really at that convent? The one in Mr. Lavigne's pictures?"

Paige shook her head. "I don't know. Probably. Why else would he have done all this? Those nuns must have treated him something horrible."

"It's crazy…" Adele said, softly. "How do you fight something like that? How do you fight those who think they're doing good?"

Paige glanced at Adele. "Define good. That might be a start," she murmured. "Your methods may be unconventional, Adele. But you pulled it together in the end." She bobbed her head once, flashing something close to a rare smile. "Either way, we may never know why he did what he did. Things happened in that convent. Things buried. Some secrets remain though. He's dead. His motives too."

Adele shivered, shaking her head in frustration. "If walls could talk…" she murmured.

"Even if they could, those old ruins were wiped away, replaced, built over. Even the convent is gone." Paige shrugged. "I wouldn't think about it too long. You did your job. That's all we can ask."

Adele shivered, staring off. "He was dressed like a monk. Kept talking about… it was so strange…"

"Honestly, I don't think I care. He's the bad guy. The woman you saved was the victim." She patted Adele on the shoulder. "Which makes you the good guy."

Adele winced at each of these words. She wasn't sure that any of them were true. The man had been tortured… No doubt. Mentally ill but treated as something monstrous. Was it his fault he'd turned out how he had? And as for Mrs. Danis… she'd simply been in the wrong place at the wrong time with the wrong name.

What about the nuns at the old convent? They'd been born in a harsh time, in a harsh world… Adele swallowed, shaking her head. The last thing she felt like was the *good guy.* She was someone with a badge and a gun slowly descending into turmoil. Something had to change… But she didn't know what.

If Paige could sense any of the emotional toll of her words, she didn't show it. She nodded once in approval and in a brusque tone said, "Good job, Adele. I'm heading back to the city—going to report. Foucault wants it in person."

Adele blinked, snapped from her morbid contemplation. "I—you sure? I can come too."

"No. That's fine. You rest. Take it easy, won't you? The world won't burn if you take a vacation. Maybe even in Southern France." Paige nodded once more, then turned and walked away, heading toward the parking lot.

Adele listened to the sound of the older woman's footsteps click against the sidewalk. As she did, she felt another slow shiver spread across her back.

Case closed, she supposed.

Jonah Baresi dead, though. He took his own life rather than surrender. Three others also dead. Adele winced, closing her eyes at the thought. It was all so horrible. She didn't know what to do with any of it.

Agent Paige seemed to have changed her tune… Commending Adele's unconventional methods. Then again, Adele knew the truth. Her methods had only seemed unconventional because she'd missed the clues. She'd bulldozed past obvious signs… She'd almost arrived too late.

She'd been slow this time around.

Very slow.

She shivered again, still leaning against the hood of her car, staring sightless now across the road and the roundabout out front the hospital.

Should she go in? Say hi to Candace? It might be nice just to see someone who'd survived all of it… To see the fruit of Robert's training. Trusting his words as well as her instincts.

She shivered.

Maybe she was best suited to stop at the church chapel. Offer a prayer of her own on behalf of the victims… In the face of such violence, such horror, such death… was there anywhere else to turn?

She pictured the missing knuckle on the killer, the rips and tears along his flesh. The sheer fury and rage with which he'd been trying to strangle the life out of Mrs. Danis.

He'd seemed convinced she was his childhood tormentor—convinced she was this Mother Candela.

What all had those old nuns done to make him hate them so much?

Adele shivered, shaking her head and pushing off the car now, her fingers pressing to the cold glass as she rounded the vehicle and moved toward the driver's side.

Perhaps some questions were best left unanswered.

She'd nearly missed it, this time. She'd been slow, fearful—trapped in her own thoughts. Would she ever recover? Would it ever be like it used to be?

People like Mrs. Danis needed her… But Adele wasn't sure how much longer she could keep going. Not now… Not with her own business out there—business she knew she needed to take care of.

# CHAPTER THIRTY SIX

Adele sighed softly as she exited the taxi, waving goodbye to the driver and coming to a halt outside the main doors to the lobby of her apartment in Paris.

She stood on the sidewalk, beneath the moonlight in the nighttime streets of the beautiful city. The air hummed with the distant sound of traffic and the swish of a wind funneled by the buildings on either side of the wide streets. She passed a row of bus stop advertisement space and approached the glass doors to her lobby.

In the night, as she moved, she felt an odd sense of nostalgia, approaching the old building she had once lived in with her mother all those years ago. For a moment she paused on the steps, not quite smiling, but allowing something akin to a contented look to cross her face as she peered up at the large building.

Another gust of wind swept through the street, causing the scraping of a wrapper discarded behind the bus stop to dislodge with the breeze.

Her shadow stretched and spun as the headlights of a passing car turned up the opposite road and moved on its merry way.

Back home.

Was it home?

Now wasn't the night to decide.

With Robert's passing it was certainly less home than it had been.

Still, part of her had missed this place. As she stood outside her apartment, turning toward the buzzers, she paused, frowning briefly as she did.

For a moment, she glanced one way and then the other up the street, looking for any pedestrians. No sign of anyone. Night was complete, Paris slept save in the clubs and river walks throughout the city.

And yet still…

Adele shivered, feeling a chill that had nothing to do with the breeze.

For the briefest moment, it felt like she was being watched.

She turned, surveying the opposite street, her eyes darting across a couple of businesses and office spaces lining the structures facing her old home.

No sign of anyone in the windows. No sign of anyone at all.

She shivered again, feeling another tremor at the sensation of being watched.

Maybe she was just being paranoid.

Adele shook her head, turning back and quickly punching in her building code, waiting a second for the doors to buzz before stepping out of the wind and back into the apartment lobby.

Home.

She glanced toward the mailboxes lining the entryway and paused. A single brown parcel was left below her mailbox. She leaned in, peering at the parcel.

Robert's niece had sent it…

The items her uncle had left Adele in his will, no doubt.

Her fingers traced the tape, the rough cardboard, and for a moment she shivered and shook her head. Did she even want to know what was in the will?

She sighed, picking up the box and hefting it beneath one arm. She supposed she didn't much want to know. At least not tonight.

She took the parcel, and feeling far more burdened now than when she'd been standing out in the night, she approached the stairs, taking them slowly, one at a time, moving back up the building.

As she reached her floor, for a moment, Adele thought she heard the sound of the buzzer again below, followed by the noise of footsteps. Quick, confident steps. She paused, glancing over the railing and watching a neighbor's hand trail the rail below. She looked away, turning back to her apartment door and, finagling the box, pushed into her small space.

She stowed the box of items from Robert's niece in the closet where she normally kept winter jackets. She pushed the box deep into the darkest corner, folding one of the jackets over the top and then closing the closet with a quick jerk of her hand.

She turned away from the closet, despite herself, feeling a bit better for it.

She faced her old home, faced the large windows across from the small kitchen. The drapes were open, allowing the moonlight to reflect through and off the glass.

Tomorrow, she would go for a jog.

She nodded. Maybe an hour, maybe two… She shivered in delight at the thought. Maybe even a three-hour run. She felt a flash of gratitude that Agent Paige had been willing to report back to Foucault on their behalf.

A small, nastier part of her wondered if perhaps Paige would use the opportunity to slander Adele's name… But a more reasonable part of her chimed in. Paige wasn't a friend… hardly. But, following the case, perhaps there was at least some sort of mutual respect earned over the course of the investigation.

At least, Adele liked to think so.

She was jarred from further consideration by a sudden knock on the door.

Adele jolted, spinning to face the door as another knock resounded.

"Hello?" she said, tentatively, her hand moving slowly to where her service weapon still rested on her hip beneath her suit jacket.

"Adele?" a low, gruff voice called.

She froze, her tongue ever so slightly wetting her suddenly dry bottom lip.

"Adele?" the voice said, louder now. "I know you're in there. Look—we need to talk!"

She closed her eyes, tilting her head back and staring sightless at the ceiling in defeat. She held back a groan of frustration if only to avoid letting him hear it.

"John?" she said, her eyes still closed, her voice coming strained with exhaustion.

"Adele, we need to talk. Please. Open up."

"I…" She trailed off. What could she say? She was tired? Go away? Both might work. But knowing John, he wouldn't leave. As if to emphasize the point, the tall Frenchman's hand slammed against the door again, louder now.

"Adele?"

She sighed, her eyes fully open again and she reached out, shaking her head in defeat. He was incorrigible and relentless. Perhaps it was simply best to get this over with.

Whatever *this* was.

"One second," she said.

She unlocked the door and pulled it open, stepping back and facing her old DGSI partner standing in the doorway.

Agent John Renee looked like a James Bond villain. He was traditionally handsome, with slicked back hair and a burn mark stretching up his neck and to the base of his chin. He was taller than most men, with a straight-postured bearing that collapsed only in the need for violence. He was also the single best shot she knew. He'd saved her life on more than one occasion. Though she'd managed to return the favor as well.

"John," she said, softly.

"Adele," he replied, jerking his head in a stiff nod.

"I'm tired," she said, softly, not quite meeting his eyes.

"Hmm," he grunted.

"No, really. Can't this wait?"

"You mean like all my calls you've been ignoring? I even threw in a text or two, just for you," he said, sarcastically.

Adele's gaze rotated about his feet, crossing over his chest, making an effort for eye contact, but failing just as quickly.

"Look, really, I'm tired. If you knew the day I had," she said, trailing off.

"Yeah, you look rough."

"What every woman wants to hear," she said, softly.

"Wouldn't know. You haven't been giving me much in the way of feedback recently."

"John… look… This doesn't have to—I don't want to…"

He stood looming in the frame of the door, his large form stretched now, his arms over the top of the doorway as if he were embracing the exit, or perhaps blocking it.

Adele frowned at this, swallowing and shaking her head. "I'm serious. I've had a long day."

"Not entirely sure I give a damn."

"What do you want, Renee?" she said, her eyes flashing up now, fixating on him.

Didn't the idiot understand? He was putting himself in danger by being seen with her. Didn't he get it? She was trying to keep him safe. Everyone safe. If they got near, they would die. Simple. She huffed a breath, shaking her head and swallowing back a retort.

"You can't ghost me," he said, simply. "You can't come in, make nice, then ghost me. It doesn't work like that." Shadows played across his handsome features, and his burn mark along his neck to his chin seemed brighter now, caught by moonlight through the landing window.

Adele looked away again. "I'm not," she said.

"Damn lie."

"Look… I'm grieving."

"Bullshit. You're cutting yourself off. There's a difference."

She turned on him, eyes wide. For a moment, she just looked at him, stunned as if he'd slapped her.

But John had never been one to mince words. He lowered his arms now, sliding them from the top of the door and crossing them over his muscled chest. "I know Robert's dead," he said, softly, his tone gentler now.

"Don't."

"I know he's dead," John repeated, louder, overriding her objection. "But that doesn't mean you can just vanish. You're not acting like yourself, Adele. Look at you, you look like a ghost. Have you been eating? Sleeping?"

"You're one to talk about diet," Adele muttered.

Instead of responding harshly, though, John just shrugged. "I guess I am. That's why I'm here. I know what self-destructive grief looks like. Hell, I'm the king of it. Just here to warn you—the further down the rabbit hole you go, the less pretty it gets."

Adele watched her old partner. John spoke with nonchalant language, shrugging as he did. But she detected something else behind the words… Something in his eyes. A hidden pain… A hurt. The hurt only seemed to intensify when he looked at her and held her gaze.

She glanced off once more. Part of her wanted to react in anger.

An easy choice, especially given John's ability to push her buttons.

But she was just too tired… What would anger help with? Didn't he get it? Didn't he understand how much danger he was in?

"I… I don't know what to tell you," she said, softly.

John shook his head, sighing now, the sound like a creaking door. He looked like he'd weathered a storm, his countenance cloudy and dark as he murmured, "Remember who you are, Sharp. Remember what you do. You gotta take care of yourself. That grief, it comes with friends. I know it too. Best you can do is draw your own friends close. That way at least it's a fair fight. And it's a fight."

"I know," she said, softly. "This isn't my first time either."

"Well… You can't ghost me."

"It's not me I'm worried about," she said, still soft.

She wanted to get angry still, but now another emotion was rising in her… Perhaps more a sense than an emotion.

Inevitability.

Part of her knew John was right. She needed to remember who she was…

Was she really able to keep everyone safe? John, Paige, Leoni, Foucault, her father, her friends… Could she do it all?

She'd barely managed to stop the killer this time. And he hadn't been targeting her loved ones. Already, she'd lost *two* of her own to the Spade Killer. Two people she loved.

She swallowed, her voice rasping.

"I, I think I need a break," she murmured, softly. "I still have some bereavement leave…" Her voice was quiet as she spoke, but her will was hardening even now beneath the words. She could feel it forming, going rigid, could feel it strengthening. She nodded once, frowning even more deeply. "Yes… I think I need to take a break."

"A break? From work? Good call," John said. "You deserve a vacation."

Adele stood in the doorway, facing her old partner, not quite asking him to leave, but not inviting him in either. Maybe they would talk for another few minutes, maybe hours. Either way, he'd already put himself in harm's way by coming here. The more people drew close, the worse it would get.

She knew that.

Inevitability.

She could feel her resolve hardening even now, half-listening as John continued to prattle on, encouraged by her seeming willingness to be persuaded.

But he didn't get it.

Even as she pretended to listen, her own mind was elsewhere, whirring, planning, plotting.

She would take bereavement leave. Take a break from work. Not for vacation though.

Her eyes narrowed and she felt that same chill she'd had entering her building. As if she were being watched. Adele glanced toward the open windows, still hearing John's voice as if it were coming down a dark well. She couldn't make out now what he was actually saying.

But what he'd said earlier was right.

She needed to focus. To remember herself. Not only for her mother, not only for Robert, but also for anyone else the Spade Killer might want to hunt.

Yes, she would take some time off.

Inevitability.

She would use the bereavement leave gifted her by the murderer so she could hunt him. Foucault wouldn't bring her on the task force—she was too close to it all. She didn't blame him. If she was in charge, she might have made the same decision. But the task force in charge of finding the Spade Killer wouldn't turn up anything. No one ever did.

She would have to solve this herself.

She nodded to herself, no longer paying any attention at all to the handsome man in her doorway. She could feel the determination settle full and complete now, like an iron anchor dropped off the prow of a ship.

She was going to hunt the hunter. She couldn't keep anyone safe.

But she wouldn't need to. Not if she found *him* first.

***

The Painter smiled, leaning forward in the desk chair at his computer, watching the entrance of his favorite friend's building. She'd been followed inside not long ago by the lanky Frenchman.

The Painter flicked his fingers absentmindedly over the ticket he'd printed. It rested beneath his small hand, the date and destination just visible past his frail knuckles.

Next stop, Germany. The ticket booked, the hotel as well. Under a different name, of course. Goodness, he hadn't used his real name in quite a spell.

He continued watching the closed circuit camera he'd installed across the street from Adele's, watching the grainy footage like a soap opera.

On a spare sheet of paper, next to the ticket, the Painter traced loops and swirls, around and around. He paused for a moment, holding his pencil firmly and focusing. Then, in a quick motion, he created a spiral in the center of the page.

He stared at the thing, glanced at the ticket, and frowned.

The Painter sighed, then shook his head. "No, no, no," he murmured. "That won't do."

He reached down, crumpling up the paper and tossing it in the corner of the small, bare apartment he'd rented.

The crumpled paper landed amidst a pile of other discarded attempts.

Not just any old pattern would do. Not for this one. This one had to be… special. Adele's father was special. The ticket booked, the hotel booked, now all that remained was a finalization of the design he'd use.

When he'd first started, he had cut and gouged into his canvas without practicing. But he was no longer an amateur. Practice made perfect. Perhaps a swirl by Joseph Sharp's cheek… then maybe down to his chest, over his arm… Yes… yes, perhaps that would do.

The Painter leaned in, his brow scrunched in concentration, but his lips still twisted in joyful delight. He pulled another piece of paper and, once more, the booked ticket still just within sight, he began to trace another pattern.

This time, the design would have to be perfect.

## NOW AVAILABLE!

**LEFT TO HUNT**
**(An Adele Sharp Mystery—Book 9)**

"When you think that life cannot get better, Blake Pierce comes up with another masterpiece of thriller and mystery! This book is full of twists and the end brings a surprising revelation. I strongly recommend this book to the permanent library of any reader that enjoys a very well written thriller."
--Books and Movie Reviews, Roberto Mattos (re Almost Gone)

**LEFT TO HUNT is book #9 in a new FBI thriller series featuring Adele Sharp (the series begins with LEFT TO DIE, book #1) by USA Today bestselling author Blake Pierce, whose #1 bestseller Once Gone (a free download) has received over 1,000 five star reviews.**

**When masked victims turn up dead at midnight balls in Venice, FBI Special Agent Adele Sharp—triple agent of the U.S., France and Germany—is summoned to find the killer before he can strike again.**

As Adele navigates the historic canals of Venice in her hunt for a killer, she wonders if there is an unseen pattern to the murders. Is it a nod to history? Or merely the work of a deranged mind?

An action-packed mystery series of international intrigue and riveting suspense, LEFT TO HUNT will leave you turning pages late into the night.

Book #10 in the series—LEFT TO FEAR—is now also available!

## Blake Pierce

Blake Pierce is the USA Today bestselling author of the RILEY PAGE mystery series, which includes seventeen books. Blake Pierce is also the author of the MACKENZIE WHITE mystery series, comprising fourteen books; of the AVERY BLACK mystery series, comprising six books; of the KERI LOCKE mystery series, comprising five books; of the MAKING OF RILEY PAIGE mystery series, comprising six books; of the KATE WISE mystery series, comprising seven books; of the CHLOE FINE psychological suspense mystery, comprising six books; of the JESSE HUNT psychological suspense thriller series, comprising nineteen books; of the AU PAIR psychological suspense thriller series, comprising three books; of the ZOE PRIME mystery series, comprising six books; of the ADELE SHARP mystery series, comprising thirteen books; of the EUROPEAN VOYAGE cozy mystery series, comprising six books (and counting); of the new LAURA FROST FBI suspense thriller, comprising three books (and counting); of the new ELLA DARK FBI suspense thriller, comprising six books (and counting); of the A YEAR IN EUROPE cozy mystery series, comprising nine books); of the AVA GOLD mystery series, comprising three books (and counting); and of the RACHEL GIFT mystery series, comprising three books (and counting).

An avid reader and lifelong fan of the mystery and thriller genres, Blake loves to hear from you, so please feel free to visit www.blakepierceauthor.com to learn more and stay in touch.

## BOOKS BY BLAKE PIERCE

**RACHEL GIFT MYSTERY SERIES**
HER LAST WISH (Book #1)
HER LAST CHANCE (Book #2)
HER LAST HOPE (Book #3)

**AVA GOLD MYSTERY SERIES**
CITY OF PREY (Book #1)
CITY OF FEAR (Book #2)
CITY OF BONES (Book #3)

**A YEAR IN EUROPE**
A MURDER IN PARIS (Book #1)
DEATH IN FLORENCE (Book #2)
VENGEANCE IN VIENNA (Book #3)

**ELLA DARK FBI SUSPENSE THRILLER**
GIRL, ALONE (Book #1)
GIRL, TAKEN (Book #2)
GIRL, HUNTED (Book #3)
GIRL, SILENCED (Book #4)
GIRL, VANISHED (Book 5)
GIRL ERASED (Book #6)

**LAURA FROST FBI SUSPENSE THRILLER**
ALREADY GONE (Book #1)
ALREADY SEEN (Book #2)
ALREADY TRAPPED (Book #3)

**EUROPEAN VOYAGE COZY MYSTERY SERIES**
MURDER (AND BAKLAVA) (Book #1)
DEATH (AND APPLE STRUDEL) (Book #2)
CRIME (AND LAGER) (Book #3)
MISFORTUNE (AND GOUDA) (Book #4)
CALAMITY (AND A DANISH) (Book #5)
MAYHEM (AND HERRING) (Book #6)

**ADELE SHARP MYSTERY SERIES**
LEFT TO DIE (Book #1)

LEFT TO RUN (Book #2)
LEFT TO HIDE (Book #3)
LEFT TO KILL (Book #4)
LEFT TO MURDER (Book #5)
LEFT TO ENVY (Book #6)
LEFT TO LAPSE (Book #7)
LEFT TO VANISH (Book #8)
LEFT TO HUNT (Book #9)
LEFT TO FEAR (Book #10)

**THE AU PAIR SERIES**

ALMOST GONE (Book#1)
ALMOST LOST (Book #2)
ALMOST DEAD (Book #3)

**ZOE PRIME MYSTERY SERIES**

FACE OF DEATH (Book#1)
FACE OF MURDER (Book #2)
FACE OF FEAR (Book #3)
FACE OF MADNESS (Book #4)
FACE OF FURY (Book #5)
FACE OF DARKNESS (Book #6)

**A JESSIE HUNT PSYCHOLOGICAL SUSPENSE SERIES**

THE PERFECT WIFE (Book #1)
THE PERFECT BLOCK (Book #2)
THE PERFECT HOUSE (Book #3)
THE PERFECT SMILE (Book #4)
THE PERFECT LIE (Book #5)
THE PERFECT LOOK (Book #6)
THE PERFECT AFFAIR (Book #7)
THE PERFECT ALIBI (Book #8)
THE PERFECT NEIGHBOR (Book #9)
THE PERFECT DISGUISE (Book #10)
THE PERFECT SECRET (Book #11)
THE PERFECT FAÇADE (Book #12)
THE PERFECT IMPRESSION (Book #13)
THE PERFECT DECEIT (Book #14)
THE PERFECT MISTRESS (Book #15)
THE PERFECT IMAGE (Book #16)

THE PERFECT VEIL (Book #17)
THE PERFECT INDISCRETION (Book #18)
THE PERFECT RUMOR (Book #19)

**CHLOE FINE PSYCHOLOGICAL SUSPENSE SERIES**
NEXT DOOR (Book #1)
A NEIGHBOR'S LIE (Book #2)
CUL DE SAC (Book #3)
SILENT NEIGHBOR (Book #4)
HOMECOMING (Book #5)
TINTED WINDOWS (Book #6)

**KATE WISE MYSTERY SERIES**
IF SHE KNEW (Book #1)
IF SHE SAW (Book #2)
IF SHE RAN (Book #3)
IF SHE HID (Book #4)
IF SHE FLED (Book #5)
IF SHE FEARED (Book #6)
IF SHE HEARD (Book #7)

**THE MAKING OF RILEY PAIGE SERIES**
WATCHING (Book #1)
WAITING (Book #2)
LURING (Book #3)
TAKING (Book #4)
STALKING (Book #5)
KILLING (Book #6)

**RILEY PAIGE MYSTERY SERIES**
ONCE GONE (Book #1)
ONCE TAKEN (Book #2)
ONCE CRAVED (Book #3)
ONCE LURED (Book #4)
ONCE HUNTED (Book #5)
ONCE PINED (Book #6)
ONCE FORSAKEN (Book #7)
ONCE COLD (Book #8)
ONCE STALKED (Book #9)
ONCE LOST (Book #10)

ONCE BURIED (Book #11)
ONCE BOUND (Book #12)
ONCE TRAPPED (Book #13)
ONCE DORMANT (Book #14)
ONCE SHUNNED (Book #15)
ONCE MISSED (Book #16)
ONCE CHOSEN (Book #17)

**MACKENZIE WHITE MYSTERY SERIES**
BEFORE HE KILLS (Book #1)
BEFORE HE SEES (Book #2)
BEFORE HE COVETS (Book #3)
BEFORE HE TAKES (Book #4)
BEFORE HE NEEDS (Book #5)
BEFORE HE FEELS (Book #6)
BEFORE HE SINS (Book #7)
BEFORE HE HUNTS (Book #8)
BEFORE HE PREYS (Book #9)
BEFORE HE LONGS (Book #10)
BEFORE HE LAPSES (Book #11)
BEFORE HE ENVIES (Book #12)
BEFORE HE STALKS (Book #13)
BEFORE HE HARMS (Book #14)

**AVERY BLACK MYSTERY SERIES**
CAUSE TO KILL (Book #1)
CAUSE TO RUN (Book #2)
CAUSE TO HIDE (Book #3)
CAUSE TO FEAR (Book #4)
CAUSE TO SAVE (Book #5)
CAUSE TO DREAD (Book #6)

**KERI LOCKE MYSTERY SERIES**
A TRACE OF DEATH (Book #1)
A TRACE OF MUDER (Book #2)
A TRACE OF VICE (Book #3)
A TRACE OF CRIME (Book #4)
A TRACE OF HOPE (Book #5)